CAST NO
SHADOW

CAST NO SHADOW

JULIE NEWMAN

Urbane
PUBLICATIONS

urbanepublications.com

First published in Great Britain in 2019
by Urbane Publications Ltd
Unit E3 The Premier Centre Abbey Park Romsey SO51 9DG
Copyright ©Julie Newman, 2019

A CIP catalogue record for this book is available from the British Library.

ISBN 978-1-912666-50-8
MOBI 978-1-912666-51-5

Design and Typeset by Michelle Morgan
Cover by Michelle Morgan

Printed and bound by 4edge UK

URBANE

urbanepublications.com

For Richard

prologue

A thin streak of light illuminates the pitch dark of the forest floor. It lifts the darkness. A darkness enveloped in sound; a hypnotising chorus led by night birds and crickets and other insects that inhabit the forest. With purpose she walks on, keeping her head toward the sky in order to use the faint light that is filtering through the trees to guide her through the blackness. She is exhausted and scared. The cut on her face - gained when a small branch resented being pushed aside and so swung back with a vengeance – is beginning to sting. She gently touches her cheek with her fingertips; it feels sticky, but also crusty where the blood has started to congeal. She is tempted to pick off the hard pieces but knows it is unwise to do so. The glimpses of moonlight begin to fade as the space between branches lessens. She is no longer able to see what is underfoot. Tentatively she continues moving forward. The tangled undergrowth tries to trip her so she shortens her stride. She presses on. With each step the ground becomes softer. She decides to rest, fearful that she may be heading into a morass. Her legs welcome her decision, they are desperate for some respite from the relentless march. For days they have carried her onward: walking and running and climbing and walking some more. How many days, she cannot say. She has been trying to keep track by counting the sunsets and sunrises. The dense vegetation hasn't aided her task; at times the sky has been completely hidden, as though a huge blanket has been thrown across the treetops stealing both the sunlight and the moonlight. But now, with exhaustion outweighing fear she allows her legs to fold beneath her and she succumbs to sleep.

A clatter of cicadas stir her from her slumber. Sunlight cascades through a gap in the canopy above, telling her that a new day is replacing the night. Fresh sounds fill the air as the forest awakens.

Slowly she rises to her feet, stretching her tired body. Reluctantly she sets off once more. She hopes that today will be the day she will leave this labyrinth of trees and all that it conceals behind her and reach somewhere more civilised. Somewhere inhabited. Somewhere full of people who may accept her. A busy town; that is what she seeks. She needs to move among others. There is safety in numbers; which is what she was told. Mingle with the masses to avoid capture, travel with others and you may stay safe. Blend in and do not draw attention to yourself. These instructions, along with a warning, were hastily given before her long dark hair was roughly hacked from her head, a rucksack placed on her back and she was pushed into the 'outside'. Thrust from the only home she had ever known because 'it is your time, little one, they are coming for you'.

The words had made no sense to her, but they were delivered with such urgency it was clear they meant she was in danger. Mahima wasn't her mother but she had always taken care of her and looked out for her just as a mother would. The rucksack Mahima had given her held a change of clothes, water, some fruit, some bhajis, (although she preferred them hot) and a few rupees. Before she sent her off into the night Mahima had held her tight and told her to seek out people; the wanderers and nomads, follow them and act as they do.

"Become one of them little one, forget this place and all of us here. It will not serve you well to remember."

She would do as she was told. Heed the warning and follow Mahima's instructions. But she would never forget Mahima, of that she was certain.

chapter one

There are stories out there. Unheard. Unseen. Unwritten. Important stories that should be documented. Very often they begin with an insignificant detail. Perhaps an unsubstantiated rumour, a snippet of overheard gossip, or a reimagined theory. But look closer and sometimes the insignificant leads you somewhere else. Follow these threads and they may lead to a glorious tapestry of stories. Not just any stories, but interesting, informative and heart-warming stories. Human stories. Stories that need to be told. Stories that should be shared. Newsworthy stories.

That was meant to accompany her plea to be allowed to follow her instincts. She knew the tapestry analogy wasn't the best, although it sounded okay in her head. But in the end it went unsaid. She sat through her appraisal, or as Paul liked to call it, performance evaluation, fingering the sleeve of her blouse; saying nothing. Occasionally she looked at him as he droned on about working your way up, earning your stripes and being part of a team. He applauded her enthusiasm, particularly when she came across something that interested her. However, he then negated that comment when he said she showed an astonishing lack of discernment over what was and wasn't worth pursuing. Her writing is good. Her time-keeping erratic, although he acknowledged she always makes her time up. His conclusion; overall there is room for improvement but she shows promise. Considerable promise, he added. His advice; listen more, pay attention to those around you who have been in this game a long time.

"Do you have anything to add?"

Samantha opened her mouth, briefly, but then shook her head. He looked at her then cast his eyes toward the door as he picked up the telephone and began punching in numbers. She stood up and exited his office; cross with herself for not speaking up.

Back at her desk, feeling somewhat deflated, she is mulling over the key points of her 'performance evaluation'. Her initial reaction was that it couldn't have gone worse, but then, on reflection she realised it wasn't so bad; after all, she still has a job, for now. But she is still cross with herself for not speaking up. She should have explained that when people think she is late for work she is very often looking into something. She should have explained that she often undertakes research in her own time. And she definitely should have explained that she is very good at spotting a good story. She concedes that some of her hunches and ideas have been a little off in terms of journalistic content, but then some have proved to be quite interesting. Okay they weren't going to garner headlines; they were mostly human interest pieces, but still not without merit. After all, when others had been allowed to pursue them they all ended up being printed somewhere, often as fillers, but they were published.

Her musings are interrupted as she spots Gregory approaching her desk; a pompous arse whose air of superiority grates on her.

"So, Sammy darling, still here I see. Must have gone well then."

Samantha grins at him, expertly hiding her irritation at his abbreviation of her name. Gregory Johnson: a vain, conceited prig. Her nemesis. He is her complete opposite; public school educated, Oxbridge graduate, family worth millions. Yet here he is working in a London newsroom, supposedly harbouring the same ambitions as she does. To give him his dues, he does work hard, which some people think odd because he can afford to fail. An ample trust-fund is his safety net. But he won't fail; he has connections and he is respected. And annoyingly for Samantha, he has gained a level of autonomy in the office that she is denied.

"It was fine. So what delights have you got for me today?"

"Usual trivia I'm afraid. Although you may well spot something that the rest of us have missed." He dumps a file on her desk and does an about turn before Samantha can respond. She flicks open the folder, wondering as she does what her father is working on at the moment. Like her he is a journalist, unlike her he is taken seriously. His work takes him right around the globe, to far flung places, often little heard of. He has investigated corrupt governments and organised crime families. Serious issues that all carry a great deal of risk, which is why he often works undercover and under assumed identities. He cites the long absences as the reason he and her mother inevitably divorced. Samantha lets out a huge sigh as she recalls the last time she saw him. It was a while ago, six or seven, actually eight months earlier. He had a short stopover in London before flying on to wherever, he didn't say. They managed to have lunch and a couple of drinks in Soho before he had to leave. He had looked rather unkempt on that occasion; an unruly beard and bloodshot eyes had led her to be concerned. But he had allayed her fears by claiming the facial hair growth was due to being in the Columbian forest - he couldn't tell her why - and the bloodshot eyes were simply down to tiredness and jetlag. 'I find it impossible to sleep on a flight, even in business class.' Their time together had passed quickly and as usual much was left unsaid between them. They spoke a little of work and the rest of the time was filled talking about the mendacities of life: the weather, the traffic, holidays. It was like having a conversation with your hairdresser, not a parent you hadn't seen for a long time. He had asked after her sister and mum but wanted to know no more than that they were well. It saddened and angered Samantha that her sister had no interest in their father whatsoever. She had more understanding regarding her Mum's indifference toward him, after all, they were divorced and had been for many years now. Mum had brought them up single-handedly, working hard to ensure they never went without. And she did this without complaint, or apportioning blame. Samantha had never heard her badmouth Dad, not once. Her Mum's stoicism and forbearance were admirable.

Gregory is right, the folder doesn't contain much of interest. Anything worth following up has already been removed by reporters far more senior than her. She pushes the file aside and begins sorting through her in-tray and getting on with the scheduled tasks that she is responsible for. A great deal of the day is spent looking at the clock. The seconds feel like minutes and the minutes feel like hours. The time crawls by at a snail's pace giving a whole new meaning to the phrase slow news day. It's almost five when her phone whistles, letting her know she has a text message. It's Justin, asking her to meet for a drink after work. She hadn't been planning to see him today, but the offer of a drink is appealing. Especially after her day so far. She would have to make it clear that it is to be only a drink. The last thing she needs is the evening spreading into the night and the night spreading into the morning. What she does need is a good night's sleep and that won't be the case if Justin persuades her to go home with him.

"Sweetpea," says Justin. "You are only a junior reporter. Your time will come and when it does I'm sure you will write a headline making, award winning story, until then…"

"I know, but…" she tries to interrupt him.

"No buts. You have to toe the line. You can't go off on a tangent, trying to build a story when there clearly isn't one just to satisfy yourself. If that's what you want to do perhaps you should try your hand at fiction. Become a novelist rather than a journalist."

Samantha lets him prattle on. Pretending to listen. Occasionally she hears him; putting emphasis on phrases like office politics and words like hierarchy and corporate. All blah blah blah as far as she is concerned. What he doesn't seem to understand is that she is almost twenty-six years old and had expected to be further along her career path than she is at the moment. She just needs someone to trust her, give her more of a free rein, like Gregory has been given. Justin should see that and support her, instead he lectures her. She wonders if it's because he doubts her ability; or worse is it because she is a woman. Either way, when he begins preaching like this she almost forgets what attracts her to him. His charm, wit and incredible good looks become irrelevant and he is quite simply another condescending, sanctimonious bore. Still at least this will make it easier to walk away from him this evening.

ℵ

Justin kisses her lightly on the head as they part company at the end of his street. Despite her protestations he did convince her to spend the night with him. As always, it was a wonderful night. He certainly knows his way around a woman. But now she is tired before the day has even begun. She thinks about attempting a power walk to work, perhaps it will imbue her with energy. Instead she settles for dragging herself to the tube station accompanied by a double strength latte.

She arrives at her desk earlier than usual, a surprise to herself and others around her. Gregory is watching her and as she catches his eye he gives her a thumbs up accompanied by one of his smug grins. She turns in her chair, opens the top drawer of her desk and pretends to be looking for something. As she aimlessly moves the contents of the drawer around, she can feel his eyes on her. In the end she roughly closes the drawer and spins her chair round to face him.

"What?" She speaks loudly and aggressively. Her tiredness coming into play. "I'm early, yes. Get over it and get over yourself." Gregory snorts as he laughs at her. "And what is so bloody funny?"

He stands up and saunters over to her.

"I'm sorry," he says, with all the sincerity of a politician on the campaign trail. "Yes, you are early. But that wasn't to what I was alluding."

"And to what were you alluding?" Samantha asks in an exaggerated plummy accent, intended as satirical mimicry.

Gregory smiles at her before explaining that his thumbs up was a crass attempt at enquiring whether she had enjoyed the previous evening.

"What has my evening got to do with you?"

"I was simply wondering if your evening had been a good one. I assume so. It normally is the case when one comes into the office in the same outfit one was wearing the previous day and said person looks particularly jaded." He winks at her before turning tail and heading back to his own desk. Samantha stares at him, silently seething at his insinuation; even though he is right. It is him being right that makes what he said all the more annoying. That and the fact that he uses at least twice as many words as a normal person to say what he means. She looks around the newsroom, convinced that everyone there has come to the same conclusion as Gregory. She is sure they are all watching her, judging her. She wants to say, yes I am wearing the same clothes, not underwear though, – – she does keep spare underwear and some toiletries at Justin's – and yes I did have a great night, thank you. But she says nothing, obviously, instead she gets up and goes over to the coffee machine. Another shot of caffeine is required.

At lunchtime Samantha stays at her desk. She buys a chicken and avocado wrap from the sandwich man and browses online. She is mostly looking at news websites; following links to the strange and wonderful. The kind of stories that appeal to her. Some are quite outlandish; exaggerated and hard to believe, but often funny. Some are just dull, attention seeking drivel. Of course some are fake news. That is the downside to the internet. The web is a fount of information but equally it houses disinformation which it spews forth quite readily. And then, very occasionally something different comes along that piques her interest, like today. A short piece that is no more than a footnote at the bottom of a web page arouses her curiosity.

'HOTELIER EXPOSED'
Businessman is really a woman – truth revealed following rape accusation.

Amit Joshi a successful Indian hotelier from Amritsar in the Indian state of Punjab had the perfect defence when accused of rape – he is a she. The respected entrepreneur asked the arresting officers to find a female to carry out a physical examination. This proved that it was impossible for Amit to have been responsible for the attack. When faced with this conclusive evidence the police had to release 'her'. Amit Joshi has apparently gone into hiding as staff and friends alike come to terms with the revelation. They are all asking the same question. Who is Amit Joshi?

४

Not just who but why, thinks Samantha. Why pretend to be a man? As far as she knows there is no law preventing women from owning businesses in India. After all they were one of the first countries to have a female Prime Minister. She googles it to be sure. She is right. Although it's rare, it's not prohibited. So why the pretence. There has to be a reason for it. She plays over possible scenarios in her head. After much deliberation, the most likely answer is that 'Amit' is running away from something or someone. Again why? She surfs the net some more, trying to find out as much about Amit Joshi as possible. It takes a while to discover the Amit Joshi she is interested in. It appears that name is very common in India. When she finds the correct one, what she reads are tales of a very generous and well respected 'man', thought to be of Brahmin origin but with no known family. Samantha is really surprised by how little she is able to uncover. Normally the web throws up a great deal of information about a person. We all leave digital footprints. She decides to look more when she gets home. For now she needs to complete the article she is working on. She has to file copy by the end of the day.

chapter two

Samantha has been sat at her laptop for a couple of hours and has discovered no more about Amit Joshi. The constant dropping off of her connection is making it a slow process. When the signal goes again she decides to go and dry her hair. She has been sitting in her bath robe with a towel wrapped round her head like a turban ever since getting out of the bath. As she dries her tresses she considers what sort of person has no social media presence. Everyone she knows has either Facebook or Twitter or Instagram these days. Even her Mum has Facebook, although Samantha is sure she only got it in order to spy on her and her sister. Her Mum rarely posts anything herself. When she finishes with her hair Samantha puts on her pyjamas and then returns to her laptop. She studies the picture of Amit carefully, wondering how he was a convincing 'man' for so long. To her he looks incredibly effeminate. But perhaps that is because she knows he is a she. After exhausting the social media options and finding no useful information on LinkedIn either, Samantha shuts down her laptop. She will look some more tomorrow. Now she needs to catch up on some long overdue sleep.

The alarm on her phone sounds, but she is already awake. Initially she wonders if she has slept at all. But she must have done for she has dreamed. A strange dream she can only recall in part, flashes. A young girl sleeping beneath jagged trees on damp ground. The same girl running; her long, dark hair blowing across her face, obscuring her vision. Sounds and lights that have no discernible shape are pursuing her. The girl trips and falls. When she stands she is no longer a girl. The person standing is Amit. An odd dream not helped by Samantha's vague recollection; clearly a product of what she had been looking at and thinking about prior to going to bed. For Samantha has concluded that Amit was running away from something. But she pictured Amit running away as a woman, not as a girl. Still, it is a possibility. Although a runaway girl going on to become a successful male entrepreneur was a bit of a stretch, even for Samantha's imaginings. No, she thinks the most likely scenario is that Amit was destined for an arranged marriage and ran away to escape that. Becoming a man was a perfect disguise, but why become an hotelier. Meeting and greeting a constant flow of people. That is still a puzzle. She swings her legs out of bed and heads for the bathroom. She steps into the shower and begins planning a day of research when she suddenly remembers she has arranged to go home for the weekend. And she can't get out of it either as it is her Grandma's birthday.

"Fuck."

"You alright?" the voice of one of her housemates asks from the other side of the door.

"Yes, I'm fine. Sorry," replies Samantha sheepishly. She thought her expletive would have been lost under the flow of running water.

Samantha knows she won't be able to spend the weekend on her computer so decides to use the train journey to see if she can uncover anything. It takes just over an hour and a half to get to Woodbridge, with a change at Ipswich, a journey that when it was her daily commute she found tedious and tiring. She makes a few notes, which are more speculative than fact as she really isn't able to find out anything about the mysterious Amit Joshi. An attempt to access the Election Commission of India website to see if Amit was on the electoral roll was also unsuccessful. Clearly a different approach is needed so she closes down her computer and puts it into its bag. The next stop is Woodbridge anyway; her stop. As she exits the station she spots her mum's car. It isn't her mum sitting in the driver's seat though, it's Maxine, her sister. Samantha is a little disappointed. She waves as she approaches the car. Maxine either doesn't see her or is ignoring her, probably the latter Samantha suspects. Good start, she thinks, but as she nears the car she can see Maxine is on her phone. In her head she admonishes herself; she must stop making rash judgements and presumptions where Maxine is concerned. Maybe this visit will be different and they will get through the weekend without the bitching and sniping. Samantha opens the rear door and places her overnight bag on the seat and then gets into the front placing the laptop bag at her feet.

"Don't know why you've brought that," says Maxine. "Mum's got things planned and she won't appreciate you sitting on your computer all weekend."

"I had work to do on the train. And hello, it's nice to see you too."

Maxine doesn't respond. She starts the car and pulls away sharply. An uneasy silence accompanies the ten-minute drive home. Thankfully Samantha's mum is pleased to see her. Although she does bombard her with questions and instructions before her feet have made it over the threshold.

"We're taking Grandma to Seckford Hall for afternoon tea and tonight we are going to a concert at Snape Maltings," says Mum. Samantha smiles and nods, trying hard not to show her true feelings. Afternoon tea is fine, she doesn't mind that, but she is not so keen on the concert. Classical music is not her thing. She catches Maxine's eye; her expression says it all. "I know what you two are thinking, but it's not your birthday, it's Grandma's and we are doing what she wants. Not every day you celebrate your 80th."

"Its fine Mum, we'll cope." Samantha takes her headphones out of her pocket and waves them at Maxine who nods enthusiastically.

The two sisters laugh out loud.

"What are you two plotting?"

"Nothing Mum," the girls reply in unison and laugh again. Their Mum just shakes her head at them. She is not going to probe any further. She is relieved they seem to be getting along. Although she doesn't hold out much hope that this shared bonhomie will last all weekend.

"You haven't heard the best bit yet," says Maxine. "Tomorrow Michael and Anna are coming over for Sunday lunch so we will be able to hear all about our super, successful cousins."

"That's enough. Just go and get yourselves ready and we can go and pick Grandma up."

Two hours later the four women are sitting in the grounds of beautiful Seckford Hall, enjoying a sumptuous afternoon tea. The Hall, now a hotel, is a Tudor manor house where Queen Elizabeth I once held court.

"This is lovely. Afternoon tea with my three favourite girls, in beautiful, peaceful surroundings. Bit different from London, eh Sammy?" Grandma is one of only two people Samantha allows to call her Sammy.

"Yes, it's very different."

"Do you miss it?"

"Grandma, I'm not that far away. I come home quite often."

"Not that often," snipes Maxine.

"Stop it Maxie," says Grandma. "Your sister can't be expected to come home every week. Newspaper reporters are very busy."

"Oh, of course. What big story are you working on at the moment 'Sammy'?" asks Maxine. Samantha ignores her sister and helps herself to a scone. "Come on, do tell. Must be something important, you've had to bring your laptop with you this weekend," presses Maxine. Samantha's mum shoots an irritated look towards Samantha which she duly passes onto Maxine.

"You know I have my laptop with me because I had to finish up something on the train. Which I did."

"Glad to hear it," says her mum. "Look at that beautiful wisteria," she continues, keen to change the subject.

"Everything here is beautiful. So much history too," adds Grandma. "You know they've had royalty and members of parliament and even pop stars stay here. I bet over the years the staff have seen some things."

"Of course," mumbles Samantha.

"Sorry dear."

"Grandma you're a genius."

"I am?"

Samantha is surprised she hadn't thought of it herself. Who would know more about the goings on at a hotel than the hotel staff? Someone who had worked at Amit Joshi's hotel must know something. At least more than what she has been able to find out. But she is getting ahead of herself. How does she find out who works at the hotel? And how does she get in touch with them? And wouldn't someone have done that already?

Y

Samantha steps outside during the interval of the concert. She tells her Mum she needs to give Justin a quick call. Her Mum is fine with that. She likes Justin. Outside Samantha googles Amit Joshi once more. The links to the relevant web pages come up; many of them she can see she has already visited. She scrolls down until she finds the link to Amit's hotel then clicks on it. The home page comes up, in the corner is a drop down menu. She clicks on that and reads the options. She is disappointed. Her hope was that there would be a 'meet the team' option. Too easy. She looks up, someone is walking towards her frantically waving their arms. It's Maxine. The second half of the concert is about to start, so she switches off her phone and goes back into the concert hall.

It's almost 10.30pm by the time they get back home. Once indoors Samantha feigns tiredness and heads off to bed. Her room is still the same as it was when she was a child. Well almost, her Mum has given it a coat of paint to freshen it up and replaced the curtains with a blind, but the furniture is still the same. Things that she decided against taking with her when she moved to London are dotted about the room. Photo frames adorn the window sill alongside ornaments from holidays and outings. Fridge magnets cling to the radiator. Cuddly toys sit atop an old pine chest that is in the corner of the room. There is a small book-case housing some of her favourite childhood reads; Harry Potter, His Dark Materials trilogy and her favourite, Alice in Wonderland. Like Alice, Samantha is unthinkably curious and the story of Amit has got under her skin. She has to learn more, especially if she is to convince Paul to let her write it up. She sits on the bed, cross-legged with her laptop in front of her and begins a new search.

She wakes with a start. It's cold. The laptop is still on the bed, the screen is dark as the battery has run out. She was dreaming again; same dream; same girl; still running. Samantha moves her computer on to the dressing table, undresses and gets into bed. In the darkness she thinks about the girl in her dream. Does it mean anything? Probably not, she thinks. Her training tells her to follow facts, not imaginings. Which after all, is all a dream is. But, she is confident that there is much more to this story than meets the eye. Call it a hunch. A hunch that she needs to support with evidence though. And she will, she tells herself as she drifts back off to sleep.

The next day's lunch is just as Maxine had suggested it would be; dominated by tales of how well their cousins are doing. Promotions, house purchases and forthcoming nuptials are all talked about with glowing pride. Maxine is finding it particularly hard, especially when Uncle Michael suggests to her that at 28 years old surely she should be thinking of settling down and not continuing to avail herself of her Mother's care.

"I like having her here," interjects their mum.

"Of course you do sis. It gives you an excuse not to get back out there. I mean, how long has it been now since you and that waste of space parted?"

"Leave it Michael."

"Okay, okay." Michael puts his arms up in mock surrender before leaning forward and picking up his glass. Red wine is boosting his belligerence. He drains his glass before adding, "Best not say anything bad about Walter."

"Who is Walter?" asks Samantha.

Michael smirks, aware his comment has invited awkwardness to the table.

"I think it's about time I had my presents." Grandma's interruption diffuses the tension – for now – and reminds them all why they are there.

With neither the inclination nor energy to do anything else Samantha spends the duration of the journey home gazing through the window of the train, daydreaming. The battery on her laptop is dead anyway. She wonders if everyone finds family occasions as draining as she does. For the first time in a few days Amit is not dominating her thoughts. Instead she is thinking of chilled prosecco and a hot bath.

chapter three

The newsroom is much quieter than usual, but then Samantha is here much earlier than she usually is. She is hoping to talk to Adrian before the rest of the staff come in. Adrian Miller, award winning journalist and writer. Responsible for uncovering an insider trading scandal and exposing an under-the-counter drug network, among other things. Sadly, ill health or some sort of accident has meant he has been desk bound for some time now but his network of contacts is far-reaching and he still reports on many high-profile stories despite his incapacity. It isn't always clear how he does it, as he never reveals his sources but his colleagues and others in the profession realise he is still all seeing and all knowing. His knowledge of the industry is second to none and he remains a journalist that many aspire to be like. He is also incredibly grumpy, prone to shouting and gives short shrift to anyone who wastes his time, which is why she wants to try and talk to him with nobody else around. If he thinks this story has no merit and is not worth looking into he will tell her in no uncertain terms. If that's the case she does not want an audience to witness her humiliation. Although a little nervous, she has to try. If anyone can tell her how to find out more about the mysterious Amit Joshi it is Adrian Miller. He may even have some contacts he can put her way. He may agree with her that this is a story worth pursuing and ask to work on it with her. That would be a feather in her cap; to have her name alongside that of Adrian Miller. As usual Samantha's imagination has set off on a flight of fancy. Tentatively she walks across the office towards his desk. The newsroom is open plan. Nobody on this floor has a desk behind walls or a door, apart from Paul. Adrian looks up and sees her approaching. When she is about six feet away and it is plain that she is planning on talking to him, he puts down his pen and says in very measured tones.

"If you are coming to see me you had better be bringing coffee with you."

"I, yes, erm… of course." Samantha scuttles over to the coffee machine. For a second she can't remember how he has his coffee. She spies a packet of chocolate biscuits and takes them over too.

"So… What do you want?" he asks as he dunks a chocolate digestive into his coffee cup. Samantha tells him the story as he lifts the biscuit and manages to pop it into his mouth just before it breaks in half. He listens patiently. When she has finished he agrees it is a little interesting, but it is most likely someone trying to escape an arranged marriage. No more than that. "If there was more to it, someone else would have followed it up by now. Someone closer. Someone in India."

"Maybe they have tried, and like me they can't find anything."

"He, I mean she, has hidden herself well, that's all."

"I still think there is more to this."

"Then go for it, but I would do it on your own time. I don't think you will be able to convince Paul to let you run with this."

"So where should I look? I was hoping to find someone who worked at the hotel to talk to me. But I don't know where to start to find someone."

"It would help if you knew someone over there."

"In India?"

"Yes, in India."

"I don't. And I don't know anyone else who does either."

"You do."

"Do I?"

"You do."

"Who?"

Adrian shakes his head as he finishes his coffee. "The man who sits at the desk closest to you has a brother who works for the British High Commission in Delhi."

Samantha turns around and looks across to her desk, then looks at the desk nearest hers. "Gregory? Gregory has a brother?"

"Call yourself a journalist. You're not even aware of what's around you, here, in this office."

"He won't help me. He doesn't like me."

"I don't think that's true," laughs Adrian. "Talk to him, you'll be surprised. And maybe his brother can connect you to someone." Samantha goes back to her desk, unsure of her next move. She absolutely wants to pursue this story, preferably without having to ask Gregory for help. But who does she look to? Adrian's advice was plain - use who you know - and ignoring him would be like the Greeks ignoring the Oracle. People are milling around now. The newsroom is a different place to what it is was half an hour ago. Noise and movement fill the space. Conversations abound. Voices are raised, all vying to be heard. Samantha leans forward, puts her elbows on her desk and begins massaging her temples with her forefingers.

"Penny for them?"

Samantha looks up. Gregory is standing over her. A fragment of a smile creeps across his face. She half-heartedly returns the smile and realising now is as good a time as any tells him she wants to chat about something with him.

"Not here though. Maybe we could grab a drink at lunchtime?"

"Sure. Yes. Great. Really?" Gregory is surprised and a little confused. His response is like that of an awkward child invited to play with the bigger and cooler kids for the first time ever. Nervous excitement forces his normally smug, assured persona to be replaced by a gentle, humbler image. Samantha watches as he walks across to his desk. His amiability confounding her. She had at least expected some sort of interrogation. And then he would say no.

Gregory listens intently, without interrupting; hanging on her every word. When she stops talking, he doesn't speak. He has nothing; no words. Whatever he was expecting her to say, this wasn't it. And what he wanted her to say, well, that was clearly wishful thinking on his part. Samantha is watching him; willing him to say something as the quiet is roaring in her ears. Eventually it is she who speaks.

"You don't think it's worth pursuing."

"I erm…"

"Or perhaps you just don't want to help me. I was surprised when Adrian said ask you."

"Adrian told you to ask me?"

"Look Gregory, it's fine. I'll ask someone else." Samantha downs her drink and stands up in one seemingly, effortless movement.

"Please sit down," said Gregory, taking hold of her arm as he speaks. "I will help you. I just thought you were…"

"I was what?"

"Nothing. Sit down, please." Reluctantly Samantha sits down again. He rubs his chin before speaking again. "I think it is a very interesting story and yes it is worth pursuing. I'll give my brother a call for you later. Now have another drink and tell me about your weekend."

She sighs before reluctantly talking about the weekend. She figures she owes him a conversation at least.

Back at her desk Samantha reflects on her lunchtime rendezvous with Gregory. Despite her initial reservations he had been easier to talk to than she expected. In fact they had settled into an easy exchange that had made them slightly late back. Thankfully nobody seemed to either notice or care. True to his word Gregory did contact his brother who said he would find out what he could at his end, although he stressed it was not a story that had crossed his radar so it was likely that it was a case of a runaway bride. Such scenarios are not uncommon, he stressed. Although he agreed, whoever she was, she seemed to have gone to a lot of trouble to conceal her gender and true identity. At the end of the day Gregory visited Samantha's desk again.

"I don't suppose you fancy a drink and maybe a bite to eat before heading home?" he asks.

"You suppose right." Samantha's reply was terse, delivered without even looking up.

Gregory walks away deflated and cross at his obvious miscalculation. Samantha hears his deep exhalation and realises she has been unnecessarily abrasive.

"Gregory, wait up." She goes over to him. "I'm sorry, I'm a bit behind today so not ready to leave yet and to be honest, if I go out on a Monday it will ruin me for the rest of the week. Rain check?" she asks, using one of her father's favourite expressions.

"Sure," replies Gregory with a smile. "See you tomorrow."

"Yes, see you tomorrow. And thanks," she shouts after him.

He doesn't turn back, he just waves his arm behind him as he leaves the office. An hour later she is on the bus, heading home. She leans her head on the window as she watches the tourists, commuters and city dwellers go about their business. She does love London. A cosmopolitan metropolis with history that can be traced back to Roman times. Its history, diversity and culture reflected in the faces flashing past her now. For a girl who grew up in a Suffolk village the city still fills her with awe. Her observations are interrupted by a text. She opens the message; disappointed that it is from Justin. He asks about her weekend and her family, particularly her sister. Her reply is short, lacking in detail. His reply is even shorter, 'cool'. A moment later he texts again, asking when he can see her. His request is accompanied by a suggestion that causes Samantha to blush. Nervously she looks around, sure that someone may have noticed her embarrassment. Nobody is paying her any mind. She replies saying she will call him later.

ɣ

He has spent the evening thinking about her. And although at the moment she clearly has no romantic designs on him, he hopes that given time he can persuade her to look at him differently. He pours himself a whiskey over ice as he goes over the day's events. He feels sure they made a connection; once they both relaxed. He needs to reveal more of himself, his true self. Not the uber-confident, pretentious arsehole who appears to dislike her. A pretence designed for self-preservation. If he can help her with this 'project' of hers, that would be a good start. Never before has he been so reliant on his brother. Growing up it had always been the other way around. As the eldest he always looked out for his siblings which include a sister and another much younger brother.

His father's insouciance and his mother's reliance on anything from a bottle – alcohol, pills, or both, she didn't care - meant he had assumed an almost parental role from an early age. He didn't mind, doesn't mind; he adores them all. And he adores her too. His love for her has led him to decline countless dates and match-making attempts by friends. He even rejected a promotion - that would have seen him move upstairs - so he could remain in the newsroom, close to her. Unrequited love; at times it feels like an illness. An illness that he is prepared to endure. His willingness to accept suffering may be called – by some – noble or stoic. In reality it is stupid. It hampers his ambition and makes him rather dispirited. Although the latter he hides behind a wall of pride and pomposity; two attributes he hates, but adopts as an effective disguise of his true feelings. He looks at his watch, it's almost 10pm. Early hours in Delhi. He isn't going to hear from his brother tonight. The ice in his whiskey has melted, he downs it anyway then pours himself another.

chapter four

Gregory never has a day off and he is never late. If he isn't here he must be unwell, very unwell, she thinks. It is not concern that first raises these thoughts, but disappointment. She was hoping he may have some news for her, from India. Some news from his brother. She silently chastises herself. When did you become so heartless Samantha? Or maybe that is me, heartless and wrapped up in my own thoughts. It is something her sister often says of her.

A dull 'Good morning' brings her from her thoughts and alerts her to his presence. He looks pale and heavy-eyed. She decides now is probably not the best time to enquire if he has heard from his brother. As she catches his eye, she asks if he is okay. She doesn't speak out loud though, instead she silently mouths the words. He nods and proffers a sad smile. Mid-morning he walks past her desk and signals with his eyes for her to come over to the coffee machine with him. Excitedly she stands up, sure that he must have heard something from his brother. Standing next to him she can see just how bad he looks. His eyes are puffy and dark. He looks washed-out; his bloodless skin in stark contrast with his dark hair.

"You look a bit rough today Gregory. Everything alright?"

"Didn't get a great night's sleep, that's all."

"Is that a good thing or bad thing?"

"What do you mean?" he asks, somewhat confused.

"I wondered if perhaps there is a lucky lady walking around somewhere today, equally as exhausted as yourself." Samantha accompanies her reply with a cheeky wink.

She said 'lucky lady' thinks Gregory. He wonders if she meant it, although he is sure she didn't. It's probably just a turn of phrase.

"Sadly not. Anyway," he says, eager to change the subject. "I've just had an email from Simon."

"Simon?"

"My brother."

"Oh right."

"He hasn't been able to find out anything either." Samantha's heart sinks. "But he is not giving up. In fact he absolutely thinks that there is more to it." In hushed tones Gregory explains that his brother believes the story has been covered up.

"What makes him think that?"

"He was told in no uncertain terms that he had no business asking questions about it."

"He was warned off?" Samantha is incredulous.

Gregory nods. "And it seems that nobody knows the whereabouts of Amit Joshi. I'll let you know when I hear anything more."

Back at her station she considers what Gregory has told her. She has been sure all along that this would be an interesting story but now it sounds as if it could be a big story. Why else tell someone to back off. The story is obviously embarrassing or harmful to someone. Who? Amit Joshi? Maybe he, she, comes from a well to-do family; a powerful family, a political family. Samantha pushes aside what she should be working on, takes a notebook from her drawer and begins making notes. She writes down all that she knows so far. It doesn't amount to much. She knows she will have to wait until Gregory has heard more from India. Please let it be before my holiday she says to herself. In little more than a fortnight she is due to jet off to Barbados with Justin. She hopes that by then she will have uncovered the truth about Amit Joshi.

ϫ

Gregory's main motive for helping Samantha has been one of self-promotion. He wants her to look at him differently. He wants her to see him as he sees her. But now, well he still wants that, of course he does, but he also wants to be part of this story. He, like Adrian and Simon did not think there was going to be much to Amit Joshi. Clearly they are all wrong. A woman for years passes herself off as a man, and then when her deception is revealed someone wants the story to go away. Who could that be? Is it just one person? Unlikely, thinks Gregory. And where has Amit gone? So many questions and not a single answer. Not yet. Gregory is sure it's just a matter of time though, his brother has the same enquiring nature as he does and he will not take kindly to being warned off. If anything it will have the reverse affect and Simon's doggedness will undoubtedly uncover something.

ϫ

The email didn't give any details but the implication was that the story is big. Simon's jibe about Gregory winning the Pulitzer

Prize hinted at that. Although surely he knew the Pulitzer was an American award, thinks Gregory. The email ended with Simon promising to call at the weekend, when he would reveal what he had learned. The call won't come. Not now. Not ever.

Simon's body was discovered in his apartment in Chanakyapuri, New Delhi. A suspected drug overdose they say. An accidental death. No way, says Gregory. He categorically knows Simon did not do drugs. He never did or would. Not even when they were being freely passed around the dormitories of their boarding school. He shunned recreational drugs and was loath to partake of prescription drugs too. He had seen the consequences of a chemically enhanced diet close up, courtesy of their mother. As a result Simon rarely even took an aspirin. Gregory was certain, Simon's death was not as a result of an overdose and it was no accident either…

૪

"Murdered?"

"Yes." Initially Gregory had reservations about telling Samantha but quickly realised that if as he suspected Simon was killed because of the Amit Joshi story he had to tell her. For her own safety. "You have to promise me that you will leave this story alone, and talk about it with no-one."

"I don't think…"

"Please," implored Gregory. "Just until I get back."

"Get back? Where are you going?"

"Delhi."

"Is that wise?"

"I have to. My parents are… not fit enough to make the journey and there are formalities. Identification and… I have to see for myself. Find out exactly what happened to him."

"Maybe it was drugs. You said yourself you hadn't seen him for a while."

"No. He has never even had so much as a cigarette. He has never smoked, snorted or otherwise imbibed anything. He just wouldn't do drugs, well, not voluntarily."

"Okay, okay."

"Look. He was killed looking into a story for us. I intend to find out why."

"Perhaps I should come with you."

"No. I'm flying tomorrow and you won't get a visa in time. Besides, I'm sure Paul won't allow you to take a trip to India."

"Promise me you'll be careful and keep in touch."

"Of course. Will you miss me?" he asks. Samantha gives him a look that says neither yes nor no. It is an unreadable look that is accompanied by a silent, solitary tear. "Don't cry," he says. "I'll be back before you know it."

She smiles. "It's not that."

"Oh." Gregory says forlornly.

"I can't help feeling responsible. I started this and…"

"No you didn't," interrupted Gregory. "Whatever this is, it started a long time ago. You just happened to stumble across it."

"But, your brother, we, I..."

Gregory takes her hands in his and shaking his head he reiterates that it is not her fault, or his.

chapter five

Gregory arrives at Indira Gandhi International Airport just after 6.30 in the evening. He hopes this means he has missed the rush hour. He has been told that the roads of the city can be busy. The British Embassy has arranged for a driver to pick him up and take him to his hotel. In the arrivals hall Gregory searches for his name among the many placards and boards being held aloft. Once he has spotted it, he makes eye contact with the holder and walks toward him.

"Namaste Mr Johnson."

"Namaste," responds Gregory bowing his head and putting his palms together, perfectly mirroring the driver. The driver smiles, acknowledging and appreciating the salutation. He then places a garland of jasmine and lotus flowers around Gregory's neck.

"Welcome to India. This way please." He takes hold of the luggage and signals for Gregory to follow him. "Which hotel please?" he asks once they have reached the car.

"The Hyatt Regency."

"Very good. It is close to the Embassy."

Gregory knows this. He has chosen it for that very reason and he knows Simon frequented the restaurants at the hotel, claiming they were among the best in Delhi. He also waxed lyrical about The Polo Lounge; the hotel bar. Extolling its extensive beverage menu, which apparently included a significant collection of single malts; something he knew his brother was partial to.

The Delhi traffic is a surprise. Cars sit bumper to bumper. Buses are full of people, packed like sardines; faces pressed against doors and windows. The air is black with fumes. Motorcycles and astonishingly push-bikes weave through the myriad of motor vehicles, often performing risky death-defying manoeuvres to gain just a few feet. Some of the motorbikes carry entire families. The streets are also home to wildlife; cows wander freely while dogs forage in the rubbish that adorns the roadside. The road they are on - a four lane highway – is accommodating six or seven lines of traffic. It seems that lane-driving is a foreign custom. "It's very busy. Is it still rush hour?" Gregory asks.

The driver laughs. "Always busy. Always rush hour."

The twenty-minute drive takes over an hour and a half. Gregory checks in and is shown to his room. Once he has freshened up he heads to The Polo Lounge. It is as Simon had described it. Elaborate woodwork, an open fireplace, and a library make it very English looking; colonial. The bar, in the middle of the room does offer an extensive choice of whiskies and cognacs as well as cocktails and hand-crafted beers. Gregory opts for a single malt. It hits the back of his throat warming him from the inside out. He imagines standing here with Simon; he wishes it could be so. He orders another and strikes up a conversation with the bartender. He downs it quickly, so orders another and another. The alcohol is loosening his tongue and raising his voice and before long his conversation with the bartender is being listened to by other occupants of the lounge.

४

Gregory opens his eyes, slowly. The dimly lit room reveals indiscernible shapes among the shadows. He has an ache in his skull and a mouth so dry it feels like it is coated in sand. His first thought is that he is unwell, but recalling the night before makes him realise his symptoms are all self-inflicted. As he pulls himself up the bed into a sitting position grief taps him on the shoulder and he remembers where he is and why he is here. The alcohol may numb the pain but it doesn't change anything; Simon is still dead. As he processes the time Gregory realises he needs to get a move on if he is to have breakfast before the driver arrives. His body takes exception to the sudden movements and a wave of nausea sweeps over him. He reaches the bathroom in time; just. When the spewing stops he stands and fills the tumbler next to the sink with water. Surprisingly he feels a little better. With a towel wrapped around his waist he goes back into the bedroom. He pulls back the heavy drapes in order to see what the weather is offering up today. He can't see a thing. He laughs at himself, realising he hasn't pulled back the fire-retardant net curtain. He reaches forward, there is no net curtain. He touches the window with his fingertips, steps closer and squints as he tries to understand what he is seeing. A thick fog hampers his view. It is astonishing; neighbouring buildings are barely visible and the street below is hidden by the thick, grey blanket. When he goes down to breakfast Gregory discovers that visibility is not much better at street level.

The driver is waiting for him at the front of the hotel.

"Good morning Sir."

"Morning. Bit foggy today," says Gregory. A description that could pertain to himself also.

"Smog, not fog. Sadly pollution in my city is very bad. I have a mask for you if you wish." The driver leans across to the glove compartment and extracts a small packet which he passes behind him. Gregory gratefully accepts it, although not sure he will use it. He had heard tell of the pollution in Delhi but had no idea it was as bad as this. He asks if it is safe to drive. "As safe as it can be," answers the driver. Gregory wonders what that means but decides not to enquire further. They reach the offices of the British High Commission quite quickly considering the traffic and the conditions. Gregory is glad, he is never at ease as a passenger at the best of times and this really is something else.

Once he has gone through the relevant security checks he is shown to the office of Rupert Appleby-Jones, the assistant to the British High Commissioner.

"Your brother co-ordinated the offices of the deputy high commissioners. So he and I often had to liaise with one another. Good golfer, we enjoyed a round or two together when our diaries allowed. He was a fine chap. I'm sorry for your loss, it must have come as a shock."

"Yes he… was." Gregory pauses before continuing. Rupert's use of the past tense is upsetting. "Will I be able to see where he worked and lived?"

"I don't see why not. The police have concluded investigations at his apartment and his office is just down the hall. Once we have gone through the formalities here I'll show you his office. The apartment we can visit after you've seen his body."

Gregory nods and swallows hard. He had forgotten that he has to identify his brother's body. He listens carefully as Rupert explains the repatriation process. He signs forms acknowledging receipt of his brother's personal possessions from his desk. He then follows Rupert to what was Simon's office. It is empty save a few items of furniture and a portrait of the Queen that hangs on the wall. The desk which has nothing on it sits in front of a large window, which according to Rupert would allow you views across the compound on a clear day. The room offers Gregory nothing; not even a sense of his brother, so he exits quickly.

The body doesn't look like Simon, not anymore; but it is him. Gregory is overwhelmed, his head fills with images of Simon as a young boy: following, chasing, and copying his older brother. He was always so active, so full of energy. Seeing him laying here now, like this, in a state of permanent inertia is too much. Gregory's breakfast threatens to revisit him, but doesn't, thanks to deep breathing and mind over matter exercises. His eyes he has less control over and his emotion is laid bare. Rupert puts a hand on his shoulder before discreetly leaving the room. Left alone Gregory regains his composure. His grieving will have to wait, for now he has to discover who did this to Simon and why.

A respectful silence is observed in the car as they drive from the morgue to Simon's apartment. Gregory is only aware they have arrived when the driver opens the rear door to let him out.

"Thank you," he mutters almost inaudibly.

The apartment smells strongly of cleaning fluids: bleach and disinfectant. The smell briefly transports Gregory to his boarding school days. He looks around and is surprised how spartan and austere the apartment is. There is even less of his brother here than at the office. In fact there is nothing.

"I hadn't realised that the cleaners had been in already or that your brother's things had been removed," said Rupert sensing Gregory's shock. "Give me a minute. I will find out where everything is." Rupert takes his phone from his jacket pocket and makes a call. He turns his back on Gregory and walks into the kitchen as he speaks. Gregory can't hear what is being said so decides to look around what was until recently his brother's home. There is nothing to see. Even the bed has been stripped bare and the cupboards are empty apart from a few wooden coat hangers.

"It seems they have had to ready this place for your, erm…," Rupert hesitates. He doesn't want to use the word replacement, but that is who will have this apartment; Simon's replacement. "…the next occupant. Simon's belongings are in the storage area, downstairs. I can have them sent direct to you back in England."

"I would still like to take a look if I may."

"Of course, sure. We can go down now."

A large blue suitcase is filled with clothes, everything apart from his suits which are hanging on a clothes rail. There are two holdalls. The one that matches the suitcase is full of shower gels, deodorants and after shaves, the other has Simon's gym gear in it. There are a set of golf clubs in the corner, leaning against them is a tennis racquet, a squash racquet and a well-used cricket bat. Gregory picks up the bat and runs his hand along its length. He bought this bat for Simon, a very long time ago. He holds onto it as he looks at the other things. There are three cardboard boxes, one large and two smaller ones, all sealed.

"Okay to open these?" he asks.

"Sure. They're yours now."

Gregory pulls the brown packing tape from the top of the large box and opens it. Shoes and trainers, a fleece jacket, a tube of tennis balls and other odds and ends. He closes the box and reseals it as best he can. The second box has files and paperwork in it, Gregory pushes it aside, he will take that one back to the hotel. The final box has a number of framed photographs in it. Gregory takes some of them out, some are of Simon at sporting events, receiving trophies - he smiles as he recalls his brother's sporting prowess –

others are family photos. One is of the two of them together at a rugby match, not the most flattering of pictures but a reminder of a very good day nonetheless. He puts that one into the box with the paperwork in it and lifts the box up.

"I'll take this one with me."

"Of course. I'll need you to sign for it though."

Once he is back in his hotel room he helps himself to a whiskey from the mini-bar and empties the contents of the box onto the bed. He starts with the loose pieces of paper first. Mostly they are of little consequence: bills, letters and lists. He shakes his head at the lists. Simon was always writing lists, ever since he was a small boy. He would write Christmas lists, (of course), birthday present lists, things I'd like to do lists, things I have to do lists, places I'd like to see, places I have seen. He would list his likes and dislikes, his favourites, his wishes and his dreams. And even as a grown man it seemed he still relied on lists; these are more of the things I have to do type. There are a couple of notepads, several very nice pens and two wallets. The first wallet contains money in three currencies: euros, rupees and sterling but nothing else. The second also has money - just rupees – bank cards, membership cards and Simon's driving license. So far nothing unexpected. He begins looking through the files, they contain more bills, receipts and statements. He sighs despondently as he realises there is nothing of interest among these things. He doesn't know what he expected to find. He had hoped he may uncover a clue that would point him in the direction of his brother's killer. At the moment he has nothing. He needs a starting point like a diary entry that has a name or a number alongside it. There isn't a diary, or an address book or anything like that. Amongst all the lists there wasn't a contacts list… but of course. Gregory curses his stupidity. All of that sort of information will be on his phone. Where is his phone?

chapter six

Samantha had hoped to have heard from Gregory by now. If as he suspected his brother was killed because of the Amit Joshi story the least he could do is keep her informed. Let her know he is safe. As far as she can ascertain no-one has heard from him. And no-one but her seems concerned, but then no-one but her is aware of Gregory's suspicions. For a moment she considers confiding in Adrian, but thinks better of it. She decides that if she has not heard from Gregory by this evening she will try and contact him. For now she has work to do. She looks back at her computer and is surprised to be faced with a white screen; she had been scrolling through her emails. She presses a button, nothing happens. She presses several buttons, still nothing happens. A glance around the newsroom tells her she is not the only one facing IT issues this morning.

It soon becomes apparent that the newspaper's entire computer network has been hit by something, possibly some sort of virus. Although the IT team say it is amateurish at best and shouldn't take long to put right. By mid-morning the computers are running again but without allowing access to emails. Paul is furious and demands to know who is responsible.

"We may never know. Could just be some kid on the other side of the planet, sitting in his room, doing this for kicks or…"

"Or what?" shouts the incensed editor.

"Or, it could be some sort of cyber-attack."

"Great. When will you know and when will we be able to access our emails?"

The IT 'expert' shrugs as Paul spins round angrily and goes back to his office.

Samantha decides, along with several of her colleagues to head out of the office. Most of her co-workers are heading to the pub for an early lunch, she goes down the road to the coffee shop. She types a message on her phone to send to Gregory, typing and deleting it several times, unsure what to say, desperate to know if he has discovered anything new but not wanting to ask too many questions regarding Amit lest she seem insensitive. In the end she settles for asking how he is.

Hey. How are you doing? Hope flight was okay. X

His reply is instantaneous.

Hi. I'm good. Flight was long. How are you? How's the office, quiet without me? G x

I'm fine. Yes, very quiet… you are missed. Computer glitch today so I'm in the café at the moment. How is Delhi? X

Gregory reads her text, *'you are missed'*. By her, or by others. He would like to think she misses him. She must do, why else contact me, he wonders. For now he will hang on to that. Her text has definitely brightened his day, he won't dampen that feeling by dwelling too much on her motive for messaging him.

Delhi is awesome, I'm sure. It is full of beauty and history and vibrancy. But at the moment those things are hard to see. So for me, now, it is suffocating. G x

She can feel his sadness as she reads the message and is unsure how to respond. She certainly can't ask about the Amit story now. In the end she settles on a heart emoji and tells him to take care before she heads back to work. She'll contact him again later.

૪

Gregory is staring at his phone, at her last text. He so wishes she were here. He misses her. And although they have never touched, he can feel her. And although they have never kissed, he can taste her. She is part of his being, yet he has never even made an advance. Despite the fact that nothing romantic has ever transpired between them he knows she is the one and he is trapped by his love for her.

He needs a drink; before despair bites.

In the Polo Lounge he selects one of the artisan beers along with a whiskey chaser. It goes down a treat. He orders another pint. The alcohol lifts him. He pushes thoughts of Samantha aside and remembers why he is here; for Simon. He calls Rupert and asks about his brother's phone. Rupert assumes it would be with Simon's things and if Gregory hasn't found it then it is most likely in one of the bags or boxes he left behind.

"Is it okay if I take a look again?"

"Sorry, old chap, everything has been removed ready to be sent back to the UK."

Gregory is not convinced by Rupert's reply which was given hesitantly and he is sure he would have spotted the phone. He considers what could be on Simon's mobile that someone does not want him to see: messages, contacts or both. While supping his beer Gregory ponders over the possibility of hacking into Simon's phone records. He knows it is possible, but is unsure who to ask. It has to be someone he can trust. Of course he can trust Samantha, but he doesn't believe she has the necessary contacts to help with this. After much brain racking he concludes that Adrian is the best person to ask. For sure he will know someone and for all his bluster he is the soul of discretion.

ᛍ

Samantha is late getting to the restaurant. The computer hiatus at work meant she had to work later than expected. Justin is waiting for her at the bar, she hears him before she sees him as he is already quite lubricated.

"Ahh cupcake, at last," he says pulling her into an embrace. She delivers a tight-lipped smile which goes no way to concealing her irritation, at both his state and his use of the term cupcake. She hates such terms of endearment. Cupcake and sweetpea, to her

CAST NO SHADOW

they sound condescending and phoney. "Big story keep you at the office?"

"No unfortunately. We had computer issues. Sorry."

"No matter. You are here now. I think we should go to our table and order; I'm rather in need of some food I think."

They eat their dinner in relative silence, the only words exchanged are compliments about the food. When they have finished he tops up her wine glass and asks her about her day.

"Rather boring today and irritating on account of the IT problems."

"Oh yes, you said. Couldn't you use your laptop?"

"Didn't have it with me today. Although those who did have them were told not to use them until they had uncovered the problem."

"And did they?"

"Did they what?"

"Uncover the problem."

"I suppose they must have done."

"Did they say what it was?"

"Not to me."

"So what are you working on?"

"Nothing particular."

"Well, it really sounds like you have had a very dull day."

"Yes. A dull week so far. Quiet and…" Samantha paused.

"And what?"

"Nothing. It's just quiet, no big news stories and some people are away."

"We will be away soon. I am so looking forward to some Caribbean sunshine."

"Yes," Samantha nods unenthusiastically. She can't think about holidays. Not at the moment.

Justin settles the bill and they go outside and flag down a taxi. The taxi stops alongside them but before Justin opens the door

Samantha tells him she is going to go home; feigning tiredness. He turns on the charm, attempting to talk her round but she is adamant. His kiss goodnight is brief and hard; full of irritation and frustration. He is not happy. He falls into the taxi, his ridiculous odd socks on show - another annoying habit, the wearing of odd socks as some kind of rebellion - he doesn't even offer to drop her at the tube station, although she is relieved by that. The journey home offers her some thinking time; thinking which is mostly dominated by Amit and Gregory. When she finally walks through her front door she is met by a flurry of activity and a wall of chatter as her housemates all try to talk to her at the same time. Amidst the chaos she establishes that a man has been in her room.

"Who was he?"

"He said the landlord sent him to fix a leak and…"

"I thought he looked suspicious," interrupted Becky.

Sian glares at Becky before continuing. "He didn't like it when I insisted on staying with him and I think he heard Becky tell Mel to call the agent to see if he was legit because he went soon after that."

"And was he?" asked Samantha.

"Was he what?" asked Sian.

"Legit."

"Don't know. Mel didn't get the agent, it went straight to her voicemail."

Samantha walks into her room, exasperated. The three girls follow her in.

"Oh no."

"What is it?"

"He's taken my laptop."

"No he hasn't. I shoved it under the bed along with that nice handbag of yours. Just in case he was a thief."

Relieved, Samantha pulls the items out from under her bed. "Thanks girls," she says before closing her door. She is grateful to them but she wants to be on her own so she can try and get hold of

Gregory again. She thinks she may actually call him until it dawns on her that it is about 4.30am in Delhi. Instead she makes herself a hot chocolate and gets into bed with it. She cups the warm mug in her hands watching the swirls of steam curling upwards. She hopes that it turns out the man in her room was sent by the landlord, – although she is unaware of any leak – the idea of a stranger in her room is a bit disconcerting. She is sure he must be from the landlord, after all, it is an odd M.O. for an opportunistic thief.

chapter seven

Adrian is thrilled to hear from Gregory. Thrilled to be asked for help, thrilled to be part of this investigation. Of course, not so thrilled to hear his sad news. But to work with someone new is exciting. And although he wishes he could be out there asking the questions, chasing the leads - he still misses that - he knows he can discover quite a lot from his desk and send others to ask the questions; his questions. He will co-ordinate this one, make it his own. Show the new breed what he can do. Too many of them have either forgotten who he was and what he did or they are unaware of him completely. He thinks his disability has made him invisible. He is no longer seen, they just see the chair, not the man and certainly not the journalist. Yes he gets a pat on the back when he produces his copy, and sometimes even awards but he knows even if it is his name on the byline no-one truly believes it is his work, not really.

Not so long ago Adrian Miller was revered as the best, rightly so because he was the best or at the very least among the best. His exposés gave him legendary status. His working practices were different to other journalists. Most reporters react to the news; they have to, after all they do not set the news agenda. And seldom can they decide what they want to cover. But not Adrian Miller. He could almost initiate stories, for he saw them when others didn't. Unfolding events would lead to briefings and press conferences which his fellow journalists would attend, he however, would be somewhere else; at the sharp end, at the heart of the story. He wasn't alone, there were others, very few though and now they are a dying breed. He observes closely the new batch of recruits that are taking up his profession. Rarely do they have 'it'. That curiosity, a desire to understand and uncover a truth coupled with the sheer bloody mindedness that it takes. Except her. He thinks she has it. Sure it needs some fine tuning, but she has it, in spades. And why wouldn't she.

૪

Until he hears from Adrian there is nothing more Gregory can do. There is nobody in Delhi he can trust, not yet. While he waits he decides to explore the city, discover what Simon loved so much about this place and its people.

He wants to visit Old Delhi; to walk the streets his brother did, to eat the food and see the sights. Chandni Chowk sounds like a good place to start, in the heart of the old city. A bustling area full of colour and life. The sights, sounds and smells are an instant assault on the senses. The area is criss-crossed by narrow lanes, home to shops and stalls selling every conceivable thing you may need. The streets are full, all manner of people and vehicles and animals jostling for position. Hawkers, traders, shoppers, tourists, beggars, cyclists, carts, rickshaws, motorbikes, dogs, cows, chickens, monkeys. Gregory stops on a corner and takes in the intoxicating aromas that are wafting through the air. Nearby a huge smoking pan of hot oil is spitting and sputtering like a rabid auctioneer. Although he is not particularly hungry he buys a bag of freshly cooked vegetable pakoras before hailing a rickshaw. He instructs the rickshaw driver to take him to the nearby Red Fort and as the driver navigates a path across the busy marketplace Gregory eats the pakoras. They are delicious; he can't recall the last time he tasted something this good.

At The Red Fort he has to haggle with the rickshaw driver for several minutes as he had broken a cardinal rule and had not negotiated the fare before the journey began. The driver tries hard to charge an exorbitant price, Gregory doesn't blame him for trying. Eventually they agree a figure. The driver seems quite happy and Gregory wonders if he has still been had. He lets it go and walks towards the entrance of the fort. As he enters the main gate he is aware of someone not far behind him. He surreptitiously glances over his shoulder, there is someone there, taking photos of the fort with a phone. Probably just a tourist thinks Gregory, dismissing his paranoia. The Red Fort is an amazing building and although quite busy offers a stark contrast to the chaos of Chandhi Chowk. It reminds him of a conversation he had with Simon, who had been explaining the rigid dichotomy between peace and pandemonium that India serves up. Poverty and wealth, shadows and colour, stillness and activity, silence and noise. He called India a country of contradictions, balanced by its faith and beauty.

Gregory completes his sight-seeing tour by visiting Humayun's Tomb and Raj Ghat, the latter a memorial dedicated to Mahatma Gandhi. He has enjoyed the day despite not being able to fully shake off the feeling that he is being followed. He is sure he spotted the man from The Red Fort at the tomb but then of course most tourists would be visiting the same things. Back at the hotel he pops into the Polo Lounge before going to his room. As he exits the lift his phone vibrates in his pocket, the hotel Wi-Fi has kicked in and his emails are coming through. There are a couple from Adrian and he hopes they contain some leads for him to follow up, since, as beautiful as Delhi is, sight-seeing is not his priority at the moment.

He prints off the PDF attachment at the hotel's business centre, astonished by how much Adrian has been able to find out. As well as a list of Simon's contacts, he has also been able to get a detailed log of his phone activity for the past three months. Some of the numbers have been highlighted for Gregory's attention; one in particular appears frequently in the week before Simon's death. Initially Gregory isn't surprised by this until he reads Adrian's second email, in which he points out that prior to that week this number only appears five times. Four times as a text message and just once as a phone call. The email ends with Adrian suggesting the guilty may be closer than you think. Gregory thinks that sounds a touch dramatic and he is sure the increase in the number of calls from the person in question will most likely have a simple explanation, after all they did work together. He could speak to him, enquire more about the work they did together, but then again… what if Adrian is right. Could it be Simon's murder is related to his work and not the Amit Joshi mystery? In which case he needs to tread carefully and not disclose what he suspects regarding his brother's death; alerting Rupert Appleby-Jones at this stage would probably be foolish.

ϒ

"Appleby-Jones, Appleby-Jones, Appleby-Jones." Adrian is muttering the name over and over under his breath. He can't recall why it is familiar to him. He has looked online and nothing that comes up has offered an answer. He curses his memory which on occasion lets him down. There was a time he was so sharp that a detail like this would not have him flummoxed. He is not sure whether to blame the stroke or his age. Both have the propensity to interfere with his recall these days, not a lot, after all no-one else seems to notice, but enough to annoy himself. The stroke was a cruel blow. After recovering from the accident, defying the doctors and finally walking again, a cruel twist of fate saw him laid low once more, but this time he did not fully recover.

He castigates himself for allowing self-pity to visit him, albeit briefly. It is a quality that was never part of his character before and he will not allow it to take root now. It would help if he could remember what he knows – if anything – about Appleby-Jones. For now he needs to talk to Samantha, she deserves an update. A hurried look catches her walking back into the newsroom. He signals for her to come over.

"Hi," says Samantha. "Everything okay?"

"Grab a chair and sit here," barks Adrian nodding to the space next to him.

She duly obeys.

"Have you heard from Gregory?" she asks.

"Of course. Why else do you think I want to talk to you?"

Samantha is crestfallen. Why has he been in touch with Adrian instead of her? He senses her disappointment and explains that Gregory required his expertise.

"He could have asked me." Samantha's response is rather petulant.

"Oh really. And I suppose you know someone who can access phone records. It's not something you can just google." As he says this he wonders if it is actually something you can google; the internet is full of surprises. Even if you could it wouldn't be as discreet or effective as his guy. Samantha concedes this point and listens earnestly as he tells her what he has discovered.

"So you think Simon's death is work related and nothing to do with Amit?" she asks.

His response is gruff and rather contradictory. "I think no such thing. Although it is a possibility. But I don't believe in coincidence and neither should you. Take that as a bit of free advice."

"So is Rupert Appleby-Jones our prime suspect?"

"I don't know what he is yet. The extra communications may

well have been work related but I'm not convinced. The only thing we know for certain is that Simon had been warned off looking into the Amit case and then he winds up dead."

"What can we do?"

"Find out what we can about Appleby-Jones."

"There was an Appleby-Jones lived in our village. I used to deliver his paper. Well, I used to help my sister, Maxine. It was her paper round. I remember him because I used to call him Apple-pie Jones. He was really old. I used to think he was a wizard or something similar. Turned out he was a judge I think. Dead now."

"What did you say?" asks Adrian.

"I said he's dead now."

"Before that."

"I used to call him Apple-pie…"

"No, you said he was a judge." Adrian has a light bulb moment. "Look go back to your desk before people wonder what we're talking about. I have my reputation as an unsociable grump to maintain you know."

He watches her walk away and when he is sure she is out of earshot Adrian picks up his phone.

Y

Back at her desk Samantha is feeling more than a little pissed off. She thinks she is being side-lined. Gregory should be contacting her, not Adrian, it's her story. Of course Gregory has a vested interest now, but he should still keep her in the loop. But then, maybe he doesn't want to talk to her. Maybe he blames her, despite what he said. She went to him with a story and now his brother is dead. As she considers all that has happened she begins to worry what she has set in motion.

She finishes writing up her copy and then starts to do a little research on Mr Appleby-Jones, Rupert Appleby-Jones, wondering as she types his name if he is a relation of old Apple-pie. She clicks the first link and begins to read, mostly its biographical stuff. She makes notes before following links to other sites. LinkedIn, Twitter, Facebook, Instagram; he has them all. Most of the posts appear to be golf related. God, he does love himself thinks Samantha. Not a shred of modesty comes across. She openly sneers at one photograph of him holding aloft a trophy; the caption below reads 'winning the family cup'. She flicks through some more photos and then stops, some of the places are familiar to her. Closer inspection tells her they were taken in her hometown: at the golf course, at the pub, at the church. It would seem Mr Rupert Appleby-Jones has been to Woodbridge, several times. Therefore it is not inconceivable to think that possibly he is related to Apple-pie, her Appleby-Jones. Adrian did tell her not to trust coincidences. Further digging confirms this; Rupert is Apple-pie's Great Nephew. Apple-pie is actually Stanley Appleby-Jones QC, a barrister and former High Court judge. He was highly respected, mostly, although some quarters suspected him of interfering with cases and miss-directing juries. They believed him to be a part of a clandestine network that was protecting high profile – the wealthy and the noble – people. Their suspicions were never substantiated and notwithstanding an attempt to leak some of the concerns to the media he was never accused of anything. Ultimately he never received the knighthood that his supporters thought he deserved and so with the help of colleagues and a compliant press at that time he slipped quietly into retirement before passing away a few years ago. She emails what she has learnt across to Adrian.

ϒ

The screen of his computer flickers annoyingly as he reads the email she has sent him. When he finishes he allows a rare smile to play on his face. As soon as she had said the word judge it had come back to him. He came across the story when he was about the same age as her, or maybe a little older; not that he was allowed to do anything with it. Stanley Appleby-jones had a lot of influential friends and the story quietly disappeared, as did he. His phone rings, he picks it up hoping its Gregory returning his call. It's not so he lets it go to voicemail and goes back to the email and re-reads it. Could it be that a deceased judge has something to do with this case, long-shot really. But however improbable it's not impossible. To rule out any connection he needs to take a look at the court records pertaining to the time Judge Appleby-Jones was on the bench.

The email from Adrian is short and sweet. 'Good work.' The two words give her a little boost and for a moment they eliminate her irritation caused by the wobbly screen she has to contend with every time she accesses her emails. The irritation soon returns when she gets a text from Justin saying he wants to see her later. No apology. He can wait. A second text turns her irritation into anger. The text is from Mel, one of her housemates saying their visitor had not been sent by the landlord and the agent suggests that they report the incident to the police. Samantha texts back saying she will do it as it was her room that was targeted.

When she leaves work she is surprised to see Justin waiting outside for her. Initially she wishes she could sidle away but it is obvious by the big smile he flashes her that he has spotted her and knows she has spotted him.

"Sweetpea," he says as he folds in a huge embrace. She doesn't respond. "Oh has my baby had a bad day at the office?"

"No, not a bad day, just a long one and I need to go to the police station on the way home."

"Why?"

Samantha tells him about the visitor. "I could do without it to be honest, but I said I would do it."

"I doubt the police will do much," says Justin. "They will tell you to improve your security, put a chain on the door, something like that."

"We have a chain."

"Then they will tell you to use it. Your dopey housemates shouldn't have just let him in."

"I think he was very convincing." Samantha jumped to the defence of her friends, although she did actually agree with him.

"Whatever. I still think going to the police is a waste of time."

"Well I have to do it. I said I would."

"Phone them."

"They will probably tell me I have to go in."

"I doubt it. Look I thought we could do a spot of shopping for our holiday, then grab a bite to eat."

"Not tonight."

"Yes tonight. It's not long now."

"I …"

Justin is undeterred by her protests and takes hold of her arm, deftly manoeuvring her across the footpath to the kerbside where he hails a cab. They spend a couple of hours shopping and a considerable amount of money. Well, Justin does. He is being incredibly generous but also rather forceful. He pays for the final purchases then suggests they go to a little bistro just off Oxford Street. She nods her agreement, she is rather hungry now. They place their order and while they are waiting she excuses herself and leaves the table. She is gone a little while and when she returns to the table Justin asks if she is alright.

"Yes fine. I called the police, they said I could fill in a form online or go to a station and report it."

"I thought you weren't going to report it."

"I never said that."

"We discussed it." Justin's face belies his anger but his tone of voice reveals it.

"What difference does it make to you?" she asks, surprised by his reaction.

"Nothing. I just think it's a waste of time."

"Well I don't."

Their food arrives and they both tuck in, each seemingly forgetting they are not dining alone. It is Samantha who speaks first. "That was nice. I didn't realise how hungry I was." Justin's reply is barely a grunt.

"What is wrong?" she asks.

"Nothing."

"Clearly there is."

"Leave it."

"Are you still cross because I contacted the police?"

"I'm a little surprised that you don't value my opinion."

"I do. This time, however, I don't agree with you."

"Fine."

Outside the restaurant he hands her the bags that contain what he has bought for her. She is surprised that he is making no attempt to persuade her to go home with him. He kisses her, tells her he will call her tomorrow and walks away. She watches him go, sees him take his phone from his pocket and place it to his ear. She turns and heads toward the tube station.

chapter eight

Gregory re-reads the letter that has been sent to him at the hotel. It is from Rupert and it details the arrangements for Simon's repatriation. He has four days left. Four days in which to discover what happened to his brother. It isn't long enough, of that he is sure, but what can he do. To ask for a postponement will provoke questions and he has no answers; yet. It would also reveal his suspicions, even alert the guilty, especially if they are as Adrian's email suggests 'close at hand'. He has managed to find contact details for the person who broke the story here, so he will try and get hold of him today. He also hopes to pay a visit to the hotel owned by Amit Joshi.

The Indian journalist is based in Amritsar. He is happy to talk to Gregory, either in person or on the phone but he can't come to Delhi. Gregory would rather meet in person but Amritsar is quite a distance; over six hours by car, longer by train, however he could fly there in little over an hour. He googles flights.

Thankfully the flight is a short one thinks Gregory as he lowers his six-foot frame into the very uncomfortable seating. The seats are so close, they barely offer legroom. The flight isn't full but there doesn't appear to be any seats left at the front where he may have been able to stretch out his legs. At least there doesn't appear to be any delays. Before he left the hotel he emailed his plans to Adrian; he thought it prudent to keep someone apprised of his movements. He will text Samantha a little later when it is a decent hour in the U.K. As he walks through the arrivals hall at Amritsar airport he spots his name on a card held aloft by a gentleman even taller than himself. He goes over and introduces himself and follows the man out to a waiting car. They drive a short distance to the man's apartment, where they settle down in the living area to talk.

Arif Chopra is not only the journalist who first told the story of Amit Joshi he was also his friend.

"I mean her friend," he corrects himself.

"How did you feel when you discovered that Amit was a… female?" asked Gregory.

"Upset. Betrayed. I always knew he, she, was different. We all did. Maybe gay, that was fine. But this, this is a lie."

Gregory nodded sympathetically as Arif continued. He talked of the intimidation that Amit had endured from developers who he believes were responsible for setting him up for the attack on the woman.

"So you think it was planned by people who wanted his hotel?"

"I know so. There were many offers, legitimate offers made for the hotel but Amit was never going to sell. Then they tried other tactics, bad publicity, harassing staff and guests. The rape accusation was another part of the plot by them."

"Who are them?" Gregory asks, trying hard to conceal his scepticism regarding Arif's claims.

"A faceless corporation, shrouded in secrecy. I learnt many things about them but never who is actually behind the group. They have another hotel in the south and more properties in other countries. I had been looking into them for quite a while, trying to help my friend. The police took all the information I had gathered."

"That's a shame. I would've liked to have seen that."

"Why is this case so interesting to you?"

Gregory thinks carefully before answering. "It is a fascinating story. For someone to have lived a lie like this for so long, fooling friends and family."

"No family. He... Amit had no family."

"I see. Why do you think she lived as a man? Was she running from something?"

"Or someone, most likely someone. An arranged marriage, abusive family, past criminal activities. There are many things to run from."

"And do you know where she is now? Asked Gregory, although he is pretty certain of the answer.

"No idea. This is a vast country and Amit has proved to be very adept in the art of deception and disguise."

"Thank you for your time," Gregory says as he stands.

"One moment." Arif leaves the room and returns with a memory stick which he gives to Gregory. "This contains all I learnt about the company who wanted to buy the hotel, perhaps it will help you with your quest. I sense you have other reasons to be interested in this case. I do not believe you would fly halfway across the world just to discover more about a cross-dressing Indian."

"I thought you gave it to the police?"

"I did but kept copies. What kind of journalist would I be if I had given everything away?"

"Quite. Thank you."

Gregory refuses Arif's offer of a lift back to the airport. His flight isn't until tomorrow. Tonight he has a reservation at Amit's hotel.

Ɣ

"CAN SOMEONE PLEASE SORT THIS OUT?" Adrian's deep timbre reverberates around the newsroom and an embarrassed hush descends. Some look over at him, although they avoid eye contact, others ignore him completely.

"What is it Adrian?" asks Paul who heard his angry plea from his office.

"The computers, the flickering. It is driving me mad."

"Yes, I agree it is a bit annoying."

"A bit annoying? It has gone way past 'a bit annoying'. I need it to stop."

"Okay, I'll get on to IT myself."

"Now?"

"Right now." Paul placates him, he doesn't want his mood to impact the rest of the team. And it does need sorting, although Adrian is over-reacting. Paul assumes it is because he spends more time at his computer than most.

Adrian continues reading Gregory's latest email. He is impressed when he reads about the memory stick. He says he will upload its contents and forward to Adrian when he is back in Delhi. He also says he is going to the hotel owned by Amit and he has no intention of returning home until he discovers who killed Simon. He can understand that, this is more than a story to Gregory, it's personal. He sends a reply urging him to be careful and to continue sending details of his movements.

A couple of hours later and the IT problem is solved, but it's not good news.

"You mean someone has been intercepting our emails?" Adrian asks.

The IT guy and Paul both nod. Paul's expression is even grimmer than normal.

"Spyware," says the IT guy.

"Spyware?"

"Yes, it's a …"

"I know what bloody spyware is," shouts Adrian. "Don't we have anti-spyware on our system?"

"Oh, we do, but when we had that problem last week, I think that's when our anti-spyware was disabled and …" he lets his voice trail off as he realises neither Paul nor Adrian are listening to him any longer. "I'll leave now," he mumbles apologetically.

"Do we know who is responsible?" Adrian asks Paul once they are alone.

"No, could be a competitor I suppose. Who knows? Not really sure what someone would have to gain from accessing our system. Most likely a kid, simply because he can. Anyway, the flickering screens are no more."

"That's good. Let's hope no-one here has anything in their emails that they wouldn't want made public."

Paul swallows hard and Adrian uses all his self-control to prevent himself from laughing as he steers his wheelchair out of Paul's office; for he is well aware of his colleague's extra-marital activities. He is still chuckling to himself when he reaches his desk where Samantha is waiting for him.

"I've come for an update."

"Nothing much to report at the moment," lies Adrian.

"Oh. Gregory said I should ask you to fill me in."

"You've heard from him?"

"Yes."

He reluctantly brings her up to speed. He tells her the computer issue has been dealt with too.

"Our emails have been read?"

"Possibly, but I shouldn't worry. Unless you have something to hide?"

"Adrian we have plenty to hide."

"Like what?"

"This investigation."

"Oh I think that's a bit of a stretch. No-one knows what we are doing."

"Except maybe those who killed Simon," she whispers. "And the computer problems have only been since Gregory went to India."

"Yes, but…"

"And you told me never trust coincidences."

He stares at her, he did say that didn't he and he was right to say that and she was right to listen. And he has been an idiot. His amusement at Paul's discomfort - who is clearly worried about revelations regarding his extra-curricular activities – has clouded his vision.

Ɣ

The taxi ride to Amit's hotel takes about half an hour. The roads in the city are quite busy, although nowhere near as busy as in Delhi.

When he reaches the hotel he is pleasantly surprised. It genuinely is as its website says, 'an oasis in the city'. It occupies a large plot, the main building encircled by beautiful, well-kept gardens that have been meticulously landscaped. The gardens lead on to a rich and verdant lawn that sits in front of a wooded area which conceals six lodges, available to those who are looking for a quieter stay. Gregory is staying in the main building which was once a haveli. It has an inner courtyard with a fountain at the centre, the gentle sound of running water a pleasant contrast to the hustle and bustle of the city. It is mesmeric, instantly evoking a feeling of peace and tranquillity that transports him somewhere else entirely. Indeed it is a few seconds before he realises that a member of the hotel staff is actually speaking to him.

"Namaste Sir."

"Sorry. Namaste," replies Gregory.

"Are you checking in?"

"Yes I am."

He is directed to the reception area. As he fills in a form he has been handed he casually asks the receptionist if Amit is available.

"Amit is no longer at the hotel."

Gregory glances up but the receptionist has her eyes set on the monitor in front of her. He completes the form and his key is given to a young man who shows him to his room explaining where the restaurant and pool are located on the way. Before he leaves, Gregory tips him and asks if Amit is around.

"Amit is no longer at the hotel."

"Will he be back today? We met a few years back and he said I should look him up if ever I come this way." Gregory deliberately refers to Amit as 'he' hoping it makes his lie sound more plausible. He is sure the staff have been asked many questions by the police, reporters and curious members of the public.

"Amit is no longer at the hotel," repeats the bellboy as he backs out of the room.

Clearly it isn't going to be easy to garner information from the hotel staff. They have obviously been scripted an answer which they must adhere to. He decides to explore the hotel and have a wander around the grounds; he may locate someone who is willing to talk him, especially if his pockets are laden with rupees.

chapter nine

Adrian and Samantha are sitting together at a table in the corner of Ye Olde Cheshire Cheese pub on Fleet Street. He claims it is London's best pub as they serve real ale, do great fish and chips and he can get his wheelchair through the door without the usual struggles. He wishes it didn't attract quite so many tourists though.

Samantha sips her white wine and shakes her head when Adrian asks if she has heard from Gregory yet.

"Me neither. But then I wasn't expecting to hear from him until he gets back to Delhi so I don't think there is any reason to worry."

"I suppose not. I just thought he would have responded when I told him no more emails."

Adrian thought so too, but he doesn't tell her this.

"You did give him that alternate email address?"

"I did."

"Good."

An uneasy pause is ended when she takes her notebook from her bag and suggests they look at what they know so far. She has compiled a detailed biography of Rupert Appleby-Jones, which includes associates, friends and family members and has also listed places he has visited in the last six months. Adrian is mightily impressed, although he knows much of the information will be superfluous. Her notes about Amit Joshi are left wanting by comparison. For his part, he has been looking at cases presided over by Rupert's Great Uncle but for now it is just a list of names which on the face it have no relevance, but they are worth noting in case they crop up later.

"We don't have much," she says despondently.

"I think we need to see what is on the memory stick and hear what Gregory learns at Amit's hotel," he responds. "This was never going to be easy."

"Perhaps we need more help."

"From who?"

"We could tell Paul."

"Paul won't sanction this. And he will be pissed when he learns we have been spending time on it. No. We tell no-one until there is something to tell."

"Okay. Then I suppose we just have to wait."

Y

Gregory is relieved to discover that bribery is still recognised by some as an acceptable way to earn money. The person whose tongue became considerably looser at the sight of a few rupees was one of the gardeners.

"No-one asks what I know. They speak to my boss, but not me. Out here, we see it all. No-one sees us though, we are invisible."

"What do you mean?" Gregory asks.

"We work and you don't notice us, so you walk through the grounds talking about your business. Your private business. And we hear. Sometimes it means nothing, but sometimes it means everything."

"So what have you heard lately?"

The gardener raises his hand slightly and rubs his fingers together. Gregory extracts some more crumbled notes from his pocket and hands them over.

"Well Mr Amit, he was a good man, although he wasn't even a man." The gardener laughs at himself. "I have to call him he, that's how I knew him. He was a good boss, fair and decent. Not many like that. He was funny too and kind. He was helping me with my English."

"You knew him well then?"

"Better than most. I looked after his garden and house too. Although that was a private arrangement because he helped me."

"Where is his… her…, where is the house?"

"Here, in the grounds. Amit lived in one of the lodges. I'll show you."

Gregory follows him. They veer off the path and through a small pocket of trees beyond which is a wooden cabin. It is smaller than Gregory expected it to be, a little shabby looking. The gardener as if reading his mind tells him it was due to be painted.

"Does anyone live in it now?"

"No."

"What will happen to it?"

The gardener shrugs. "We don't know what will happen to any of it." He sweeps his arm through the air indicating all that is around them.

"Someone must know," suggests Gregory.

"Maybe. For now we carry on. Amit could come back everything is still here. I hope he comes back, but maybe they wear him down."

"Who?"

"Those who want to have the hotel. They try many times to persuade him to sell. He always said no."

Gregory points at the cabin and asks if he can go inside. The man rubs his fingers together again and gives a gap-toothed smile as Gregory hands over some more rupees.

"It is not very tidy; the police made a mess."

As the door opens the cabin emits a stale, fusty smell. It badly needs ventilating. The kitchen and living area all occupy one space, a door leads off to the bedroom and bathroom. It is a mess. It has been searched thoroughly. Gregory notices a picture on the wall is not straight. He can't abide a wonky picture. He has previously had to straighten pictures at dinner parties and restaurants, even his doctor's surgery once. As he straightens this picture the gardener tells him it is a painting of the city of Jodhpur.

"It is where Amit comes from."

"I see. And could he, I mean she, have gone back there?"

"Maybe, but probably not."

"Why do you say that?"

"There was nothing to go back for."

"Did anyone ever visit?"

"Not really. Nisha used to come."

"Where might I find this Nisha?"

"Now, I think Gujarat."

"Is that far?"

"Yes very far." The gardener laughs. "And Gujarat is a large state. I don't know where Nisha is. The others may know."

"Others?"

"The Hijra."

The two men are alerted by a sound outside. The gardener looks worried and puts his finger to his lips and waves at Gregory to move away from the window. After a few seconds the gardener exhales deeply - unaware he was even holding his breath – when he realises it is just a colleague. He goes outside and Gregory can hear the two men talking, in Hindi, so he is unable to understand what passes between them. The gardener comes back inside and tells him he must leave now. He asks about the Hijra. The gardener tells him he will find them at the temple.

Gregory heads back to the main hotel building intent on visiting 'the hijra' at the temple but first he needs to find out who they are. It is a term he has not come across before. He assumes it is a religious group or sect if they are located at the temple. Which temple? The gardener did not say. He is aware of the Golden Temple of Amritsar, but something tells him it is not that one. As he walks through the lobby on the way back to his room, he passes a familiar face but is unable to say why it is familiar and looks back over his shoulder as he steps into the lift in order to get a second look but the man has gone.

In his room he types in Hijra. The search results are surprising and not what he expects. Hijra refers to India's transgender population; although transgender is a seldom used term in India. There are many terms used to define this group, but hijra is the most common. The Hijras have a history that can be traced back many hundreds of years. They often live in distinct communities and in April 2014 the Supreme Court of India recognised them as the third sex. Gregory is quite ashamed that his knowledge of India and its people goes way beyond just geographical ignorance. He clearly knows very little of the country his brother loved enough to make it his home.

While he is online Gregory checks his mail. He is surprised not to have anything from Samantha or Adrian, but then realises he has an unread text. The text is from Samantha telling him not to email either her or Adrian via the newspaper. She explains that the system had been hacked into and although the problem has supposedly been fixed they think it's best that they use an alternative email address. Gregory sends a reply, acknowledging what she has said - although he thinks the pair are being a little paranoid – and he tells her he will update them once he is back in Delhi.

ϗ

Samantha is relieved to hear back from him, it's a brief reply, but a reply nonetheless. Her relief though is matched by her disappointment at the lack of new information. She lets Adrian know that she has heard from Gregory, he too is visibly relieved. Sensing her frustration he urges her to be patient and suggests the memory stick may give them a lead. He hopes it will, otherwise he is unsure how they progress further.

Concentrating on her day job is a hard ask and it's not just because she would rather be doing something else. She misses him, which is a surprise. But then Gregory Johnson is a big presence. A presence that fills the newsroom. Not just physically. Often with his supercilious attitude and imperious lording. His empty desk is in her eye-line. Normally if she can't see him she can hear him, but today, nothing. It dawns on her that Gregory Johnson is one of the few people who does talk to her. He may not like her, but he talks to her. And so she misses him.

ϒ

The following day, he learns little from the Hijra, once he locates them. They have a sympathetic spirit and listen to him carefully but none reveal where Nisha has gone. Nor Amit, although it is patently obvious that they know of both. Rupees do little to persuade them to give him more than their blessings. What he does learn, however, is that he is being followed. The familiar face from the hotel lobby is also at the temple. Initially Gregory dismisses his suspicions – not wanting to succumb to paranoia like Samantha and Adrian - until he recalls where he has seen him before. He is 'the tourist' from The Red Fort, and other attractions in Delhi. To be sure he sets off on foot to nowhere in particular, wandering the streets of Amritsar. When he is convinced that the man is indeed following him he realises he may need to take precautions regarding the memory stick and the scant notes he has made based on his chat with the gardener.

Back at the hotel he asks the receptionist if there is a computer he can use. He is directed to a small business suite on the first floor. He has decided to send whatever is on the memory stick to Adrian's alternate email address which he hopes is safe. He has no reason to doubt Adrian. Or Samantha. In fact, they are the only people he can rely upon; sadly they are over 4,000 miles away.

Suddenly he feels quite alone. He shakes his head in an effort to gather his senses; feeling sorry for himself is not an option at the moment. Whoever is following him may well be responsible for Simon's death, so he needs to keep his wits about him. Once the email has gone he sets about taking screenshots of the notes he has on his phone. These he sends to Samantha and when he is done, he collects his few belongings from his hotel room and checks out. Outside the hotel he is directed to a taxi and as he opens the rear door the gardener steps out from behind a large shrub that he is tending to and bids Gregory farewell. They shake hands and as they do the gardener presses a piece of paper into Gregory's hand.

"Have a safe journey Sir."

He looks at the man, his eyes imparting his thanks. In the car he unfolds the piece of paper. Written on it in a spidery scrawl are the words: Bahucharaji, Gujarat. This must be where Nisha has gone. He slides the piece of paper into his pocket and contemplates his next move. He wants to stay here, continue the search for Amit, or travel to Gujarat but he thinks he should return to Delhi to accompany his brother home. He continues chewing over his options as the taxi heads to the airport in a steady stream of traffic that emits a continuous hum. In Delhi the byways and highways reverberate with an unending roar.

A glance out of the window alerts him to the car which is clearly on a collision course with the taxi. It gives him a precious couple of seconds to brace for the impact. The noise isn't as loud as he anticipated. He had expected a monster wall of sound like you hear in the films. What he got was a dull thud, followed by a harsh scraping sound accompanied by splintering glass. Then an eerie silence before he is wrenched from the car and everything turns black.

chapter ten

The Cheshire Cheese pub has become Samantha and Adrian's meeting place where they freely discuss things without being observed. Today there is no discussion. Samantha has made a decision and she won't be swayed.

"I'm going and that's that."

"Don't be stupid."

"Don't call me stupid."

"I didn't. I said don't be stupid. There is a difference."

"Adrian, we know he is not taking time off because of Simon, no matter what Paul may have been told and he sure as hell is not exploring India. He is missing and God only knows what has happened to him but we have to find out, I have to find out and I have to bring him home."

"Have you thought he may already be…"

"Do not say it. I have thought that, yes. But I can't accept that. I have to find out."

"It takes a while to get a visa."

"No it doesn't. Anyway I've already got one."

"How? When?"

"I got it when Gregory went, just in case."

"I doubt you'll get time off."

"Already have. I was due to go to Barbados next week."

"You think you have it all figured out then?"

"Pretty much."

"It is not safe. Simon is dead, Gregory is …"

"Missing. He is missing and I am going to find him. I have to, this is my fault."

"Leave guilt aside. Where would you even begin?"

"Gujarat."

"Why there?"

"Because Gregory sent me a text when he was en route to the airport for his flight back to Delhi. He said someone at Amit's hotel had told him he would find Nisha there and I should add it to the notes he sent earlier."

"He never got to the airport," says Adrian.

"Are we sure about that?"

"Absolutely. I had someone very reliable access the flight manifests, he did not take the flight he was scheduled to, and he has not been on any flight since."

"Then I reckon I'll find him in Gujarat. He probably decided to visit Nisha himself."

"Then why hasn't he been in touch to tell us that? Eh Samantha, why hasn't he done that?

"I will find him and I will get to the bottom of this whole story. You can keep going through the file that he sent to you. Look deeper. You might have missed something."

He throws her as stern a look as he can muster in an attempt to convey his offence at her last comment. He hasn't missed anything. It might be better if he had. He can't tell her what he has uncovered. She would insist on telling someone else and then she could jeopardise everything. Yet he knows it is impossible to keep her here.

"You'll need to travel light," he says.

"Yes, I know."

"That means not lugging that thing around with you." Adrian nods at her laptop which is in a bag at her feet. "I don't know why you take it everywhere. You have a computer at work and you have a smartphone."

"I keep it with me because I almost lost it recently and I have a lot of stuff on it that is not on my computer at work or my phone."

"That doesn't make sense. How could you almost lose it when it's always with you?"

Adrian sits, open-mouthed as she relays to him the story of the uninvited guest at her house. She clearly hasn't thought to link it to other events. But he is, as soon as she said it was only her room that was targeted. He chooses not to alarm her and keeps his thoughts to himself.

"I'll leave it at my mum's. I'm going there tonight to get what I need and she will take me to the airport."

"I expect you to keep in touch, on a daily basis. You hear me. A daily basis."

ɣ

"Of course I tried to stop her. But let's not forget I'm a middle-aged man in a fuckin' wheelchair. It's up to you now."

ɣ

"Mum, it is work. I have to go. But it's a freelance job, not with the paper which is why I'm doing it during my holiday."

"Is that allowed?"

"Yes. Well kind of. Probably best not to say anything about it."

"Sounds a bit dodgy to me." Maxine pronounces.

"It is not dodgy."

"Then why all the secrecy? Why can't you even tell Mum what it's about?"

"Its fine," says Mum. She can sense the beginning of an argument between the two girls. "What did Justin have to say?"

"Well he wasn't pleased to say the least. I think Justin and I are done. I think we've been done for a while."

"That's a shame. I like him."

"I know. He is a charmer. But to be honest he's a bit of a control freak. And he really isn't that interested in what I do. Although he had a million questions about my trip to India and didn't understand that I couldn't tell him anything."

"Here she goes again, her top-secret mission. This family doesn't need another bloody Walter."

"Maxine, that's enough," shouts Mum.

"What is this Walter thing?" asks Samantha infuriated that her sister is intent on spoiling the evening.

"Walter Mitty."

"And?"

"The book and film character, the daydreamer."

"Yes. I know all that but I don't get your comment."

"It's Dad. Dad is Walter Mitty. He's off investigating this, and that, and saving the world. All in his head though."

Samantha looks from her sister to her Mum and back again. Her Mum's expression is a strange mix of rage, sadness and embarrassment. Maxine's is one of pure malice.

"Is that what you think too?" Samantha asks her mum.

"I ..."

"She doesn't think it, she knows it. Our dad is a useless shit who lives in fantasy land. But you know what, it suits him. Because in his world he doesn't have to hold down a job, he doesn't have to pay his way, he doesn't have to be a husband and he doesn't have to be a father. And you know what you are becoming just like him."

"Mum?" Samantha's eyes implore her mum to say something to counter what Maxine has said.

"When I met your dad, he was a journalist. A good journalist, like you. But then he was away, working, and then something happened."

"What?"

"Something, I think. I don't know what, but it changed him and he was never the same man. Never again the man I married."

"Okay. I understand that, but it doesn't mean what she says is right." Samantha points an accusing finger at Maxine.

"He never gave Mum a penny, just upped and left, no forwarding address nothing."

"That's not entirely true Maxine. He sent money in the beginning."

"He forgot us. He forgot us all."

"He used to write," said Samantha. "I loved his letters and cards."

"All full of nonsense."

"STOP IT, both of you."

The two girls look toward their mum who has her head in her hands.

"Look, have a good trip and keep in touch, let Mum know you're okay. I'm going to bed," says Maxine softly. The two sisters exchange tight-lipped smiles and Maxine gently squeezes Samantha's shoulder as she passes by.

"Take no notice of your sister. She took it hard when your dad went. She was that bit older than you and… well back then she was the one who was closer to him."

"Really? I don't remember."

"You didn't seem to notice that he wasn't here. Not immediately. And then one day when you did ask and I told you he had gone away, well, you just accepted it. You loved the letters though. That was when your relationship with your dad began. Through his words. It wasn't enough for Maxine, she needed actions. She is still like that now, promises and pledges mean nothing to her; she judges people by what they do not what they say."

chapter eleven

India is a revelation to her. Regardless that she has been reading extensively about the country -from the minute the Amit story first came into her consciousness- nothing has quite prepared her for it. In truth, nothing could. First impressions are overwhelming; a slew of sights and sounds astound her. Aromas and scents assail her. And later the tastes seduce her. It is chaos and confusion, that like so many before her, she sees first. However, it becomes obvious that this is a country that should not be defined by this, for soon the chaos is pierced and India's serene beauty filters through. She can think of no single word to describe this glorious country; it is every word. Incredible, vibrant, frenetic, exuberant, astonishing, beautiful, graceful, colourful, humbling, dignified, sparkling. Alive.

She looks like any other tourist, not quite the naïve young backpacker, but a tourist nonetheless. This is exactly what she wants to look like, as she hopes to move freely without revealing her actual purpose. Adrian briefed her on how to blend in, although the term brief is a misnomer. There was nothing brief about his brief, It was a lecture; a long one at that. But, he is a man who has travelled extensively, often facing extreme situations in hostile countries. Therefore she accepts his advice readily. He has printed her an itinerary that adds to her cover. He also suggested that despite a direct flight to Rajkot in Gujarat that she should fly first to Delhi and visit some of the sights.

"Your arrival in India may well be noticed and you could be followed. If for a couple of days you behave as a tourist they may think that's all you are. I have arranged for you to join a group. The guide among them is someone I know and trust. Stay with them for a couple of days. He will then arrange for you to go to Gujarat."

"But I'll be wasting time. Surely it will be better if I fly direct…"

"Samantha, please trust me."

His tone had told her that her protestations were a waste of time and now that she is actually here, she is glad to know that there is someone here she can trust. Adrian's guide is a local man called Gopal. He is hard to age, but Samantha is sure he is considerably younger than Adrian. Very knowledgeable and passionate about his country, he has an easy manner that puts the whole group at ease. He speaks to all but is far more animated if the conversation touches on his favourite subject; cricket. The visits are interesting but as at so many tourist attractions across the world, you must run the gauntlet of beggars to reach them. These people, they stir something in her; especially the children. She watches them playing in the gutter or chasing tourists with palms outstretched. Their poverty so visible; yet the faces they wear are so full of hope. Deep brown eyes and engaging smiles hijack her heart and she wants to help them all. In the end she helps none. At the end of the day Gopal approaches her, he tells her he has booked her flight for the day after tomorrow.

"I have arranged for a friend to meet you at the airport, you will stay with her."

"I can stay at a hotel, it's no problem."

"It is all sorted. My friend's family offer homestays to visitors. It is becoming popular for travellers who want an authentic experience and for you it is a good idea and it is close to the temple that I understand you need to visit."

That evening she goes to dinner with some of the people from her group. A motley crew of people of varying ages, nationalities and considerably different backgrounds. She sits next to an Australian woman who is happy to declare that everything she owns is in her backpack. The woman is at the very least in her late thirties and has never had a regular job, proudly stating she has travelled across every continent, bar Antarctica, working her way around the world. Samantha is mightily impressed, although knows that an itinerant lifestyle like that would not suit her. After dinner she finds time to text Adrian and her Mum. She tells her Mum she is fine. She tells him her plans and is rather pleased that he was unaware of them. She was beginning to wonder if he is arranging her investigation from London.

In bed, sleep is eluding her, despite feeling physically exhausted. Her brain does not want to shut down. The images of today are still fresh; especially the children. The contrasts are so stark. Poverty and squalor side by side with opulence and grandeur.

Never before has she seen this; not on this scale. But maybe that is it, the scale. Everything here is concentrated. She wrestles aside these thoughts and thinks about the coming days and her trip to Gujarat. Excitement and apprehension fill the empty spot in her brain as she tries to formulate a plan of sorts, but it is impossible. She can't foresee what Nisha may be able to tell her; and what if Nisha isn't there. Then what? She pushes aside the negative thoughts. Nisha will be there and lead her to Gregory. And, maybe even to Amit for although her priority is to locate Gregory she does still hope that she can solve the Amit mystery too. In doing this she hopes she will bring the person responsible for Simon's murder to justice. A big ask. But she has to sort this. She started it.

ৼ

Two days later she is met at the airport by Aisha. A very pretty girl, dressed simply in jeans and t-shirt which flatter her considerably. She extends a traditional greeting to Samantha and places a garland of flowers around her neck. The airport is a little way from Aisha's home, but the time passes quickly as the car journey is punctuated by Aisha's well-rehearsed commentary on her hometown. When they arrive she is introduced to other members of the household and then shown to her small but comfortable and light room on the third floor. A sliding glass door leads to a small balcony, too small even for a single chair. Standing on it does however give a wonderful view across the street. The houses all have a distinctive architectural style. All are at least three stories; tall, narrow and deep, many painted in various colours giving them a slightly European feel which is at odds with the hot, dusty street and the people on it. She takes some photographs before freshening up and heading back downstairs.

Aisha's mother offers her tea, which she accepts gladly. It is somewhat sweeter than she is used to, but it is refreshing. As she sips it Aisha's mum asks if her journey has been pleasant and if she is enjoying India.

"Very much so. It is a beautiful country."

"Thank you. You are happy to be traveling alone?"

It takes Samantha a few seconds to realise this is actually a question.

"Sorry. Yes, I erm, actually find it freeing to travel alone." She is regurgitating answers given to her by the Australian lady she met in Delhi.

"I see. And you feel safe?"

"Completely. People have been very kind and helpful."

"That is good. Here is very safe. Some places, in the cities, not always."

Aisha comes into the kitchen and she and her mother converse in their native tongue. She then turns to Samantha and asks if she would like to go out.

"I can show you some interesting things here, we can go to the shops and also plan what you would like to see tomorrow."

She hesitates, she had hoped to go to the temple alone. Her hesitation is noticed by Aisha's mother who interjects.

"Aisha is a proper guide. Mostly it is men who have this job but things are changing. Even here women are starting to do what men do. And she is very good."

"Of course, but I wouldn't want to take up her time."

"Nonsense. This is her job, she is the guide for our guests and you are our guest."

"Then, thank you."

The two young women converse freely as they walk down the street and seem to have much in common. They are the same age, their fathers work away, (Samantha doesn't say this is because her parents are actually divorced), and they both have an inquisitive nature. She has many questions and Aisha is happy to answer them.

"Did you always want to be a tour guide?"

"Not especially. I have always wanted to travel, meet new people and experience different things. Travel is not so easy but by being a guide I meet many interesting people from all over the world. I share with them my knowledge of my country and very often they do the same. It is not the same as actually visiting other countries but it is the next best thing."

"What countries have you visited?" she asks.

"None, yet. As I say it is difficult. It is expensive and I am needed here."

"Do you take holidays?"

"We do. Often as a family, and only in India. North for the mountains. South for the beaches."

"India has so much to offer, I suppose you don't have to go abroad."

"It would be nice, one day." For the first time Aisha's smile falters. "I would settle for being able to work in one of our cities, Delhi or Mumbai."

"You should do it. What's stopping you?"

"Many things. Family, responsibilities."

"Your family would stop you?"

"I would stop me, because my family need me." Aisha's tone becomes suddenly defensive.

"I'm sorry. I didn't mean to…"

"It is fine. It is just our culture is very different. What I do has to be for the good of my family, not just for myself. And my mother would worry if I was in the city. Perhaps when my father returns I may be able to pursue my dream. For now I am needed here." Aisha pauses before continuing. "I think the opposition from my family is borne of fear. The prospect of change can be frightening. And although they don't always support my ideas initially, very often they come round. Take driving for example, my mother did not think it was a good idea and not necessary. I did it anyway and she was not pleased, thought it was a waste of money and unseemly for a young girl to drive. But then, my father had to travel for his work, so when she had to go somewhere I was the only one who could drive her."

"So you proved to her it was a good thing."

"Not really. I think her dislike of buses was greater than her dislike of female drivers," laughs Aisha. "Over time though she has accepted it and now when she talks of it, you would think it were her idea all along."

As the young woman explains her situation, Samantha realises that the commonalities between them are superficial. She was able to take a job and move to London without any consideration for anyone else. She hadn't sought her mum's approval. Didn't need to. Did she? Her sister on the other hand, still lives at home and works locally. Her choice, thinks Samantha. Or was it? Not for the first time something she has learnt in India makes her look at her own life.

Y

Adrian answers his phone, his other phone, gruffly. He knows who it is. Only one person calls this number. A barrage of questions are fired at him, no how are you or other such pleasantries. Yes, thank you very much, I'm fine, thank you for asking, you tosser; of course this he just thinks, he doesn't say it out loud. He answers the questions as best he can and says he will forward what he has discovered based on Gregory's last email. He is about to hang up when a final question is put to him.

"No I haven't heard from her yet. I will let you know as soon as I do. She is supposed to contact me daily. Not that she plays by the rules. I wonder where she gets that from."

chapter twelve

They leave early in the morning as the Bahucharaji Temple is quite some distance away. Although the night has passed, the sun is held behind a veil of mist. As they begin their journey, joining other early risers on the pot-holed street that leads to the main highway, the early morning mist begins to clear and another hot and humid day announces itself. To help pass the time Aisha tells Samantha the history of the temple. Some of the information is hard to process as she is preoccupied with thoughts of Nisha and Gregory but her ears prick up when she hears Aisha mention the Hijra.

"Do the Hijra live at the temple?"

"No. A small community of them live in the town. Mostly the Hijra make pilgrimages to the temple."

She tries but fails to hide her disappointment.

"Are you wanting a blessing from the Hijra?"

"Sorry?"

"A blessing. Some people like to be blessed. I can arrange it."

"No. Actually maybe. Are the ones who offer blessings those that live in the town?"

"I'm sure any of them would bless you, but I will ask one that I know."

"You know some of them?"

"Yes. I come here often and many visitors ask for blessings or photographs. You will have to pay."

"That's fine." She wonders what a blessing from the Hijra entails and hopes it is conducted in private as that may give her the opportunity to ask some questions.

The temple is not one single building, it is a complex consisting of three temples. Entry through a huge gateway reveals the beautiful white buildings, decorated with intricate carvings on their stone walls. The concrete underfoot is inlaid with tiles that form symmetrical patterns and overhead, prayer flags in an array of colours gently sway in the breeze. It is busy, despite still being relatively early. Samantha comments on this and is amazed when Aisha tells her that the temple is often visited by up to 20,000 people daily. In an effort to seem like a regular tourist she busies herself taking photographs and asks questions. They walk around the complex for a few minutes and then Aisha points to a group of women sitting on a low wall at the side of one of the temples explaining that they are the Hijra and she will arrange a blessing. A price is agreed and she receives the blessing. A positive feeling washes over her. Buoyed by this she begins asking questions and initially the group are happy to talk but as her questioning becomes bolder they become more reticent with their answers. The offer of more money is accepted but slowly the group disperse leaving her alone with Aisha, who is looking at her strangely.

"You ask a lot of questions."

"It is for something I'm writing," says Samantha.

"What, exactly?"

"I'm a student."

"Studying what?"

"I'm looking at equal opportunities among minority groups," she says, surprising herself as the lies are flowing quite steadily. "The Hijra have recently been recognised as the third sex in India, it is interesting."

"It is and you should have said so earlier, I can take you to the town where there is a house that is home to the Hijra. They often live together as a community and are led by a guru, an elder Hijra who looks after the younger ones. The elder here, Nisha, she will answer your questions."

She can't believe it. She was beginning to wonder how she would ever find Nisha and now she is being taken to her.

The house is large and white, but the cracked and flaking paint give it a rather decrepit look. A veranda at the front is covered with pots containing jasmine and roses which exude a wonderful scent. They are met at the door by a tall, slender woman wearing a glittering sari and light make-up. She acknowledges Aisha and lets her and Samantha into the house.

Nisha is not as Samantha had expected. For a start she is quite a bit older, although her movement would rival someone much younger. Her heavily lined face however, cannot conceal the advancing years but her delicate features hint at how she would have looked in her youth. She is quietly spoken, polite and unassuming and Samantha's initial thought is that this person cannot help her. Yet, when she speaks, Nisha's words convey a mental agility and alertness that belie her age and she soon realises that this is someone not to be trifled with. This is someone clearly in control. Not for the first time Samantha has made the error of observing stereotypes and letting them inform her opinions.

Aisha was right; Nisha is happy to answer her questions. She tells Samantha about the history of the Hijra and about her own personal journey. She talks a little of the community in which she lives and her travels that finally brought her to Gujarat. She mentions Delhi, Rajasthan and Amritsar. Samantha sees an opportunity to ask more pertinent questions when Amritsar is brought up and at first Nisha continues as she had; answering everything with great detail. But Samantha is too eager to learn more about her time there and this does not go unnoticed and Nisha's responses become shorter: she is clearly more guarded. And then, she suggests they stop for tea. She asks Aisha if she could go to the kitchen to organise this. When she is sure Aisha is no longer able to hear them talking Nisha sits tall in her chair and with great authority asks Samantha some questions.

"Who are you? And what do you really want?"

She looks directly at Nisha but does not answer her; she doesn't know how. The two stare at each other for a few seconds. The weight of silence unsettling them both and Nisha suggests that it is probably time they left.

"Please don't ask me to go. I'm sorry," she pleads.

"Then tell me what you want, the truth."

Her gut instinct is to trust Nisha. She doesn't believe this is a bad person sitting in front of her, yet… she must be careful. She wonders what Adrian would do. And then she knows. He wouldn't lose the only lead he has, that's for sure.

"I'm looking for a friend, he has gone missing."

"And who is this friend?"

She rifles through her backpack and pulls out a photograph of Gregory. Nisha looks at the picture and shakes her head.

"I do not know this man."

"Are you sure? Please look closer." She presses the photo into Nisha's hands. Her desperation is clear.

"I do not know him," repeats Nisha. "But I should like to know why you think I would."

She explains that Gregory came to India following the death of his brother.

"Simon was murdered and now Gregory is missing and…"

"And you think I know something of this, how dare you." Nisha's offence is plain to see. "We are peaceful people. You should go."

Samantha pleads with Nisha to let her stay. She promises to explain, properly, everything. She feels she has nothing to lose and in her heart she is sure that Nisha is no more a murderer than she herself is. She starts at the beginning: the Amit story, Gregory, Simon.

"It is my fault," says Samantha through tears that had been held back for too long.

"Not really," says Nisha consolingly. "You have unfortunately ventured into something involving very dangerous people."

"Why?" she asks. "Why kill Simon? Why kill anyone?"

"Money. Greed. Power," says Nisha. "Always the same. Money, greed and power."

Aisha returns with the tea, surprised to see Samantha in tears she looks at Nisha who motions for her to sit. The three of them drink the sweet, warm liquid which soothes Samantha enough for her to begin questioning Nisha once more.

"You clearly know Amit. Why did she pretend to be a man for so long? And what does it have to do with the people who want her hotel?"

"My hotel."

"What?"

"The hotel belongs to me, well us." Nisha waves her arm to indicate she means those who live alongside her. "Amit ran the hotel for me, and very well too."

"Is that why she lived as a man? Is it easier to be in business as a man?"

"It is much easier as a man, as are many things. But no, that was not the reason. And it is not for me to divulge why. You must ask her that yourself."

"I will. When I find her. Unless you are able to lead me to her?"

"I will see what I can do."

Nisha turns to Aisha, they talk in Hindi. Aisha looks stunned by what she is hearing and turns and stares at Samantha who shrugs apologetically. Nisha stands and bids the two women farewell, not before promising to be in touch soon.

۲

Awkwardness sits between them on the journey home, like an unwelcome passenger. Samantha apologises to Aisha, explaining she had not meant to mislead her but it had been hard to know who to trust. Her apology is accepted - kind of - but it does little to diffuse the tension. Rather than explain further Samantha decides to remain quiet. The quiet speaks to Aisha who eventually concedes that she was right to be cautious.

"I would have done the same thing, but I hope that now you feel you are able to trust me and you will allow me to help you."

"Yes I do and thank you."

"Tell me about Gregory. He is obviously someone who means a lot to you."

"He is just a work colleague."

"Really? You have come a long way for a work colleague." The scepticism in Aisha's voice is something Samantha wants to respond to but Aisha's mobile phone rings before she has a chance.

When the call is over Aisha looks at her.

"It is done. Amit will see you tomorrow."

chapter thirteen

Exiting the highway the sun finally peeps above the horizon. It is another early start. Samantha doesn't mind; she has barely slept anyway with the anticipation. For her, meeting Amit takes her a step closer to finding Gregory and for the first time in weeks she is in a state of looking forward. She accepts that what has been done can't be undone, but now her hope is that a time is approaching when she can put things right. Make amends. Bring Gregory home. And discover what really happened to Simon. In her head she is predicting how today will go, as usual anticipation is breeding expectation; thus her initial excitement is morphing into anxiety.

A glance out of the window reveals the changing landscape, the surrounding area much drier and dustier than before, if that is possible. She remarks on this to Aisha, who explains that this part of India is quite arid and the sun brutal, even when the rain comes it offers little respite. From drought to earthquakes, this part of the world often has to respond to the extraordinary power of nature.

As they drive on, the road becomes busier. The swathes of dusty land, barren and lifeless apart from the odd lone cow or tree, miraculously clinging to life, are joined by badly erected stalls offering refreshments and souvenirs. Women and children sit on the kerbside while men hawk their wares. Samantha spots a small stone temple beneath a banyan tree, and later another and another. The stalls and tents and people and temples keep appearing at regular intervals like a video being played on a loop. And then, very suddenly Aisha turns the car sharply to the left into a much narrower road, more like a lane which very quickly stutters and stammers before disappearing entirely. Samantha looks across at Aisha who is removing her seat belt.

"Now we walk," she says.

She removes her seat belt and gets out of the car, following Aisha along a barely visible footpath. The ground underfoot begins to feel slightly softer and the vegetation becomes larger and lusher. A short incline means Samantha is unable to see what is ahead, but once she reaches the brow of the hill the view that opens before her is simultaneously breath-taking and utterly surprising.

An oasis of blue and green. The shimmering surface of the water along with the clear blue sky above and the variegated colours of the bankside vegetation, is quite simply, beautiful. Aisha noticing Samantha's expression allows herself a smile. She is so very proud of her country and all it has to offer and very much enjoys the look of wonder that it so often evokes. She explains that although India has many natural lakes this one was actually manmade several centuries ago.

"It is amazing and so unexpected."

"Yes it is. And a lovely place for a meeting too."

"We are meeting Amit here?"

"We are. We need to walk a little further yet, over there." She points at a small thicket and indicates the building just beyond it, which is yet another temple.

The temple - although relatively small in size compared to others – is quite spectacular. Indian temples all seem to exude grace and beauty, but this one's existing charm is magnified by its beautiful surroundings. The still surface of the lake is like a giant mirror and the sun reflects off of it creating dazzling patterns all around. The water and light and pristine white marble have a kaleidoscopic effect which is simply jaw-dropping. The temple and its surroundings are a perfect blend of history and nature. Inside, the walls are adorned with intricate carvings and drawings which Samantha would ordinarily take time to study, but she is mindful she is here for another purpose.

It is much cooler inside and Samantha stands still for a moment trying to absorb the cool, fresher, unheated air. Aisha goes past her and stands in front of one of the statues, where, a few seconds later she is joined by a tall, slender woman wearing a light purple sari, a scarf in the same delicate purple covers her head. The two women stand side by side facing the statue; their backs are toward Samantha. Slight movements suggest that the two women are talking to each other. Samantha watches and waits, uncertain whether to approach them and just as she decides to venture closer they move towards a bench and sit down next to each other. They are still looking away from her. What feels like an age, (but in reality is probably less than a minute), passes by, and then Aisha stands and beckons her over. She motions for her to sit in her place.

"I hear you have been looking for me," says the woman as Samantha sits.

"Amit?" she asks.

"Not anymore. Now I am Mahima."

"It is good to meet you Mahima. And thank you. I understand you are taking a risk seeing me."

"Possibly I am, but Nisha felt you are someone to trust."

"I am and I hope I can help you… but first I am here to ask you for help."

"Yes Nisha explained you are looking for a friend. Although, I don't see how I can help."

Samantha repeats her story and Mahima listens carefully, but reiterates that she does not know anything that will help.

"Perhaps you could start by telling me your story. Why you pretended to be a man. It could be the people you are running from have my friend and are even responsible for Simon's death too."

"If that is the case, then I think it is too dangerous to speak with you. I should go."

"No please don't." Samantha places her hand on Mahima's arm as she pleads with her to stay. "You are the only lead I have. You really are the only one who can help me."

"I don't know how."

"Tell me who you are running from."

"I have been running. Running and hiding for a long time now, but from who, I don't know."

"You don't know who you are running from?" She is incredulous.

"No, I don't. My pursuer is both faceless and nameless."

"I'm sorry, you must know something. Please tell me. Something or someone must have scared you. Who are you afraid of?"

"I promise you, there was nothing. One day I was told to leave the only home I had known. I was very young and was sent out alone. I was told someone was coming for me, but I didn't know who or why, I just knew they must be bad for her to push me out."

"Your mother?"

"I have never known my mother, but it was the person closest to me; she was like a mother, she cared for me and others. My instructions were simple, to run and hide. To conceal myself always. Become invisible. Cast no shadow, she said. I never knew who was coming, why they were coming or what would happen if they found me, but I understood enough to know it would be bad. So I ran and ran and ran and eventually I became Amit."

"And then they found you at the hotel?"

"No."

"Didn't they try to frame you for attacking a woman?" Samantha prompted.

"That was the people who wanted to buy the hotel."

"Yes I know."

"Different people."

"What? This is ridiculous. Are you saying the people who framed you are not those you are running from?"

"Exactly."

"So why are you hiding now?"

"What if the people I ran from saw the story?"

"Is that likely?"

"You did."

"Yes, but…" Samantha has to concede this point, but she is still mightily confused. "How long have you been running from… whatever or whoever?"

"Fourteen years, no fifteen."

"You don't know?"

"No, not exactly. When I was younger, days merged and blended into one another."

"How old are you?"

"Twenty-eight, I think."

"Do you really think you are in danger after all this time?"

"I don't know. That is the problem. I don't think I will ever know."

"So, there are two sets of people who one way or another wish to do you harm?"

"Yes."

"I'm sorry, this is all rather odd," says Samantha.

"Not odd, just a coincidence."

"Someone once told me not to believe in coincidences, and I'm inclined to agree with them."

Someone approaches them, he bends down and whispers in Mahima's ear. Her body tenses.

"It would seem you have brought the danger with you."

"Oh no, I'm so sorry. What should we do?" Samantha looks at Mahima, who appears perfectly calm.

"They will not do anything in here. The temple is a sacred place."

"But they will when we go outside and we can't stay in here forever." Despite looking perfectly calm Samantha's fear is revealed by her voice as it has risen an octave.

"The trick is not to let them see us leave," says Mahima. "Follow me."

Aisha and Samantha follow her. They walk past the offering table and go behind the altar, down a few steps before passing through a small doorway. The wooden door is closed and locked behind them by the same priest who spoke to Mahima earlier. They are in a narrow passageway; so narrow they are only able to get through in single file. The passage is unlit so Mahima uses the light from her phone to navigate their way through. Samantha hopes they are not underground for too long as she is beginning to feel a little claustrophobic and the scratching and scuttling sounds that she can hear tell her that this tunnel is home to some of her least favourite creatures. A minute or so later and the women are ascending a stone staircase.

"This was once a monastery," says Mahima. "Now it is a museum and art gallery."

Samantha blinks and squints as her eyes adjust to the light. "Now what?" she asks.

"Now you should go."

"Go where?"

"Go home Samantha."

"Absolutely not. I am not leaving India without Gregory." Tears sting her eyes, but they are not sad tears, they are angry tears. "I'm not," she repeats.

"I fear your friend may already have met the same fate as his brother and I do not wish that for any of us here."

"You cannot hide forever."

"I have managed so far."

"They will find you. I found you."

Aisha who has been standing patiently, listening to their conversation suddenly interjects. She speaks very fast and Samantha cannot catch what she is saying, then realises she is talking in Hindi and is addressing Mahima. Samantha watches as the conversation between the two becomes more animated. Although unable to understand the words, their body language suggests that the debate is becoming heated. Samantha is mindful that the room they are in is beginning to fill with people and signals for them to keep their voices down. The two women fall silent for a few seconds then Aisha speaks, just one word that Samantha understands.

"Well?"

Mahima nods. She is stony-faced, but has conceded. Samantha wonders what Aisha has said to make her change her mind.

"Come," says Mahima. The three go outside and get into a waiting car.

४

So, as he suspected, he is not the only one following her. These men, however, look far more menacing than he does. What to do now, he wonders. If they make a grab for her he will have to intervene, obviously. There are three of them, two of them positioning themselves by the entrance to the temple, the third is behind the building, presumably covering a rear exit and is now out of sight. He decides the best course of action is to stay put and see what happens. A good deal of time passes; he is used to watching and waiting, surveillance one of his many skills. But he does consider the possibility that she is not going to come out. Maybe she has some sort of sanctuary within the temple walls, sensible if she knows she is being followed. Or perhaps someone has already gone inside and got her or…worse. He dismisses this idea. Of one thing he is sure, these men, whoever they are, will observe the sanctity of the temple and besides it really is far too busy to cause a commotion. The three men have regrouped and are heading back towards him, faces thunderous. He runs to his car and watches as they get into theirs, wondering if they have been called off or come to the same conclusion as him. He has a decision to make, stay here in the hope she is still around or follow these three. He chooses the latter.

૪

Mahima's current home is a house on a busy street in a busy town. Samantha cannot conceal her surprise; she expected something in the middle of nowhere, in a remote location. She tells her she has learnt it is better to hide among people than in isolation.

"You are far less likely to be noticed in a crowd."

She shows them into the sitting room before excusing herself. She says she will return shortly with some tea and then they can begin formulating a plan. Once she has gone Samantha turns to Aisha, she is curious as to how she persuaded Mahima to change her mind.

"I told her to think of the others."

"What others?"

"She said there were others. What if they are still there?"

"You guilt tripped her. That's a bit mean."

"It worked."

Mahima returns with refreshments and once they have all had something to eat and drink they begin to discuss what to do next. "I think it is time to tell us all you can about your life before you became Amit," says Samantha.

"Very well." She takes a deep breath before beginning. "I think I was happy. Well, I don't remember being unhappy, not as a young child. I had everything I needed. We all did. Food and clothes and friends and school and medicines. We never went anywhere, but then we didn't need to."

"Sounds like some sort of commune," suggests Samantha.

"Yes, I suppose it was."

"No family?"

"No. I did not know my mother or father. Mahima, whose name I have taken, she took care of me. And not just me, as I said there were others too. She looked after us all until we were old enough to go to the big house. But I never reached the big house, she sent me away before it was my turn and then, everything I knew was gone."

"What was the big house?"

"It was just where you were sent as you got older. Before going to work."

"Work? What sort of work?"

"I don't know. As I said I never went to the big house. I was sent away and then, for me, everything changed. The only thing I am certain of is that I was in some sort of danger. Mahima would never have made me go otherwise."

Aisha and Samantha exchange a look. They are both forming their own conclusions as to the type of place Mahima was running from.

"What happened next?" Samantha asked. "Once you were out on your own?"

"I will tell you. I will tell you everything, as best I can."

Amit's Story

Noise. New noise. As unfamiliar and disquieting as the forest had first been. The origin was far off but a trace of it was drifting through the air; atop a warm, delicate breeze. It was indeterminable. Nothing at all like the symphony of sounds I had become accustomed to. Although a little afraid, I pressed on. The noise was like a magnet drawing me to it. As the noise grew louder so everywhere became lighter. It is then I realised the trees were disappearing; the vegetation thinning. I stopped, turned and looked behind me. Then I looked ahead and behind and ahead and behind. Several times I did this for I had a decision to make. One more step would take me from the forest and into an unknown. An unknown that was exposed and open. I looked forward again. In front of me lay a field, mostly brown in colour but dappled with the odd smattering of green. Beyond this field is the source of the noise; I knew that. But did I want to go there, should I go there. I was afraid, but then Mahima's words came to me; 'Seek out others. There is safety in numbers.' And I knew what I had to do.

The further I got from the forest, the louder the noise became. I walked for several minutes, then the field split in two, bisected by a dusty track. Another decision to be made, left or right. I went to the right. The track meandered along, following a winding course of zigzags and bends that straightened and widened before joining a much larger road. And it is here I see him, the first person I had seen since leaving; a goat herder with his goats. He paid me no mind as he walked past, stick in hand to control his four-legged companions. I stood still, so engrossed by this spectacle that I did not hear the truck until it passed by. There were men sitting in the back. They looked at me, briefly, as they drove by, but showed no more interest in me than the goat herder had. A motorcycle was next, that too sped past without paying any attention at all. Noise was all around now, still indiscernible, but I could tell that it was not one single sound but an amalgamation of sounds, abundant and insistent. All around me things were altering. There were people and vehicles and animals and buildings. All of which I had seen before, of course, but never on such a scale. Before, the people I saw were mostly the same people and there was a van which sometimes brought more people and there were animals - there was always animals - and buildings, several small ones and the big house. But here, it was different. Many, many people. Many vehicles, some the like of which I had never seen. Animals, not confined by pens but wandering freely, in fields and even on the roads. And the buildings, there were lots, set in rows along the roadside and beyond. But most importantly, there was an energy. I could feel it. Each of my senses was aroused by it. If it were a colour, it would be red. Bright, vivid, vibrant red. I continued walking, with each step I was feeling brighter. The weariness, along with my fear had vanished, replaced by freshness and hope. Could this be the capital, I asked myself. In lessons I had learnt about New Delhi and other cities across India and the world. I had thought that one day I might like to work in a city. Some of the girls did; so I had heard. And here I was.

My newfound optimism was tempered by an uncomfortable, gnawing feeling in my stomach. I stopped and removed my back-pack and looked through it in the hope of finding something edible, but there was nothing left. The small leather pouch that contained a few rupees was all I had to sate my hunger. I knew what money was and understood the concept of using it to get what you need - in theory at least – but I had never done that. My senses were still on high alert, confronted by this new environment, particularly my sense of smell, which was being teased and taunted by the most exquisite aromas. I had not encountered scents like these in what seemed an age. My nose soon established where the aromas emanated from and my legs led me to them without any opposition from the rest of my body. In exchange for a handful of coins a man gave me a paper bag filled with freshly cooked samosas. A large rock on the kerbside looked the perfect spot to eat them, so I sat upon it. My hunger was impatient and did not allow time for the samosas to cool and I almost burnt my mouth in my haste to devour them. They were incredibly delicious, their heat a reminder that it had been quite some time since my last hot meal. While eating, I became oblivious to my surroundings. The rock I was sat on became my world; an island paradise amid the chaos. As I put my hand into the bag to take the last samosa from it, my imaginary world began to shrink and the real world claimed me once more. A glance upwards alerted me to a ring of faces around me. A boy, slightly older than myself, lunged forward and snatched my back-pack. I jumped up and tried to retrieve it from him, the paper bag fell from my grasp and the last samosa landed on the ground. It was quickly scooped up by a rather sad looking unkempt dog, who ran away munching on it as he went. This was the final straw and despite being in a weakened state due to days of walking and under-eating, a well of strength swelled within me. It gave me not only the ability to get back my belongings but also to knock the offending thief clean off of his feet. The boy, clearly shaken, took a few seconds to comprehend what had happened. When he did, his own anger kicked in, but before he could retaliate a hand reached on to his shoulder and he was told to go. The hand belonged to a lady - not unlike Mahima, I thought - who extended it toward me. I was unsure of the lady's motive so I took a step back. This elicited a chuckle from the lady. A soft, gentle chuckle accompanied by an almost toothless grin.

"Who are you? Where is your family?" The lady began asking me lots of questions in quick succession. "Are you alone? No family? What are you doing here? I think you are alone. Maybe you can stay here, with us. A strong lad like you could be useful."

I stood still and silent. I did not know if I should answer or even how I should answer. Again, Mahima's advice returned to me, 'find others'. I had done just that, found others, and they wanted me to stay. The only problem was, they thought I was a boy. The woman called a man over and talked to him, he gave a derisory snort. "There is nothing of him. It will just be another mouth to feed," he said. The woman responded angrily and the man walked away waving a dismissive hand. The woman smiled at me, the gaps between her teeth gave a slightly sinister edge to her smile, but her voice, like her laugh, was gentle.

"You can stay," she said. "What do we call you?" She was waiting for a response but I still could not offer one. "Fine. I am sure you will speak at some point, but for now I will give you a name. You will be Amit."

γ

Every few weeks we were on the move. I longed for the day when we might stay somewhere forever. I was happy enough: glad to be with them, glad to be accepted. And because of that, glad even, to be a boy in their eyes. But the constant travelling, of that I was not so glad. I had hoped never to have to journey far again. It was exhausting, especially because 'as a boy' I was expected to carry a great deal. I never complained - well not out loud, but often in my head - after all I was safe once more. Being a boy was the perfect disguise, they were not looking for a boy.

The nomadic community taught me a great deal. I learnt about the land and the plants and the animals. And skills, so many skills: bartering, begging, building, chopping, making fires, tending livestock. But above all, I learnt how to be a boy. And, actually I began to think that being a boy was the best. A male had a position. A female had a role.

Traversing the Thar Desert was the hardest thing I had to undertake. If you have never been, let me tell you the heat in the glaring desert is oppressive. I could only marvel at how the others in the community coped, the young ones and even the old, especially the old; but to me it was brutal and unrelenting. Of course each step was harder for me as I was tasked with carrying a great deal; like all the boys. At the end of each day relief wrapped around me like a wonderful caress, soothing my aching back and massaging my tired limbs. The respite was far too short, although thankfully the division of labour was generally fair and days of heavy lifting and carrying were interspersed with days of tending the livestock. It seemed to me the longest journey we undertook, and took several days to reach our destination; Jodhpur. I am unsure whether we arrived there by accident or design, but I was nonetheless pleased. Busy and bustling over-crowded cities were where I felt safest. I still do. I learnt there is always somewhere to run to and somewhere to hide, should I need to; unlike the stark, featureless desert.

I adored Jodhpur. Home, once again, was a camp on a roadside intersection. This time on the outskirts of The Blue City. While the older members of the group established their spot and ingratiated themselves with others who lived along that stretch of highway, the younger members were sent out to try and earn a few rupees. The hope was, that there would be rich-pickings as Jodhpur was - indeed is - a popular place for tourists, especially western tourists. Some of us headed toward the old town and the clock tower that stood in the centre of the market place. I stayed with them for a while before deciding to go to the fort. It was a good choice. I was able to sell several of the red and gold thread bracelets that we had made and far more important, to me anyway, I was able to take in the view from The Mehrangarh Fort which sits above the old city. It was without doubt the most stunning view I had ever seen. Blue. Astonishing, vibrant, wonderful, beautiful bright blue. The Blue City is spellbinding. Over the coming days and weeks this became my most favourite place in all of the world. In fact it still is, although it has been a while since I have been there.

૪

No-one questioned why I always chose the fort as my patch. I always brought back more rupees than the rest of them so they let me do as I wished. Besides it was the furthest tourist spot from our camp and none of the others were so keen on walking that far. They did not realise that I had been totally seduced by the magnificence of the fort and the vistas that it offered. Sometimes, once I had earnt enough rupees, I would walk down to the Old City and wander through the narrow passageways. It was a magical labyrinth of azure. Colour was on show everywhere. In addition to the blue hues of the houses, the people too were visions in colour. Women wore glorious saris: orange, yellow, rainbow colours. And the men in their over-sized turbans in wonderful colours drew your eye as much as the ladies did.

However, it seemed my excursions into the old town had not gone unnoticed. A man who lived and worked there had been watching me keenly. He wondered who the young man was, making daily visits to his neighbourhood. Of course he was used to visitors and tourists wandering the streets, but rarely do they revisit so many times and without a clear purpose, like taking photographs. He lived in one of the turquoise houses with his mother, sister and young son. The house was next to a small hotel that he also owned. One afternoon he was sitting at the front of the hotel when he saw me and spoke to me.

"Young man. What is it that brings you back here every day?"

He stood as he asked the question and immediately I felt intimidated. Not that the man's tone was openly aggressive, but the manner of his stance across the narrow walkway suggested he would not let me pass by without first hearing a suitable explanation as to my presence there. I opted for the truth and he listened intently. I learnt it was not the first time he had heard someone wax lyrical about Jodhpur, especially the old town. But it would usually be a guest at his hotel, or a back-packer or other tourist. It was rarely heard from someone who lived there. Although, strictly speaking, I was not a local. He was also impressed by my language, apparently I used words normally favoured by those who have received some sort of formal education and not the wayfarers that pass through the city. The man asked me several more questions: Where are you from? What is your name? Where is your family? I simply responded with questions of my own regarding the area, the blue houses and the fort. "Ah, there are many theories as to why the houses are blue. Some say they are blue to keep them cool, others say chemical dyes were added to the traditional whitewash to help rid the buildings of termites and others say the blue denotes a house belonging to someone from the Brahmin caste. All very good reasons, and maybe all true or maybe not."

I asked him which version he believed.

"I rather like the Brahmin theory as it fits well with my own family history."

This exchange was the first of many conversations between the two of us. We would sit at the front of the hotel, talking and drinking masala chai. The man enjoyed sharing his knowledge with me. At that time his own son was still too young to appreciate some of the things he liked to talk about. But for me, someone who had always had a thirst for learning, it was a joy to be educated once again. As our friendship grew, a mutual trust developed between us and before long he invited me into his home and introduced me to his family. On one of the visits to his home I spotted several books that interested me. He allowed me to read them. The discovery that I was able to read, and read very well astonished him. Despite education being a fundamental right for all children he knew many were still overlooked, especially those like myself who lived in makeshift camps at the edge of the city. During our conversations he probed more into my life prior to arriving in Jodhpur. I told him I did not have parents and I had been taken in by the travellers, contributing to the community by begging and selling trinkets and things that the group make. He asked if I was happy doing that. I said happiness had nothing to do with it.

"What if I told you there was a different way of earning money, a better way. One that may offer you a future even."

I did not think it possible. A future of any kind did not figure at all. Life was lived one day at a time. Earning enough each day to survive the next. The man however had been giving it some thought as he had got to know me better. He needed help at the hotel and believed the answer was sitting in front of him. He offered me a job and a home. I explained that it was not possible. I had an obligation, to those I lived with. Despite my negative response he could see that the idea did actually appeal to me. He thought my loyalty was misguided but he understood. He then tried a different approach, suggesting I work at the hotel but not live there.

"I would give you enough money to satisfy those you live with and extra for yourself to keep. You could return to your erm… home each day as you do now. Nothing much would change, except you would no longer have to beg and plead for your money and you will learn about the hotel and maybe give some thought to the future. There are opportunities to be had here."

४

I liked the man, very much and would have liked nothing more than to stay with him and his family, but it was because I liked him that I knew I could not. You see to him, I was a boy and by accepting his hospitality I felt I would be deceiving him even more than I already was. However, the offer of work I did not feel guilty about accepting. It was a far better way of earning money. More honest, I suppose. And true to his word he did pay me enough to satisfy those I lived with and there was some left over for me. But the greatest thing about working there was what I learnt rather than what I earnt. He taught me everything about running a hotel and I was very happy. I knew one day I would have to leave; it would be time to move on. A decision that was out of my hands, but until then I would glean all I could from my situation.

When the day I feared finally arrived I was beside myself. I did not want to go, and yet, if these people had not taken me in, where would I be. Guilt can be a heavy burden. I sought counsel from Nisha, who lived not far from the hotel. As you know Nisha is from the Hijra community. She lived in a large house with others like her. The house was an amiable place which Nisha ruled over strictly, but fairly. She was quite a few years senior to me but despite the disparity in our age we had become firm friends. She told me that her life path had been dictated to her by circumstance and others until she finally said no and began making her own choices, and that it was time I did the same. My allegiance had already shifted. The man, his hotel and family were more important to me than those I lived with. The travellers had been very good to me and I was grateful to them, I always will be, but I no longer felt beholden to them. So once I understood that I did have a choice, the decision was not a difficult one.

At first I lived in a small room at the hotel. This suited me, but as time went on the man suggested I move in with him and his family, which I did. By this time I had more responsibility at the hotel as he was happy to leave much of the day to day running to me. I was a quick learner and I had impressed him, in spite of my youth. I did not realise at this stage that I was being groomed for more than just hotel management. It was Nisha who revealed to me the man's intentions.

"He is looking for a match for his sister."

I was horrified when I discovered this. Nisha understood my horror, but for the wrong reason, so I explained to her why I could not marry the sister, or any woman. She offered me a place to stay as clearly it was no longer appropriate for me to stay with the man and his family and advised me not to tell him the reason why a marriage was out of the question.

"Just tell him, you are not interested in women. It will be more readily accepted than the revelation that you are a girl who has been deceiving him all this time."

He did accept this, along with my resignation. And so ended another chapter in my life. Staying with Nisha was fine but I did feel awkward living in such close proximity to the man and the hotel, which I missed more than anything. I told Nisha that it was time I moved on. My plan was to try and find a hotel to work at, if possible, although I knew I would not be trusted with the same level of responsibility that I'd had here. It was then that Nisha came up with an even better alternative.

"I will buy a hotel."

This statement caused me to laugh for the first time in some weeks, it seemed so fanciful and far-fetched, but she did not think it funny and then it dawned on me that she was actually being serious.

"I have been considering a move for some time and I have money. Money which I would like to invest for the benefit of all of us here."

I told her a hotel might not be the best investment and her reply was the greatest compliment I have ever received.

"It will be fine Amit, because you will run it. You will be my investment."

ɣ

It didn't take us very long to find the property in Amritsar. It was already a hotel, although it had been closed for some time. The building was in very good condition but the grounds required some care and attention. Nisha was able to negotiate a very good price and before long we were up and running. Business was slow to begin with but soon we began to pick up a regular clientele. Amritsar is home to the Golden Temple, the holiest religious complex of the Sikh religion, attracting pilgrims and tourists alike which was very good for us. It is also the administrative and business capital of Punjab which meant we were well placed for the business traveller. As our reputation grew so did the interest in us, and not just from prospective guests. We received several offers for the hotel, although *it was never up for sale. A couple of the larger hotel chains wanted to add us to their portfolio, another potential buyer was interested in the land we occupied and then of course there were those who, as you know refused to take no for an answer. They tried every trick in the book to force us to sell: smear campaigns, fake guests, posting false reviews. But we didn't budge. We finally thought they had accepted that we were not for sale, only for them to switch tack and go for us personally. Nisha, by now, was tired of it all. She was getting older and could not cope with the personal attacks, so she went to Gujarat. Me, I was determined to stick it out, the hotel was my home after all. And then, well you know what happened next. What they did forced me to reveal who I really was and with that came the threat of being caught by those I had been hiding from for so long.*

chapter fourteen

Mahima weeps. Telling her story, Amit's story, has drained her. It has also brought into stark focus how little she understands and knows of her own life. She does not know her birth name, her age, her parents, or if she has any family at all. What she does know is that she is tired; tired of running and hiding and looking over her shoulder. She is weary and exhausted of constantly looking backwards in fear instead of looking forward with hope. She no longer wants to live her life like this but how to change; and who to trust?

Samantha kneels in front of the weeping woman and takes hold of her hands.

"Let me help you," she whispers.

"How?"

At this moment she has no idea how, but she knows that she must, because she is sure that Gregory's and Mahima's fate are intrinsically linked.

"I have friends in London who know people who will be able to help us and…."

"And I know people here who can help too," Aisha interrupts Samantha whose faltering voice is not conveying confidence.

"Yes," says Samantha firmly. "Between us we will find a way."

ɤ

Adrian is beginning to join the dots. The file that Gregory got from the journalist in Amritsar has been quite helpful. On its own it didn't amount to much, but when added to what Adrian and his man in the field have discovered, well it is dynamite. Front page stuff for sure. He tells himself to calm down, as exciting as this is, he needs no reminding that Gregory is still missing and Samantha is, well, hopefully not in harm's way. He last heard from her two days ago when she relayed to him 'Amit's story', which was interesting, of course it was, but not as explosive as what he now knows. He still can't believe some of the names associated with it. A girl running away from a commune in the jungle is not a headline making story - even if she did live convincingly as a man - but a chain of 'members only hotels' for the rich and powerful that cater for *all* requirements certainly is. Five-star brothels masquerading as legitimate businesses. And it will be a scoop too. As far as he knows this is not a story that is attracting the attention of any of the other dailies.

ɤ

Coming up with a plan, or a strategy of any kind is proving to be an impossible task. Samantha is convinced that what Mahima left, all those years before, is some sort of commune. A commune that has a particular interest in young girls. Mahima left before she was taken to the 'big house', but what was the big house and what happened within its walls? From Mahima's recollections, they have learnt that the girls were moved to the big house when they reached a certain age; around twelve or thirteen, she thinks. Sadly Mahima never saw the girls who had gone to the big house ever again and her understanding was that they were sent out to work. But what sort of work? Samantha and Aisha are beginning to have their suspicions, convinced the commune is the home of a human trafficking operation. And as it involves young girls, it is probably for the purpose of sexual exploitation. This seems the most plausible explanation. Samantha decides to give Adrian a call since he had seemed a bit pre-occupied last time they spoke about Mahima. Now that he'd had a day or two to mull it over she was interested in his take on it.

He answers his phone instantly and barks at her. "Daily. You are supposed to contact me daily."

"And hello to you too," she says sarcastically.

"How are you doing?" he asks, softening his tone.

"I'm good. Now listen. I've been giving this commune theory some thought and I think ..."

"Yes, yes. Forget that for a minute and listen to me. I've been going through what Gregory sent and I've discovered some very interesting things and I can state categorically that this story is about the hotel."

"Story? This is not just a bloody story. It's about Gregory and ..."

"Yes of course, sorry. Bad turn of phrase. What I mean is, the people behind Simon's death and, erm... whatever has happened to Gregory are the people who want the hotel. It is all about the hotel. The commune thing is nothing more than a coincidence."

"I thought we didn't believe in coincidences."

"We don't. But occasionally they do occur. I know who these people are and why they wanted the hotel."

"Why?" asks Samantha.

"Well. In a nutshell. Sex hotels."

"Sex hotels?"

He fills her in, explaining that these hotels are for elite businessmen; the rich and the powerful and are not the sort of hotels that come up on google search or feature on TripAdvisor. They are accessed via a member's only network and at these hotels all needs and requirements are catered for, in house: sex, drugs, anything and everything. Samantha listens to him patiently as he tells her that many prominent names have come up in relation to this, although he doesn't go as far as revealing any of them to her.

She lets him finish before asking a question. One simple question.

"Where do they recruit their staff from?"

"What?"

"I'm wondering where they get their staff from. After all, you can hardly advertise jobs like that at a job centre or employment agency. Where do you suggest they might get their staff from? Girls I'm assuming, lots of girls."

Adrian does not reply and his silence tells her that the penny has dropped. He knows where these girls come from, they are trafficked, of course, probably groomed from a young age. Possibly in some sort of camp or, commune.

"You see Adrian, you were right. There is no such thing as a coincidence." She disconnects the call before he can say anything back to her.

"Shit, shit." Why hadn't he seen this? He has become so absorbed by the idea of bringing down these people, people who use their power and privilege for their own ends and personal gratification, that he has forgotten the human cost. If she is right – and she probably is – and these things are connected then she is definitely in danger. He calls her back but it goes straight to voicemail. He tries again. Same. He sends her a text asking her to send her location and to stay put. He will send someone for her.

chapter fifteen

Are there shades of black? Gregory doesn't think so. Black, surely is a definitive colour. Although, if he remembers rightly, black is not actually a colour, according to his art teacher, it is a shade. Whatever it is, this room that he is in, is it. It is black. The blackest of blacks. He cannot see anything, neither shape nor shade, not a chink of light in the room. He has no idea what day it is, what time it is. Is it morning or night? He is disoriented. Exploration of the room has revealed a bed, of sorts, and a toilet the stench of which makes him glad it is not visible to him. The previous place he was held in had a small skylight allowing the daylight to filter through. Then he was trussed up and put in the back of a van and brought here. He preferred the other room. The light was hope. The black is despair. He considers for a moment if the emotions he assigns to the light and dark are true or driven by stereotypes? Black is bad. White is good. Red is anger. Green is jealousy. Pink for a girl. Blue for a boy. He wished he knew who actually decided that. Especially the last two. He wears rather a lot of pink and he is sure Gloucester Rugby Club have a pink strip. Clearly all nonsense really. Although, he still thinks black is bad. Because to him black represents death.

Footsteps are approaching the cell door. This could be it. There is no more they can do to him now. They can beat him and abuse him all they like, he will not tell them anything. They clearly did not find his phone based on the questions they have been asking, which is a relief. He had but a second to shove it as far down into the back of the rear seat as he could before they dragged him out. A key is put in the lock and the door opens. A faint light seeps through the doorway, barely perceptible, unless like Gregory you have been sitting in the darkest place on earth for several days. Someone takes hold of his arm and marches him along the passageway. His limbs are weak and he is squinting as his eyes adjust to the light. He stumbles as he is roughly pulled up a stone stairway. At the top of the stairs he is handed over to someone else who takes him into another room; a room he has been in before. He is pushed onto a chair in the corner. The man who brought him in here stands guard by the door, staring at him. Gregory leans forward and holds his head in his hands and looking down toward the floor he spots a dark stain at his feet. A reminder of his previous visit here. A couple of minutes pass by and he and the guard are joined by another man who walks over to him and hands him an envelope.

"For you," he says with a smirk that sets off alarm bells in Gregory's head. "Open it."

Reluctantly Gregory does as he is told, lifting the flap of the envelope and peering inside he can see that it contains photographs. He slides them out. They are pictures, several long distance shots of two girls: getting out of a car, walking by a lake, entering a temple. He studies them carefully, then swallows hard. This does not go unnoticed.

"I see you have spotted your girlfriend. She looks well, don't you think? For now."

"Where is she?"

His captor does not respond. Instead he lets the question hover between them while he picks at his teeth with a wooden toothpick.

"Where is she, you bastard? Tell me." Gregory shouts out the question with all the vehemence he can muster, as if that and the added insult will elicit a response.

"I think it is time that you told us what you have done with the file that Mr Chopra gave you."

"I do not know anyone called Mr Chopra."

"Please stop this. We know you visited Mr Chopra. We know he gave you a file. We want the file and the names of those you may have sent it to."

"We? Who is this we?"

"I don't think that is any concern of yours. Just tell me…"

"Oh I think it is. I want to talk to the organ grinder, not the monkey."

"You really are in no position to make demands. I will show you a photograph of Mr Chopra, maybe it will jog your memory, although, I'm afraid he is not looking his best in this picture."

The man reaches into his pocket and takes out another envelope. From inside the envelope he pulls out a photograph and holds it in front of Gregory. The man in the picture has been severely beaten, but it is still clear to see that it is Arif Chopra. His face is covered with blood. Lifeless eyes stare out.

"I don't know this man," says Gregory.

"Fine, have it your way. But be warned, the next photo like this may be of someone you do care about."

ᚷ

When he opted to follow the three men from the temple he had no idea they would drive this far. He hopes they haven't realised they are being followed. If they have they could just be driving randomly in the hope he will get bored or run out of petrol but he doesn't really think that this is the case. He is sure if they knew they had a tail they would have tried to lose him or they would have drawn him down some blind alley or dead end and sorted him out. He is keeping his distance but the roads are getting busier now, worried that he may lose them he overtakes a couple of cars. They are heading into a largely residential area, a quite affluent area where the car he is following pulls into a gated property. He drives past as the gates close and makes a mental note of the house number before parking a bit further down the street. He sends the address to Adrian and tells him to find out who lives there. He gets out of the car and walks back towards the house. Seeing a pathway run between it and the neighbouring property, he walks down it in the hope of gauging how many people are there and also locating a way in. He climbs over a wall and drops down into the rear garden which is large and thankfully very mature, the dense shrubbery giving him cover. When he nears the house an approaching voice brings him to a halt and he sees a man pacing as he talks into his mobile phone. Listening carefully, thanks to a smattering of Hindi, he is able to ascertain that someone is being held in the house and that they intend to use the person as bait to lure out the female reporter. His mouth goes dry. He'll need to act. But how. He has faced many difficult situations during his career, but mostly it has been himself who has been at risk. The last time he tried to help someone it went horribly wrong. He reminds himself he is not an action hero, he is a journalist, even so, he must do something, because if he doesn't it is Samantha who will be in danger.

When the man goes back inside he ventures closer to the house, tying to imagine the inside and where someone against their will might be kept. Slowly he edges forward and when he is as close to the house as he can be without breaking cover he scans everywhere once again and spots something he couldn't see before. At the side of the house are some steps leading to a basement.

Gut instinct tells him he will find their captive in the basement but if he goes in now he will be going in blind. With at least three people in the house, perhaps more, and possibly armed, entering on his own will be suicide. But if he doesn't… He rubs his chin, he always does when he is thinking. Scanning the perimeter again he notices rubbish piled high behind the house. Boxes and bags, some which have split and are leaking their contents onto the ground and close by several canisters resembling oil drums, but much smaller. An idea is forming, although its execution may depend on what is in those canisters. Carefully he goes over to the pile of rubbish, crouching behind it as he reaches for one of the canisters and gives it a shake. It is almost empty so he unscrews the cap and takes a sniff, almost releasing a cheer as he realises it is paraffin. He opens the remaining canisters and pours the residue from each of them over the rubbish then screws up some of the paper and card in amongst the rubbish and feeds it into the top of the containers. Sliding his hand into his pocket he pulls out a matchbook picked up at a restaurant. Although a non-smoker for several years now, he is grateful that his former habit has left him with a fondness for collecting matchbooks. It takes a few strikes to get a match to flicker to life and set fire to the rubbish. The fire takes hold immediately, the flames licking their way through the mound of rubbish and the smoke billowing upwards, fanned by the breeze drifting through an open fanlight. It seems an age before anything happens but then in a space of a few seconds there is a loud bang followed by the beeping of an alarm. The flames are high now and the pile of rubbish crackles and pops as the fire intensifies. He wonders when someone will notice. Suddenly, as though hearing his thoughts, a door opens and two men run towards the fire, shouting at each other without any clear idea what to do. Another bang causes them to step back, but it also lures another man out of the house, the man who was on the phone. He exits via the steps leading to the basement.

This may be his only chance. He breaks cover and runs, heading quickly for the steps, praying he isn't seen, he imagines this is like running the gauntlet. Once inside he moves silently through a series of rooms, trying each door as he passes them, then he stops, dead. Ahead of him is a man standing outside one of the rooms, guarding it, or at least that's what he looks as if he's doing. As he presses himself against the wall trying to formulate a plan the guard turns and spots him.

"Fire, fire," he screams, waving his arms and running toward the guard. "Fire, you must get out, quick go." His panic-stricken delivery coupled with the shrill beeping of the persistent smoke alarm are enough for the guard to sprint upstairs without looking back. Now for the door, he thinks. "Please, don't be locked." One shove and it swings open and he is face to face with Gregory who is looking confused and dishevelled. "Get up now and come with me, quickly. We don't have long."

"What? Who are you?" Gregory asks.

"Your fairy godmother here to rescue you. I hope."

Gregory hesitates for a moment then decides to chance it. They climb another staircase that leads into the house and run to the front door, which by luck is ahead of them.

"Can you run?" he asks Gregory.

"I'll do my best."

"Good man."

On a console table next to the front door he spots some car keys, picks them up and pockets them. Then opens the door and starts running, the released prisoner close behind. Gregory stops by the car parked on the drive.

"Are we not taking this?"

"No, now come on."

They run up the driveway towards the gate. He fumbles in his pocket for the keys and pulls them out pointing a small remote key fob towards the gate and pressing the button. The gates begin to open, slowly. A commotion is building behind them, shouts and … shots.

"Shit," he says. He grabs Gregory and pushes him through the gap in the gate and follows quickly. "This way." As he runs he searches his pocket for his own car keys. Relieved when he finds them. They jump into the car and he starts the engine pulling away swiftly, ignoring the red light at the end of the street and pulling straight across the path of an oncoming lorry. The lorry driver hoots and gesticulates, at the same time swerving violently to avoid them, as he does the rear of the lorry lurches to one side and his overloaded cargo pulls it down onto its side blocking the road.

"God. I feel like I'm in a film," mutters Gregory.

"Yes, it is all a bit surreal." His hands are shaking so he grips the wheel more tightly the adrenaline wearing off slowly.

"So, thanks for rescuing me. That whole thing back there was crazy. Who are you by the way?"

"I'm a friend of Adrian's."

"Oh, right. Is he here?"

"Adrian? Here? You do know Adrian, right, grumpy man in a wheelchair, never ventures out of London."

"Yes, sorry of course. I er… it's just I think Samantha is here and I was hoping he was with her. Do you know Samantha?"

"I do and yes, she is here."

"Oh God. They have a photograph of her."

"Do you know where from?"

"No."

"Think man. Think. Was there anyone else in the photo or a landmark, anything?"

"It was outside a temple of some sort and there was a lake."

Clive exhales deeply. That was where he last saw her and he knows they didn't get her there. "She is safe, for now. But I think we need to let her know as soon as possible that you're okay. Then she can return home."

"Yes, absolutely," agrees Gregory. "What do I call you?"

"What?"

"Your name?"

"Clive."

"I'm Gregory. So, Clive. What's the plan?"

"I want to put some distance between us and the bad guys, then we can find somewhere to stay. For now, you can call Adrian." Clive tosses Gregory his mobile phone.

Y

Samantha's phone keeps ringing. And it isn't just Adrian who is trying to call her, Justin has been calling her for the past hour or so too. She switches her phone so calls go directly to her voicemail since she needs to tell Mahima and Aisha what Adrian has told her. As she begins to talk her phone emits a text alert, then another and another in quick succession. It's Justin, begging her to call him. She can do without this right now but remembers how persistent he can be so knows if she doesn't call him he will keep on and on. She excuses herself and steps outside for a moment.

"Sweetpea."

She cringes at the greeting. She never liked it before and she certainly does not like it now.

"Justin. What do you want?"

"I would have thought that was obvious. You."

"Look, I'm sorry but…"

"Where are you?"

"In India."

"Still? Whereabouts?"

"Gujarat. Justin I have to go and …"

"I just want to talk to you."

"I can't. I haven't time and to be honest I …"

"Alright, maybe later when you're not so busy. Give me your hotel details and I'll call you later."

"I'm not in a hotel. I'm staying with a friend."

"You don't have friends in India."

"I do and I'm going now. Goodbye Justin." She ends the call, wondering what she ever saw in him. She flicks the switch to silent again and turns back to Aisha and Mahima.

Mahima is horrified that the hotel was wanted as nothing more than a glorified brothel. And she is even more appalled when she learns the purpose of the commune in which she spent the early years of her childhood.

"It is not difficult to find a prostitute so why is somewhere like this needed?" asks Aisha innocently.

"There are some men who want it all laid out for them. Powerful men who believe they are somewhat entitled."

"We have to stop them," says Mahima.

"Yes we do. But first we need to find out who they are and where they are."

"And how do you suggest we do that?" Aisha asks.

"We need to find Gregory."

"Easier said than done."

"I think it's easily done," says Samantha. "But what I have in mind is not without risk."

Aisha and Mahima exchange a nervous glance. "Go on then, tell us," says Aisha.

"I'm going to let myself get captured."

"What? No, no way…"

"Hear me out. I will let them take me and I will offer you up Mahima, in exchange for Gregory. Of course we won't actually do that. You two will follow when I am taken and then inform the authorities."

"That is the most ridiculous thing I've ever heard," says Aisha.

"Ridiculous or not I'm doing it because there is simply no other way."

"And what if he is already dead?"

"He isn't."

"You don't know that."

"If you have a better idea, let's hear it."

"How exactly are you going to let them take you? I assume they don't know where we are at the moment otherwise they would be here already."

"Yes," chips in Mahima. "They don't know where we are and we don't know where they are, so this will not work." Her relief is all too visible, which irks Samantha.

"Sorry to disappoint you but I have thought of that and I've got it covered. I will go back to Aisha's car since they are sure to be watching it."

Mahima shakes her head. "Okay, so they take you. How are we supposed to rescue you?"

"You don't. You follow and find out where I'm being held and then get help."

"No."

"With or without you I am doing this. I have to find Gregory. He is here because of me."

"And you are here because of me," adds Mahima. "We could go on like that, but it doesn't help. We need to stop being foolish."

"What we need to do is find out who these people are, because right at this moment there may be young girls sitting in a forest somewhere being prepared for a life as a rich man's plaything. We cannot let that happen."

They know she is right, they have to do something. And right now they are on their own, but her plan is not a good one. Samantha has reservations too, but she also believes they can do this. Women across the world and across history have faced challenges, many far more dangerous than this, and they have succeeded. And those who didn't, well at least they tried.

chapter sixteen

Clive and Gregory have checked into a roadside hotel. It is not the sort of establishment that Gregory would have chosen. 5-star luxury is his natural habitat whereas this place is more akin to a hostel, but as he has no money or means of getting any he doesn't really have a say. Clive senses Gregory's discomfort and it brings a hint of a smirk to his lips.

"I'm guessing you never took a gap year."

"On the contrary," says Gregory. "I did travel extensively following university."

"Really."

"I wasn't a backpacker though so my accommodation was a step or two up from this."

"Of course. Funded by Daddy, no doubt."

Gregory opts not to respond. He has been used to this type of goading most of his adult life and he stopped apologising for being the son of a rich man many years ago. In recent times he has set about forging his own path and is not reliant on the funds available to him via the family trust. Despite this he has continued to be the target for abuse and ridicule, believing sometimes that people have a lower opinion of him than someone at the other end of the spectrum who has opted for a life of crime. Excuses seem to be offered on behalf of that person, somehow justifying their actions, whereas he has led a law-abiding life, hurting no-one intentionally yet is vilified because he comes from money. He will never fully understand human nature. He glances at Clive who is trying to access the hotels Wi-Fi and feels a little sad that this man has already made assumptions about him.

On the third attempt, the password that he has been given is accepted and Clive is able to connect to the internet, searching through local news items to see if there is anything regarding the events earlier. There is nothing, no house fire, no shooting, no truck accident. Although he realises the latter is probably commonplace. He calls Adrian, hopefully he has got in touch with Samantha and told her that Gregory is safe.

"What do you mean she isn't answering her calls?"

"Exactly that. I've called several times and I just get her voicemail. I've sent her messages telling her to call too, but so far, nothing."

"No matter. Tell me where she is staying and we'll go there."

"I can't."

"Why?"

"Because I don't know where she is staying."

"Jesus Adrian. You are meant to be keeping tabs on her."

"Don't start with me. I can only tell you what she tells me and quite frankly that is next to nothing. Although she…"

"Although she what?"

Adrian tells Clive what Samantha had told him and with what he has learnt he warns that it paints a rather unpleasant picture.

"Yes it does. Let me know as soon as you hear from her and make sure you get a bloody address." Clive turns and looks at Gregory.

"You need some new clothes."

Gregory looks down at himself. He is filthy. Mud and dust and grime and sweat and snot and blood and probably even tears have left unsightly stains across his trousers and his shirt. He nods his agreement and follows Clive from their hotel room. Once downstairs Clive asks directions to the shopping district, the man he is asking shakes his head and then beckons for the two men to follow him. Outside the front of the hotel the man whistles loudly, a young boy appears from the side of the hotel acknowledges the man then disappears again. A few seconds later he returns to the front of the hotel in a tuk-tuk. Clive and Gregory get in and the boy delivers them to the local marketplace. Although busy, it is nothing like the market of Chandni Chowk in Delhi. Here it is possible to navigate the streets in a fairly civilised manner and browsing is made much easier. Within half an hour Gregory has acquired a new pair of trousers, a couple of polo t-shirts and some underpants. When Clive asks if there is anything else he needs he asks for some basic toiletries, although what he would really like is whiskey. Clive tells him he has enough toothpaste for the pair of them and then buys him a toothbrush and some deodorant, claiming he never uses the stuff. They hail another tuk-tuk and head back to the hotel. As they walk through the entrance a smell that Gregory recognises but can't place hits him. The lobby area is busier, several young people are sitting around smoking. It is indeed a back-packers hotel.

"Aah smell that," says Clive breathing in deeply as they walk across the lobby to the stairs. "Those were the days."

It is then Gregory realises the familiar scent is marijuana, which is being openly smoked in the hotel. At this moment, in the absence of whiskey, a couple of tokes on a joint would be most welcome. Back in the room Clive suggests he take a shower.

"No offence, but I think you're due for one."

"None taken," laughs Gregory who is finding it hard standing in his own skin at the moment anyway.

"Give me your dirty clothes and I'll pop them downstairs and ask for them to be laundered."

"Will they do that in a place like this?"

"Of course, they are perfectly civilised here you know. Didn't you get things laundered when you were travelling?"

"I did. But I wasn't staying somewhere as basic as this. As you correctly observed, I was no back-packer."

"This may be basic but I guarantee you will enjoy a lovely hot shower, have freshly washed clothes waiting for you in the morning after you have slept like a baby in that bed and tonight you will eat a meal that in terms of taste will rival anything you have ever eaten before. Nothing wrong with this. Cheap and cheerful works for me."

Gregory throws his dirty clothes through the bathroom door then steps into the shower. The water is hot. He hopes it remains so for some time as he feels he has a lot to wash away. He closes his eyes so he is not put off by the tiles edged in mould and the slightly scummy shower screen. The water cascades over him, running down his head and neck, across his back and shoulders, cleansing him of the detritus that has adhered to him since his capture. Physically he is fresh, energised and clean. Emotionally he is stale, exhausted and stained. So it is no surprise when the flow of water from the shower head mixes with his tears. Tears for Simon, first and foremost, but also for Arif and Amit and himself. He does not try to stem his tears, he allows them to come. The tears, he knows, are as necessary as the shower. After several minutes he switches off the water, which is still hot, and steps out of the shower. He dries himself with a towel that is surprisingly soft, despite being a shade of grey rather than the white that it should be, then wraps it around his waist and goes into the bedroom. Clive is laying on the bed nursing a glass of brown liquid; there is another on the bedside cabinet that sits between the two wooden single beds. Gregory hopes it is what he thinks it is.

"Don't know if you're a fan of whiskey. It's my tipple I'm afraid. Either way I reckon a shot of anything alcoholic will do you good."

"Thank you."

Clive goes into the shower and Gregory sits down on the bed and picks up the tumbler of whiskey. He holds the glass by its base and raises it in front of him. Ordinarily he would have disposed of this by now, but today he wants to savour this moment. Never before has he so looked forward to the taste and warmth that he is expecting. He brings the glass towards his nose, searching for a hint of oil; an oily scent is often the mark of a fine whiskey. It has a pleasant buttery scent. Perhaps to the connoisseur in him, not a fine whiskey, but right now it is very fine indeed as it has come to him at precisely the right moment. Before anticipation threatens to overshadow the actual experience Gregory raises the glass to his lips. The warmth plays on his tongue before slipping gently down his throat. He closes his eyes as he swallows, and in an instant he is transported to a better time and place. Whiskey can do that to him; evoke a memory, just as food or music can for others. In reality, it is not a great whiskey. It has a harsh after taste that on any other day would leave him cold, but here today, it is perfect. An antidote to his ills and relief from recent trials. Quite simply it has helped him feel a bit more himself.

He is still holding the now empty glass in front of him when

Clive emerges from the shower.

"You look like you enjoyed that."

"Yes, I did, very much. Thank you."

"You're welcome. It's not the best but in the absence of anything better, it does the job. Are you a whiskey man?"

"I am. Maybe we can get another at dinner."

"Afraid not. Gujarat is a dry state. I have a personal supply."

"Is that allowed?"

"For visitors, yes. If you get the necessary permit."

"And have you?"

"I did, once."

Gregory decides not to ask anymore. Dinner is at the restaurant next door to, but not part of the hotel. Its décor is unappealing and the long tables with bench seats either side put Gregory in mind of his school refectory. He doesn't think the seating arrangement offers much privacy and he and Clive have much to discuss this evening, but it isn't busy and in the end they do not have anyone sitting in close proximity to them. There aren't any menus. Instead there is a very extensive buffet to choose from. Gregory follows Clive and selects much the same as him as his knowledge of Indian cuisine is limited. The first mouthful is astonishing. An abundance of tastes; spicy, rich and creamy. He goes back for seconds and thirds. His appetite restored.

When they finish eating the two men begin discussing events that have brought them together. Gregory relating the story of his abduction and answering Clive's many questions as best he can and the latter in turn telling him what he knows and also what Adrian has discovered. What emerges is, for Gregory a rather unpalatable truth. He is sickened to hear that people of privilege and power are abusing their positions in this way and although Clive claims to not know the names of those involved Gregory is pretty sure that he will. He thinks it most likely that Simon uncovered names that he recognised; why else kill him.

"I am not leaving India until I find out what happened to Simon." He braces himself for opposition from Clive. After all this man put his own life on the line to rescue him but Clive agrees with him.

"I understand completely and actually expected you to say that. I'm happy to help you. I'm quite invested in this myself now."

"Thank you."

"But I hope you agree that we need to get Sammy on a plane home first. Don't need a female around."

Gregory is taken aback by this sexist and completely unnecessary remark. Clive is clearly old school, but even so. Today's social climate makes a comment like that totally unacceptable but, what is more surprising is that Clive referred to Samantha as Sammy. Was that just another way of demeaning her, or does he know her? He can't know her. If he did he would be well aware that she is rather averse to name shortening. However, despite his comments and attitude, Gregory is in agreement with Clive, for he himself would much rather that Samantha was out of harm's way, although for very different reasons.

ᵡ

Gregory wakes from a very good night's sleep, initially feeling a little guilty that he slept so well. He will never casually dismiss budget hotels again as he is unable to fault this one without being particularly pernickety. He looks across at the bed next to his and realises it is empty. Sitting up with a start, he looks about the room. The bathroom door is open and he can see Clive is not in there. He jumps up, slightly alarmed at his absent roommate, pulls on his trousers and reaches for the door handle just as the door comes toward him almost knocking him over.

"Well, if it isn't Sleeping Beauty. Good Morning," says Clive.

"Morning."

"Sleep well?"

"Like a baby," answers Gregory.

"Here, breakfast." He hands him a brown paper bag and a banana. The contents of the bag are warm. "Parathas," says Clive. "Freshly made this morning."

"Thanks." Gregory opens the bag and tears off a piece of the flatbread. It is delicious, although a coffee is what he really requires at the moment. As if reading his mind Clive says they will get a coffee to go from downstairs.

"You sort yourself out, I'm going to call Adrian."

"Won't you wake him? It's still the middle of the night at home."

"It's fine. That man never sleeps."

Gregory continues eating his breakfast while Clive steps outside to make the call. At first all he can hear is Clive's muffled voice, not the words just a soft, muted mumbling, but then he hears all too clearly as Clive begins shouting. He presumes Adrian has told him off for calling so early, or late depending on your perspective. When Clive bursts back into the room he thinks it all rather amusing until the shouts are directed at him and he is told in no uncertain terms to get himself sorted quickly.

"I'll see you at the car. Don't be long." Clive picks up his bag and exits the room without even closing the door behind him.

He does as he is told and gets dressed quickly, hurries downstairs, and as he passes through the lobby a bag is pushed into his arms.

"Your laundry Sir."

He thanks the man and heads outside, wishing it was a coffee the man had given him. Clive is sitting in the car with the engine running and jumps in.

"What's the rush?"

"Adrian hasn't heard from her."

"What? Who? Oh Samantha. I ... but you know where she was staying. Right?"

"Wrong."

"But you were following her."

"And then I came to rescue you."

"But before that. You knew where she was staying."

"She didn't go back."

Gregory's shoulders slump, he is devastated to hear this. He thought he would see her today and then see her safely home. "Do you think they have her? Oh God, she'll be terrified. Alone and terrified."

"She is not alone."

"She's not?"

"No. She is with a girl called Aisha, a travel guide."

"Fine if she is lost. Not much use if she has been abducted," says Gregory sarcastically.

Clive spins round to face him. "You know what, you need to stop thinking you are the only one who is concerned about her."

"Okay, okay." Gregory is surprised at Clive's outburst. "So what do we do?"

"We find them, that's what."

chapter seventeen

Samantha does not feel the same as she did the last time she undertook this journey. Then she was on her way to meet Amit, perhaps a little apprehensive, but mostly excited, expectant, although by the time they had arrived she was more than a bit anxious. This time she is apprehensive from the start. No, more than that, this time she is scared. And no wonder, she is intending to play a game of cat and mouse, with her as the mouse.

At the cost of a few hundred rupees Aisha has arranged for someone to drive Samantha to where they have left the car. The hope is that it will look as though Samantha has hitch-hiked back and Aisha and Mahima will follow on behind at a safe distance.

Her driver is a young man happy to oblige since it is no hardship to him as he has to travel along this road anyway and he is grateful to earn a little money. The turning that goes down to the lake is a little way ahead so she gets him to drop her at the side of the main road. She doesn't want him to inadvertently become part of what she hopes will happen. She crosses the carriageway and starts down the lake road where Aisha's car is parked about halfway down. As she walks along she passes a car with two men inside, both are asleep. She coughs loudly and the man in the passenger seat stirs. She glances back and is sure he sat up straighter when he saw her and nudged the man sitting beside him. She bends down to do her shoelace up giving her an opportunity to look again at the men who are now watching her intently. She quickly sends Aisha a text detailing the car they are in, just in case they grab her before she reaches Aisha's car.

They don't make a grab for her. Has she got it wrong, she wonders? Maybe they have a perfectly legitimate reason for being there so she gets into the car and starts the engine. At the top of the road she looks in her rear-view mirror, she can no longer see the car that the men were in, only a cloud of dust where the car was parked. She indicates left and drives onto the highway and a few seconds later the car with the men in it pulls onto the highway too. She hopes Aisha and Mahima are doing the same.

४

Clive is driving along aimlessly, not knowing where to begin which is very disconcerting. It is unlike him not to have a plan, but his options are limited, if, as he suspects, Samantha has been targeted, where is she being held? Not, in all probability at the same place Gregory was held at. If she has not been caught then where is she? Maybe she has unearthed something that he and Adrian have yet to find. He decides to call Adrian again. He pulls off of the main carriageway and onto a dusty and very uneven part of the road. The car bounces roughly as he hits a pothole before he brings it to a stop. The violent motion threatens to relieve Gregory of his breakfast.

"Why have we stopped here?"

"Because we need a plan and to do that we need to go over everything we know so far. I'm calling Adrian."

Adrian answers quickly. "I told you I would call you if I heard from her. I haven't." He does not sound happy, but then Gregory realises you would never use the word happy to describe Adrian.

"Yes okay. I want to run over things with you. See if there is some detail that might give me an idea where to start looking. I'm going to put you on loudspeaker so Gregory can hear what you're saying too."

"Fine."

Before they begin Gregory asks Clive if he has some paper and something to write with. Clive leans behind him and pulls a notebook and pencil from his beaten up rucksack. Starting at the beginning the three discuss what they know. Clive is amused by Gregory's need to make notes. His scribbling covers several pages; clearly they have gathered a lot of information, however none of it suggests a location for Samantha. Adrian says he is still trying to find out who owns the house that Gregory was being held in and he promises that he will call if he hears anything at all from Samantha.

"I think it would be prudent to get you a mobile phone," says Clive to Gregory. "We'll stop at the next town."

"And a coffee, please. I really will function better with a coffee."

It takes ten minutes to reach the next town. They buy Gregory a pay as you go phone. It is very cheap and looks it. It feels it too. Holding it puts Gregory in mind of the plastic toys you used to get free with comics or in cereal packets. He and Simon would fight over them, which one morning resulted in a box of coco pops being unceremoniously split in two, its contents showering down on the breakfast table. He smiles sadly at the memory as Clive succinctly reminds him that aesthetics are unimportant as long as it does the job. They find a small coffee bar with an extensive tea menu but coffee is either black or white. Gregory opts for white but when it comes it is neither white nor a shade of brown or beige as you might expect. Instead it is a rather striking orange making it resemble something he might have concocted in a chemistry lesson. While supping the strange brew Gregory studies his notes. They have a pretty clear picture of what they are dealing with, but who, eludes them. And more importantly where they might be.

"Can I make a suggestion?" asks Gregory.

"Go ahead."

"I think we should retrace Samantha's movements. Visit the Hijra, find Nisha, according to Adrian she was the one who arranged for Samantha to meet Amit."

"Yes, I agree. It is what I was thinking." Clive is relieved they have some sort of plan. Doing nothing was not an option.

 ৪

Samantha has been driving for fifteen minutes or so and she is still being followed. As they have made no attempt to intercept her she decides it's time to do something different. At the next town she finds somewhere to park, then calls the girls.

"Are you still following?" she asks.

"Yes of course."

"I think I need to provoke them into taking me."

"How will you do that?"

"I'm not entirely sure. Just do not lose sight of me, or them and stay on the line." She gets out of the car, a look behind reveals her pursuers have also parked. With her bag slung on her shoulder and phone to her ear she walks along the street. One of the men follows her on the same side of the street, the other crosses over and observes her from that side. She stops and browses in one the stalls. Brightly coloured rolls of material lay next to each other like a row of sleeping soldiers in full ceremonial regalia. She holds a piece of the cloth between finger and thumb, rubbing it gently as if to assess its quality. The stallholder approaches her but she shakes her head before turning away and walking back the way she has come. As she passes the man tailing her, he nonchalantly glances at his watch so as not to make eye contact. He looks across at his partner on the other side of the street who shrugs his shoulders before turning around himself. Samantha walks past Aisha's car and keeps walking until she reaches the car that the men were in.

"What are you doing?" asks Aisha.

"Exactly what I said. Getting them to take me. I'm hanging up now. Don't lose me." Samantha looks behind her and across the street. They are watching. She tries the car doors, which are locked. They are still watching. With the camera on her phone, she takes photographs of the car. They are no longer watching. They are coming.

૪

The Bahucharaji Temple is busy. It is the busiest place that Clive and Gregory have encountered in Gujarat and they are both wondering how they will spot who they are looking for amongst the crowds. They wander through the mass of people. Understanding now why the man who gave them directions said it is generally better to visit early in the morning, for now the mix of pilgrims and sightseers is at its peak. They press on with their task and before long they spot a group of people they believe may be who they are looking for.

Gregory takes the lead. He greets them politely and asks if there is someone called Nisha among them. A collective shake of their heads says no but Clive does not believe them. He is sure if Nisha isn't here, at least one of them knows where they will find her. He thrusts his hand into his pocket, and pulls out an impressive roll of bank notes. And simply by doing that he has already spotted the one who can be bought. He peels some of the notes from the roll, explaining as he does that they mean nobody any harm.

"We are simply looking for someone, a girl, my, our friend. She came here to see Nisha."

One of them steps forward, takes the money on offer and tells them to wait. They do as they're told, awkwardly attempting to make conversation with the remainder of the group while they wait. Several minutes pass by and Clive is starting to think he may have been ripped off when he spots her returning. She catches his eye and beckons for them to follow. Nisha meets them at the door of her house. She studies Gregory carefully, something about him is familiar. When they explain they are looking for Samantha, Nisha realises that Gregory is the man from the photograph that Samantha had shown her. She invites them in and explains that she has met Samantha.

"She is looking for you," says Nisha pointing at Gregory.

"Yes, we know but as you can see I'm fine and we are keen to find her and take her home."

"I see that, but she believed you were still being held so she and the others have gone to get you."

"By others, you mean Aisha and Amit?" asks Clive.

Nisha nods.

"And have you heard from them?"

"Not today, but I can call. I think they need to know that whatever they are planning is no longer necessary." She takes a mobile phone from the folds of her sari and makes the call. When it is answered she speaks quickly and in Hindi. Her face drains of colour and as her eyes widen it is easy to ascertain that all is not good.

"What is it?" asks Gregory as soon as the phone call is over.

"They have her. Samantha. They have her."

Samantha is told to get into the back of the car. Not roughly, in fact one of her would be captors holds the door open for her and slides in next to her. They head out of the town and back towards the highway. When they reach the main road the man sitting in the back tells her she must either put her head down or travel in the boot. Although she is not happy that this means laying with her head in his lap, she figures it is better than being flung about in the boot. As she lowers her head she shudders as she spots an exchange of lascivious smirks in the mirror between the two men. The man in the back holds her head down firmly. Samantha prays they do not have far to go.

Aisha and Mahima are cautiously following. It is relatively easy on the highway but soon they leave the main road and head into a much quieter area with fewer cars and a higher risk of being spotted. They hang back as much as they dare. At the next intersection the car turns left, they do the same but as they round the corner the car has vanished. With anxious expressions they continue along the road until they spot a concealed driveway.

"We can't risk driving down there," says Mahima. "We need to go on foot now."

They park their car but before they get out Mahima's phone rings and Aisha can tell it is not good news.

"What is it?"

"That was Nisha. She said Gregory is there, with her."

chapter eighteen

"I'm not sure about this," says Mahima in a low voice. "I think we should wait."

Aisha ignores her and marches on purposefully, but keeping

close to the tall trees that line the driveway. Mahima follows reluctantly. She is afraid. A noise behind them forces them to step into the trees. They press themselves against the thick trunks in the hope they will not be noticed. The crunching sound is getting closer, the source is revealed when a black car with tinted windows passes by.

"Aisha please, let's get help. We cannot do this. I cannot do this." She is pleading now.

"Be quiet. Your whining is not helpful." Aisha's response is sharp and tears threaten the back of Mahima's eyes. "There is no time to wait. And I think you underestimate your ability. You escaped from these people when you were only a child. You survived in the jungle. You trekked across the desert. You lived as a man. All of those things took courage. Find that courage once more, for Samantha."

They reach the point where the driveway widens to unveil a large house, rather unattractive and despite its size, lacking in both grandeur and character. The car that passed them is parked outside, alongside the car that brought Samantha here and a white van. Tall trees form a small copse at the side of the property. The women make their way towards it. From their hiding place they are able to see into the house via two ground floor windows, the first offers nothing but an empty room. But the second is a view into a room that is bustling with activity and movement. There are several people, but they cannot make out if one of them is Samantha. A line of people stand to one side, how many, they can't tell as the window is not wide enough to allow them to see the end of the line. They are moving one at a time towards a woman, at least they think it is a woman, they then raise their arms in front of her.

"I think they are being measured," says Aisha. "They are…" she is about to say girls but Mahima's grip on her arm prevents her from finishing her sentence. She turns to look at her, following her stare. A man is leaning on the white van - which she can now see is actually a mini-bus – smoking a cigarette. He is wearing a blue sweatshirt with a motif on the front. "What is it?" she asks while loosening Mahima's fingers from her forearm.

"That top. It's from the big house."

"What do you mean?" Aisha pulls Mahima so she is facing her.

"When you went to the big house you were given a top just like that one." Her lower lip is trembling. "And those who worked at the big house had them too."

Aisha looks at the man who is grinding his cigarette into the gravel with the heel of his boot and then looks at the line of girls in the room. They are all wearing the same colour sweatshirt with some sort of motif on it.

Samantha has been put into a large sitting room. It's over the top opulence fails to exude the glamour and style it is supposed to and instead the room looks gaudy and tacky. Everything is either gold trimmed or draped in velvet, the walls have a metallic sheen, and the furniture is chunky. An outlandishly large chandelier which is probably meant to be the star of the room, looks more like an alien spacecraft than an elegant light fitting. Bored with waiting she decides to explore, but as she opens the door of the room she is greeted by the man whose lap held her head on the way here. He motions for her to go back into the room and although not chained in a dingy cell she is still clearly a prisoner. She has barely sat down when the door is flung open and in walks a tall man, in his fifties, at least, his paunchy midriff hanging over his waistband in a rather undignified fashion.

He is accompanied by the man from the car, her guard.

"I hear you have a proposition for me."

Samantha swallows hard, then explains that she is here to negotiate Gregory's release. The man laughs at this. "I can bring you the person you are looking for," she continues making the man laugh harder. Through his laughter she tells him she is perfectly serious.

"I am sure you are," he says, still laughing.

"I don't see what is so funny. I can bring you the person you are looking for," she repeats.

"But you already have. You are here. We will talk later, now I have some business to attend to. This man here will look after you." The guard nods his agreement. As his boss leaves the room he looks at Samantha, grabs his crotch and delivers her a wink accompanied by a sinister smile.

Aisha knows she is fast and light-footed so when the man opens the door to the mini-bus and leans inside she is aware it is an opportunity, her opportunity. She tells Mahima not to move and before Mahima can even say why she darts out from the thicket of trees, across the drive and is inches from the minibus. The man steps back and as he does Aisha takes hold of the door and with all the strength she can muster slams it against him. A sickening crunch tells her she got him. As he falls to the ground she realises she has got him good; his head has taken all the impact. She removes the vehicle's keys from his hand and signals for Mahima to join her.

"Is he dead?" Mahima asks.

"I don't know, possibly. Probably."

"What now?"

"Do you have your phone?

"Yes. Shall I call the police?"

"No. Not yet. Send our location to Nisha."

"I already have."

"Good. Now we get Samantha."

"How? This place is huge. We will be discovered before we find her."

"I'm going to put the keys in the ignition. We can use this once we have got her," says Aisha.

"But you still haven't said how we will…"

"I know. I'm working on it."

Aisha carefully opens the door of the bus and slots the key into the ignition. Behind the driver's seat is a large hessian bag. Once she registers the contents of the bag, a plan begins to form. She looks around to see if there is anything else that may prove useful and then she spots it. Taped to the underside of the driver's seat is a handgun. Her first instinct is to leave it where it is. But then, she figures, if the driver of the minibus has a gun, chances are those inside the house will have one too. Carefully she peels away the tape and removes it from its hiding place then she takes two sweatshirts from the hessian laundry bag.

"Put this on," she says handing a sweatshirt to Mahima. She takes one for herself and puts it on, then pushes the gun into the waistband of her trousers.

"What is that for?" Mahima is shocked at the sight of the gun.

"Insurance. Right, these tops may help get us in, but we will have a limited amount of time to find Samantha. Ready?" Mahima isn't ready but nods anyway.

Samantha backs into the room. Her eyes dart around the room searching out something that she could use as a weapon. Surely amongst all these artefacts there must be something. A noise outside distracts her from her hunt and she goes towards the door. She tries the handle, this time the door is locked so she bangs it in frustration, then steps back when she hears the lock turn. The door opens slowly and the guard steps into the room.

"What?" he barks.

She's about to reply but sees movement over his shoulder, and he glances behind him. Aisha and Mahima are being ushered along the hallway by a woman. Samantha cannot understand what the woman is saying but her tone suggests she is reprimanding them. Mahima spots Samantha and gives the woman a shove sending her sprawling to the floor, the guard realising something is amiss moves toward the now prone woman, his hand reaching inside his jacket as he bends to see if the woman is alright. Samantha picks up a heavy sculpture and brings it down on to the back of the guard's head, who pitches forward, landing on top of the woman. She pushes him off, but before she can scream Aisha is standing over her with the gun in her hand.

"Let's get out of here," says Mahima.

"Gregory. I need to find Gregory first."

"Samantha, Gregory is fine. Let's go. Now. We will explain on the way." Mahima pulls Samantha along.

"Go and start the minibus," says Aisha, keeping the gun aimed at the woman. They do as they are told and as soon as Aisha hears the engine start she runs to join them. The woman's shouts and screams are loud and as they drive the bus down the driveway men pursue them. A shot is fired, the bullet ricochets off of the rear door. More shots follow, but they don't reach their target.

"Can't you go any faster," shouts Aisha. "They will be getting into their cars and catch us."

"They'll have to change their tyres first," laughs Mahima.

"You didn't."

"I did." Mahima holds up a knife.

"Brilliant"

"What's going on?" asks Samantha looking both elated and terrified.

"We'll tell you, but we need to call the police first. There are a group of girls back there destined for who knows what."

"Look out," shouts Samantha.

The minibus lurches to the side as Mahima pulls hard on the steering wheel to avoid a car heading straight towards her. It goes past at great speed followed by another. The second car is a police car. Seconds later another police car drives toward them, this one stops and officers get out pointing guns towards the women. They get out of the bus and raise their hands, Aisha desperately trying to explain who they are but to no avail. On the street several cars and many police officers are waiting for them, some are armed and their weapons are trained on them. They are roughly flung to the ground and searched. Mahima's knife she used to slash the tires is taken from her. Aisha is glad she left the gun in the bus. Then they are handcuffed and roughly lifted to their feet before being placed in the back of a police van. Again they try to explain themselves but are told in a language they all understand to be quiet.

chapter nineteen

"There was never an assassination plot?"

Gregory shakes his head and then brings the confounded civil servant up to speed. Once Adrian had discovered who owned the properties that Gregory and Samantha were held at, it was clear that persuading the authorities to intervene might prove difficult. An entrepreneur, politician and philanthropist, was not someone people would accept was involved with people trafficking, money laundering and other organised crime.

"We had no alternative. He had many people in his pocket, possibly including high ranking police officers. We had to somehow involve the police before he had time to cover his tracks."

"If what you say is correct Mr Johnson then we have to tread carefully. This could have far-reaching consequences, so it must be handled sensitively."

"Of course. But Samantha and her friends must be freed as a matter of urgency."

"I have no jurisdiction regarding her friends, but regarding Miss Wainwright I will get onto it. However, there is a process to follow."

"Fuck process. You get the three of them released, now. I'm sure neither the British nor Indian government want anything issued to the media regarding recent events. Who knows who else might be implicated?"

"I understand your frustration but really I can't do…"

"Perhaps the contents of this file may persuade you otherwise. I'm heading to the police station where the women are being held. I very much hope to see you there too."

Outside the embassy Clive is waiting. He waves at Gregory as he comes out.

"How did it go?"

"The file will persuade him."

"Good. Get in."

They drive over to the police station. Once there, Gregory opens the car door and goes to get out but Clive doesn't move and the engine is still running.

"Can't you park here?" he asks.

"It's not that. I'm not stopping. I need to get off."

"What? No. You have to come in with me. I know Samantha will want to meet you."

"Gregory I'm sure you realise that what we have uncovered here is just the tip of the iceberg. This goes far deeper and wider than we dare to imagine and before too many of those involved begin to crawl back under their rocks they need exposing."

"And how will you do that?"

"Follow the money. Well, Adrian will do that and I'll pay a visit to some of the individuals whose names we already know."

"You and Adrian are going to work on this?"

"Yes."

"Remind me again. How did you say you know him?"

"I didn't."

"Oh I erm…"

"Look, Adrian and I go way back. And we have worked on many things before."

"Aah I see. You are the unnamed and uncredited reporter who gets him his stories. You do the leg work, he writes it up."

"Don't dismiss Adrian's contribution. There is no one better at following a paper trail and seeing details that many others would disregard and he has fostered many relationships in his time so his address book includes contacts across the world."

"Okay, point taken. I should like to continue working on this too, my brother lost his life over this."

"I get that, but for now you need to ensure Samantha and her friends are freed and you need to get her home. You seem a good sort, I wasn't sure at first but you've proved your worth, but don't fuck with her. She deserves the best."

"Of course. But that's a strange thing to say about someone you don't really know."

"She came all this way putting her life at risk to save you and anyone who does that deserves the best."

"Fair enough Clive. Look, keep in touch and if you need anything please ask. If as you say, we have only scratched the surface, then maybe I can be useful in helping to unearth more, I do have a vested interest and more than anything I despise people who abuse their privilege."

"Me too," says Clive. "Me too."

The two men shake hands and embrace awkwardly before going their separate ways. Gregory watches as he drives off then heads into the police station where he has to join a slow-moving queue. In ten minutes only one person has been seen so his delight is plain to see when he spots the civil servant he was talking to at the embassy earlier.

"I take it you read the file then."

The civil servant gives a solemn nod. His intention is to arrange the immediate release of the three women, although he fears that will not be the end of the matter.

"And I should bloody well hope it isn't," says Gregory.

"Something of this nature and this seriousness cannot be swept under the carpet. We're talking human rights abuses, abuse of power, of public office and God only knows what else. This does not warrant a cover up."

"Even at the risk of destabilising political relationships that have been built up over many years?"

"Even then," spits Gregory. "Political casualties versus human suffering. Which side are you on?"

"You are an educated man. You know how these things work."

"And that makes it right?"

"I'm only a messenger, a foot soldier in the grand scheme of things. I may not like or agree with what I have to do, but I have to do it."

"No, you don't and actually, you will be wasting your time because someone has to be held accountable."

"And they will."

"Maybe a foot soldier, like yourself? No. Not this time, this is too big."

Their debate is interrupted by a police officer who shows them through to an interview room. They are joined there by an official of the Indian government. Much form filling and discussion follows, but when finally all the formalities are completed the three women are released into their custody. Samantha forgets herself as she throws her arms around Gregory. He responds in kind and holds on to her tightly. Through all his imaginings of himself holding her, he never envisaged it like this. A room in a police station in India could not be further from a romantic setting, but it is his here and now. Should he take his chance? He loosens his grip and gently strokes her hair from her face, leans forward and kisses her softly. Her lips part, ever so slightly as she responds.

"I thought you said he was just a friend," says Aisha interrupting the moment.

Gregory and Samantha stare at one another, both

acknowledging silently, that something between them has shifted. The civil servant coughs nervously before informing them that a car is waiting outside to take them to the embassy where they will be debriefed and the necessary travel documents will be arranged. In the back of the car Samantha and Gregory sit next to each other, their fingers discreetly entwined. She asks how he managed to escape.

"I didn't escape. I was rescued. By a friend of Adrian's, no less."

At the embassy the Deputy High Commissioner updates them. To their relief they hear that the girls who were at the house are all safe and one of the arrested men is cooperating and has disclosed the location of the camp at which the girls were held at. The relevant agencies are dealing with that, but as it is an ongoing operation the commissioner cannot say any more about it. The names mentioned in the file are being investigated as a matter of urgency, but again he cannot comment further.

"Are you actually able to tell us anything?" barks Gregory with more than a hint of frustration in his voice.

"I can tell you that Rupert Appleby-Jones has had his diplomatic status revoked and is at present on a UK bound flight where he will be arrested for conspiracy to murder one Simon Johnson."

"Thank you." Gregory sighs deeply at the mention of his brother but is relieved to hear that his murder has not been forgotten. He can't help feeling though that perhaps Appleby-Jones is being made the scapegoat. Ideally he would like all involved to be brought to justice but it seems unlikely that will happen.

"I'm sure it's been a long day. We have arranged accommodation at a hotel tonight and transport and flights for each of you tomorrow to your relevant destinations." The commissioner stands to let them know that the meeting is over. He shakes each of their hands in turn, leaving Gregory till last. "I trust you will exercise discretion with regard to recent events." He holds onto Gregory's hand as he speaks.

"I'm not entirely sure what you mean by that. But if as I suspect you are asking me to keep this quiet I'm afraid I can't do that. The information given to you has already been shared with others. I think it is time to do what is morally right, not politically right."

"The two are not mutually exclusive. There is an overlap."

"Please do not start talking about the greater good."

"Sometimes you need to look at the bigger picture."

"I am. And my picture is one of equality, plain and simple. It is time that the rich and the powerful and the prominent played by the same rules as everyone else."

"A naïve sentiment."

"I don't think so, not anymore."

"These type of people are masters of their game and I fear you will never beat them."

"We will. In time. We will get them all. Old sins cast long shadows."

chapter twenty

Adrian reads over his copy. It is explosive stuff and more importantly exclusive. The shock waves from this story will have many people fearing a knock on their door. Paul's initial reluctance to print the story was soon overturned once he realised how determined Adrian was; and rightly so, for this story needs to be told. And when Samantha and Gregory return it can be updated with first-hand accounts of their experience. Clive has surpassed himself too, the additional information he has garnered along with photographic evidence will keep this story running for quite some time. At times like this he can almost forgive him. Almost. For he would still rather be out there, in the thick of it. He can't achieve the same excitement and adrenaline rush from desktop research alone, no matter how clever and ingenious some of his methods are and he misses the danger: the risk-taking, the chases, the unpredictability. His safe, risk-averse, static life bores him. And makes him grumpy.

The accident was, well just that, an accident caused by neither design nor intention. Adrian knows that, but there must always be someone to blame; that he knows too. They were going too fast, unnecessarily fast. They were not being chased nor were they chasing. They were not late. There was no reason for the speed, save bravado. Adrian always had him down as a bit of show off, he liked to brag, was prone to exaggeration and of course he was angry. Maybe justifiably angry, he felt let down, his friend wasn't listening to him. He thought he was listening to her and he was beginning to wonder, was it just listening. Adrian told him to slow down, on more than one occasion. He was always telling him to slow down. But on that day, he didn't listen. In fact he responded to the slow down plea with extra pressure on the accelerator pedal. The two of them had been bickering all morning, sniping and throwing insults at one another and dinner the previous evening had seen their biggest quarrel yet. The subject of which was Clive's wife. Adrian hated how Clive treated her, how he spoke to her and of her, the casual disregard he displayed for her opinions and feelings. And now he wanted sympathy from him. Well that's not what he got. He got a lecture. Adrian had observed their relationship from the day Clive plucked up the courage to ask her out and he hadn't. When romance blossomed, he silently accepted it. When marriage beckoned he was there to support it. He was the best man on what was for him the worst day; a day on which he would have swapped places with Clive in a heartbeat. So he settled for admiring from afar and consoled himself with the fact that the two people he loved most in this world were very happy. At times, being in close proximity was torturous, but he hid his heartbreak and was the best friend he could be, delighting in their joy and sharing their triumphs. Until, the marriage started floundering.

That changed things. Then he had to speak up. He told him his indifference and reluctance to talk to her was not fair. Expecting her to understand the long absences was not fair. Not loving her as she deserved was not fair. To Adrian she was perfect, so when his best friend criticised her it was hard to hear. Unkindly and unfairly he imagined all the fault lay with Clive. The time he spent chasing a story was wasted time; he should have been at home with his wife and family. This resentment smouldered beneath the surface until, that day, fuelled by Clive's self-pity it ignited. Instead of offering advice when his counsel was sought, he berated and lambasted. He let down the man who was like a brother to him. But love was to blame. It makes the rational, irrational, the happy, unhappy and the right, wrong. Their worst argument, full of accusations and recriminations, was not resolved and the bitterness and tension followed them into the next day. Slow down, he shouted, one time too many. Clive's resentment showed its hand and they travelled faster. As the speed increased the shouting got louder and louder and louder and then the child…

Clive wrenched the steering wheel to the right, pulling it down as hard as he could. They left the road and were bouncing along rough terrain which rather than slowing them down was propelling them along and then they tipped forward and the bang silenced them both. Initially it was Clive who appeared to have taken the brunt of the impact. He was bloodied and broken and his pain was immense. The steering wheel had smashed into his chest, cracking several ribs. Blood poured from head and nose and mouth. An arm was twisted at an irregular angle. Adrian was calm. Apart from a slight metallic taste in his mouth, the result of a dislodged tooth piercing his upper lip, he felt nothing. He said he would go for help, but when he tried to move his lower limbs failed to cooperate with his brain. No response, no feeling, no movement. Something was very wrong.

chapter twenty-one

Dinner at the hotel is a somewhat muted affair. The drama of the past few days has taken its toll and the four are spent forces. The sombre tone isn't helped by Aisha and Mahima's concern that they are hampering a reunion, and Gregory wonders if he is surplus to requirements as the three women have become quite a tight knit unit. No surprise really, they had to learn to trust one another very quickly. The evening is pleasant enough, but they are all a little pre-occupied, although none realise they are sharing the same thought. What now? Must they all step back into the lives they had before. Can they? Recent events will of course leave an indelible mark on each of them.

Aisha is thinking of home. She wants to go home, for now. Her sights have always been set on greater things. The city calls her, other countries call her. And she is capable of answering the call. Her Mother has always been opposed to her venturing farther away. She wants many things for her daughter, but hopes they can be achieved within the confines of the traditional values and tenets that she abides by and also within the confines of the family home. But there is a change in Aisha; a change that will see her challenge the expectations of her family. A family she loves and respects, so she does not wish to cause them embarrassment, but she will make them see that she must be allowed to live her life. Her mother will be the one. She will create obstacles, out of love and concern. And ignorance, for her own life has been relatively sheltered and much of it preordained. Aisha wants something different, she needs to fly and cannot do that if her wings are clipped by convention or duty. A move to the city would be a start. Delhi perhaps, to begin with.

Mahima is contemplating a life without anonymity. A life as herself. Something that due to circumstance has eluded her thus far. All her adult life and a huge part of her childhood were spent living as someone else but now it is time to be herself; she wants to be. Although it is probably more dangerous now than at any other time. There are people who will see her as the architect of their downfall. Some are in custody, many are not. The latter she must be wary of but she will not hide from them, she will hide no longer. She will meet them head on, fight them when she has to. They must be brought to account and she will see it done, anything less would be iniquitous. The young girls that went before and after her deserve justice.

Gregory glances across the table at Samantha. Her eyes are cast down toward her plate, lost in thought. What now for them? They have been brought together by unusual circumstances. A roller coaster of high drama and emotions has bonded them but is it sustainable. He hopes with every fibre in his body that it is but in this moment in time he is still uncertain. When he left London he had her sympathy, nothing more. Now what. Is it love? Is that what brought her here? Or guilt? Or perhaps not him at all; perhaps just the story. They need to talk. Until then though, he will pin his hopes on love.

She can feel him looking at her. Not wanting to meet his gaze she looks down and pushes the last piece of meat around her plate with her fork. Tiredness has reached every corner of her body and sleep will ambush her very soon. She desperately wants this evening to carry on. Tomorrow they will all go their separate ways, except her and Gregory, they return to London together. Then what? Is it possible for them to have a relationship? That sort of relationship. She was sure he disliked her and she disliked him. She had always thought there was a horrible imbalance between them. One that made him look down on her. But now it seems he has feelings for her and surprisingly her for him. Or are they clinging to one another because of everything going on around them.

At the front of the hotel the three women are locked together in an embrace. None wanting to be the first to let go. Gregory is standing nearby, he has bid farewell to Aisha and Mahima but this final goodbye, he is not part of. The disbanding of their trio is hard. In a short period of time a friendship has been sealed. Mutual dependability is generally fostered over a period of time but this alliance, so quickly formed, has had to bypass such conventions. The make or break, life or death situation that they found themselves a part of hastened the process. Knowledge and details of one another that would normally be shared as a friendship grew have been spoken of much sooner. A lifetime condensed into a few days. And yet, as they part company, none are truly aware of the profundity of their meeting.

The driver who is taking Samantha and Gregory to the airport has been waiting patiently, but he signals that it is time to go by opening the car door. He looks toward Gregory for some assistance in getting the women's attention.

"Ladies, it is time to go."

They drop their arms simultaneously, not a dry eye between them. Samantha slides into the car and before the door is closed she calls out. "Come to London, soon." Gregory gets in beside her and the car heads toward the airport. She rests her head on the window; her aimless stare not registering anything. Gregory on the other hand, is alert and paying close attention to the other vehicles around them. He recalls all too well what happened the last time he was en route to an airport.

Check in is straightforward and painless. The documentation provided to them by the embassy sees them breeze through passport control without any questions. The airport is busy, so they make use of the lounge passes they have been given. Away from the hustle and bustle they feel more at ease. There is much to discuss but now is not the time, so Gregory fetches them both coffee and picks up a couple of the complimentary newspapers. Samantha sleeps on and off for much of the flight and Gregory tries to pass the time watching films but his mind is elsewhere. He watches her as she sleeps; cocooned in a blanket held in place by the seatbelt, hair masking one half of her face. Just looking at her fills him with joy. She is his ideal. She is perfect.

At Heathrow they are met by a car and driver arranged by Adrian and as they head into the city Samantha apologises for being a lousy travelling companion.

"I am utterly exhausted."

"It's fine," he says. He ventures further. "We do have a lot to talk about though."

"Yes, indeed."

"Dinner? Tomorrow?"

"That'll be nice. Yes."

"Shall I pick you up about, say 7pm?"

"That might be a little too early. I have some things to do. I'll call you tomorrow and we can meet somewhere."

"Okay." Gregory hides his disappointment. He was hoping to plan a wonderful evening at a swanky restaurant. "Actually no, I'd better call you. I need to get a new phone, mine was lost and I only have this pay as you go thing that Clive bought me."

"Clive?"

"Yes, Adrian's friend. He got me this phone and it's really not great. But then it was only to call him in an emergency when…"

"The man who rescued you was called Clive?"

"Yes."

"You didn't say."

"You didn't ask."

"I'm sure I did. His name was definitely Clive?"

"Yes."

"What did he look like?" demands Samantha.

Gregory gives a vague description he is nonplussed by her

attitude. "Is there something wrong?"

"No. I'm fine."

She clearly isn't. This has distracted her, but something about her demeanour tells him not to pursue it. He hopes whatever it is will not prevent them from going out tomorrow. They turn into her street and Gregory jumps out of the car first, gets her bag from the boot and carries it up the steps to the front door. She takes her bag from him and gives him a peck on the cheek before going inside and closing the door.

chapter twenty-two

Adrian knew this day would come. He had warned him many times but he never quite understood the need for secrecy. Quite frankly it was probably just another way for him to avoid responsibility but if his anonymity and absence were what he wanted, why tell Gregory his real name. It didn't make sense but then very little that Clive Wainwright did ever really made sense.

He can feel her eyes burning into him waiting for a response. There is much he can say, but it isn't up to him. Despite everything that has happened it is not his version of events that she needs to hear.

"Tell me about Clive," she repeats.

"Look Samantha, you have clearly joined the dots. You know exactly who Clive is, therefore it is him you should be talking to."

"I would if I knew how to get hold of him. He contacts me, generally at six monthly intervals, if I'm lucky."

"Then your mother. Talk to her."

"No Adrian. I'm talking to you. Either you explain or you get hold of him right now. I know you can do that." She picks up his phone that is sitting on the table between them and hands it to him. He places it back on the table and reaches into his pocket and pulls out another mobile phone. "You have another phone. Is that just to call him?"

"Not just him." Adrian makes the call but it is unanswered. He doesn't leave a voicemail, preferring a text instead. "I've told him to call you."

"Good. Now tell me about him. How do you know him? Why do you know him? And why don't I know you know him?"

"I have to get back to work."

"Then you had better talk fast."

He lets out an elongated sigh when he realises she is not going to be put off.

We first met at university, through the Students Union, where he was already an established member. He is a year older than me, so was in his second year. I recall him always being quite vocal at the meetings. He made an impression on me from the start. Our courses were similar as were our interests and when he said he worked on the student newspaper I knew it was something that I wanted to get involved with too. That was the first of our partnerships and the beginning of our friendship. Despite him being a year ahead he became my closest friend. Obviously he left university before I did and began working on one of the nationals. When I left I worked on a local paper and did some freelance work. I wanted to work where he did. He wanted to be freelance. He was never much good at being told what to do. And that never changed over the years. Anyway, we knew we worked well together so when he told me about an opportunity where he worked I jumped at it. He got me into trouble on more than one occasion though. He always thought he knew best so often he would disregard what he had been asked to do and go off on a tangent. Some of his writing was rather fanciful. I said to him once maybe fiction was more his bag.

Samantha winces at this as she recalls Justin saying a similar thing to her.

The thing was though, despite his lack of respect for authority, he was often right. He could sense a story. I think it has a lot to do with his inability to trust anyone. He always suspects ulterior motives or hidden agendas. We worked at that paper for a good few years, eventually enjoying a considerable degree of autonomy.

We broke a few high-profile stories in our time. It was when we were out celebrating one night that he met your mother. She was with a group of friends, all nurses as I recall and I think they were celebrating too; maybe a birthday. We were part of a very loud group and at times it seemed as if we were competing with them: to be the loudest, the funniest, to get to the bar. In the end our two groups merged and became one. She stood out among them. Not because she was a great beauty. I mean she was, but not in the classic sense. She was delicate, ethereal, with a dainty air that was at odds with her humour and confidence. And she was a little bit flirty. Her enigmatic and contradictory nature made her a challenge. He was smitten, and I don't think he was the only one, but by the end of the evening it was he who had charmed her. No surprise really; his elaborate tales of derring-do and hopes for the world always impressed the ladies. Nobody else stood a chance. Theirs was a whirlwind romance. Engagement, wedding - I was his best man – and babies followed in quick succession. He had it all and still for some inexplicable reason it wasn't enough. I suppose domesticity lacked excitement. It was then he decided to go freelance, as a foreign correspondent; walking away from a salaried position with benefits just to satisfy his wanderlust or ego. Whatever it was, it certainly was not the best idea when you have responsibilities and people who depend upon you.

I continued to work at the paper for a short while after that but he persuaded me to join him and become a freelancer too. I did, because I missed working with him and because I also craved the excitement but more importantly I thought I could persuade him to visit home a bit more frequently. I knew how much your mum missed him and she was finding things hard. I did manage to convince him to take a *few trips home and it was when he returned from one of those trips that he said things between him and your mum were not so good. I wasn't that sympathetic and we argued and said some unpleasant things and then...*

Adrian's silence is unnerving so Samantha speaks. "You must have resolved your differences, after all you work together now."

"I think you should ask him for the rest of the story."

"No I want you to tell me."

Adrian reluctantly continues. He tells her about the accident, but without too much detail and he explains their current working relationship.

"So you blame Dad for the accident?"

"He was driving."

"But you were arguing, you were both arguing. Some might say that was a distraction."

"Some might," concedes Adrian.

"But not you?"

"Look it hardly matters anymore. We have an amicable relationship now that suits us both."

"It matters to me. I want to get everything straight in my head. Clive, my father is responsible for the accident that put you in that chair."

"Not exactly. The stroke put me in this thing."

"A stroke?"

"Yes. I had a stroke sometime after the accident."

"As a result of the accident?"

"I don't know. Most likely."

"Did your doctor say it was the accident that caused the stroke?"

"No. Not definitively."

"So maybe not Dad's fault then."

"Following the accident I had several operations and then endless physiotherapy. I worked so bloody hard and I got myself back on my feet, literally and then boom… one morning I wake up not feeling so good and the next thing I'm back in hospital, back to square one. I know it was all the stress and anxiety I was under that caused it. That's why I decided I was not going through that again. The stress would have probably finished me off."

"You mean you didn't even try to walk again?"

"Don't you dare lecture me, you hear me. Don't you dare…"

"Oh, don't worry, I shan't waste my time." Samantha stands up to go. "Just one more thing though. My job. Does that have anything to do with you or Dad?"

"Samantha you're good at your job."

"That's not what I asked."

"I'm not answering that question."

"I think you just did." Samantha sweeps out of the door before Adrian has a chance to say anything more to her. Outside she marches along the road at quite a pace and doesn't stop until she has rounded the corner. She leans on the wall and breathes deeply. She has the beginnings of a headache, and no wonder, her head is full, and there is still so much she doesn't understand. The wind purses its lips in her direction, the cold blast of air making her pull up the lapels of her jacket around her neck. She considers going home but with so many questions looking for answers she knows that is not an option. Adrian can tell her no more, she doesn't know where her father is, that leaves only one other person who may be able to cast some light on the situation. Samantha heads towards Liverpool Street. She has been walking for a few minutes when her phone rings. It's not a recognised number. Her thumb hovers above the decline button for a second, but what if it's him, dad. If Adrian has two phones maybe he does too. She accepts the call.

"Hi Samantha. It's Gregory."

"Oh hi."

"I'm back in the 21st century."

"Sorry?"

"I have a new phone."

"Oh yes. That's good."

"So where are you? Still okay for dinner?"

"Oh I… Look I'm sorry, something's came up. I need to go home."

"That's fine. I can pick you up from there later."

"No, I mean home to Woodbridge. I have to speak to my mum."

"Oh I see." His disappointment is audible.

Samantha hates to let him down. In truth she had actually forgotten about their arrangements but she needs to see her mum. Her head is full of her dad at the moment, something Gregory can't help with. "I'm really sorry."

"It's fine. With all that's gone on I can understand you wanting to see your family. Another time."

"Yes, I…" But of course, Gregory has seen her dad recently. Not that he can answer questions about the past but he can tell her how he is, where he is. He may know of future plans. Unlikely but… "Look, I'm heading to Liverpool Street now. We could grab a coffee there while I wait for my train and arrange another day for dinner."

"Yes sure. See you shortly."

She saves the number.

Liverpool Street station is busy for this time of day, the overhead display board tells her why; cancellations. She isn't surprised. Still, it will give her time to have a chat with Gregory. As she approaches the coffee shop she spots him walking toward it from the opposite direction.

"Perfect timing," she says as she reaches him.

They choose a table on the concourse so she can keep an eye on the departure board.

"How long are you going to be in Suffolk for?" he asks.

"I'm coming back tomorrow. I need to get to work. If I don't I fear Adrian will hijack this story completely and make it his own."

"I think he has done that already."

"I understand him writing up what happened in Gujarat. It had to be done quickly but there is a follow-up story which I want to do."

"Good luck with that."

She detects a hint of annoyance in his voice. "I want you to do it with me, of course."

"I'm not going back to work just yet. I have other things to do."

"What could be more important than this story?"

"Simon's funeral."

"Oh God. Gregory I'm sorry. I erm, I, with everything going on…"

"It's fine."

"No it's not. I'm being incredibly insensitive. There are far more important things."

"Ordinarily I would love to work on this with you."

"I know."

"I do wonder how much input you or I will be able to have though. Adrian and his sidekick have already claimed this one. At the most we may be given a credit for assisting."

"That's not going to happen. I found this story."

"The problem is, it is a far bigger story than anyone imagined and Adrian does have a network of people to tap into." "That isn't fair."

"No it's not, but there is not much you or I can do about it. I imagine he and Clive are already looking into others that are involved."

"What's this Clive like then?"

"My rescuer? He's okay. Bit of an oddball, but a good guy."

"Oddball?"

"Not really odd, different. Well different to me."

"So maybe you are the oddball."

"Very likely, in his eyes. In many eyes I shouldn't wonder."

"What did you talk about?"

"Not much really: Adrian, India, whiskey, you." He pauses for a second, just to gauge her reaction at being a subject of conversation. "Actually I got the impression he knew you, but I think it was more that he knew of you, from Adrian I suppose."

"I suppose so. Did he say anything else? Where he was going or what he had been doing."

"Not that I can recall. We really just spoke about what was going on at the time."

"He must have said something."

"Nothing of any significance. If you're trying to find out if he knows anything more than we do, I can't really help. Keeps his cards close to his chest I would say." He can tell she is disappointed in his answer. "I'm sorry I can't say more about him, perhaps you should talk to Adrian."

"I have," snaps Samantha.

"Oh, okay." Gregory is surprised at her tone. "Am I missing something?"

Samantha lowers her head and raises her coffee cup to her lips. "This is good coffee. You should drink yours while it's still hot."

Her crass attempts at changing the subject have not gone unnoticed. "Samantha. What is it?"

"He's my dad. Clive is my dad."

He is gobsmacked, and yet, it makes sense. Clive's concern for her was clear, looking back. Gregory hopes he didn't reveal his affection for Samantha; he thinks he did. That's why Clive gave him a warning, "Shit," is all he can say.

"I don't see much of him. I had no idea he was in India or knew Adrian until you mentioned his name yesterday. I spoke to Adrian earlier, he provided more questions than answers."

"Have you tried calling him? Clive?"

"No point, he never answers my calls. He may reply to a text now and then. I have to wait for him to contact me; that's how it's always been, which is why I'm going to see Mum." Activity behind her causes her to turn around. The departure boards are showing a time and platform for her train. "Time to go."

"I'll walk with you". At the ticket barrier by the platform he takes hold of her hand. "We haven't fixed a dinner date yet."

"I'll call you when I get back." She leans forward allowing their lips to meet. Their kiss is brief, but tender and full of promise.

He turns away, pushing his hands deep into his jacket pockets, feeling a phone in each. He turns back. "Samantha, wait," he shouts, running back to the ticket barrier. She hears him and makes her way back. "Take this," he says pushing the phone he got in India into her hands.

"I have a phone." Her expression is one of confusion.

"Not like this one. This is the phone Clive bought me. It has only one phone number stored in it. His."

chapter twenty-three

Mahima watches everybody. Should someone so much as glance at her, she studies them, trying to determine whether they are friend or foe? In truth, they are neither. Most people she passes are going about their daily business none the wiser as to who she is. But, there may always be that one person who is more interested in her than she would like. More interested in her as a result of recent publicity, that is okay. But, if their interest is more sinister she needs to recognise it instantly.

She is staying with Nisha for a few days. Nisha has always offered a safe space; a sanctuary. And it is with her that she feels most at ease, generally and they have much to discuss, like what to do with the hotel. Mahima does not feel she wants to return there. Now that she has learnt the true nature of her early years and what she was being prepared for she is thankful that she was able to escape but coupled with this is guilt and sadness. Many of her first ever friends and playmates were not so fortunate and what of the first Mahima, she who helped her to flee, whose name she has taken. What happened to her? If her complicity was discovered, no doubt the punishment would have been severe. With that in mind, she knows she must do more with her life.

Her need to right wrongs and stand and be counted worries Nisha, whilst also filling her with immense pride. Her feelings for Mahima go beyond that of friendship, she is like a daughter to her and as much as she wants to support and encourage her to do what she feels she must, she is more concerned with keeping her safe.

"I understand Nisha, of course I do. But I have to do something and I cannot be confined anymore. Besides, if there is someone who wishes to find me and do me harm I'm sure they will."

"But putting yourself in full view will only make it easier for them."

"Perhaps, then again perhaps not. Either way it's a risk I am prepared to take. Too many people in this world are marginalised. You more than most should understand that."

She does, of course. Her whole life she has been denied so many things that others take for granted, on account of being different. Much of her life has seen her relegated to the fringes of society. Viewed as an underclass. And does she not want better for the younger members of her own community. Recent events will give her a platform, her status will be elevated and people will listen. But reprisals are likely.

The requests for interviews are numerous, mostly from news and media outlets, although there are some from dubious organisations and individuals. Separating them into those worth serious consideration and those that should be ignored will be time consuming. Mahima enlists Nisha's help with this task and between them they draw up a list of those worth talking to. They are all based in India; despite offers from international newspapers and publications Mahima has chosen to talk only with those in her home country, besides if she does decide to tell her story she has already promised it to Samantha.

chapter twenty-four

Her head is full of her father, so once her mum releases her from a vice-like embrace Samantha only has one thing to say. "Tell me about Dad."

"Tell you what about him?"

"Everything."

Her mum has nothing to say, instead firing a barrage of questions at Samantha about her time in India along with trying to elicit a promise from her that she will not be going back there or anywhere else equally as dangerous. Samantha will not be swayed, she is determined to get her mum to talk.

"Alright, alright." Her mum's exasperated tone tells Samantha she has won this battle. In truth her mum is not that surprised. She always expected to be questioned but thought it would be much sooner. "Where shall I start?"

"The beginning is a good place."

"Well I'm sure you know how we met."

"I know a lot of things Mum. I've had Maxine's version, Uncle Michael's version, along with his sarcastic comments about dad over the years and I've even had Adrian's version. Now I want yours."

At the mention of Adrian, Samantha's mum snaps her head back. She stands up and goes over to the window. "How do you know about Adrian?"

"I work with him. As does my father."

"What? Still?"

Samantha can see her mum is genuinely confused by this revelation. "I know about the accident, although I'm not entirely convinced that was Dad's fault."

"What else do you know?"

"Not much. That's why I need to hear your story and Dad's."

Her mum knows this is not going to be easy; her words need to be chosen with care. Although no longer a child, Samantha may still find some things hard to hear.

I probably haven't said enough that we were happy in the beginning. I should try and remember that more than I do but it is sometimes difficult to look back on the delight of those days. Recalling a past happiness makes its loss harder to bear. We met at a bar in London. I was with friends celebrating one of their birthdays. Clive was with Adrian and other work colleagues. They were very loud. We both ended up at the bar at the same time and just started chatting. He was easy to talk to; full of boyish charm and youthful optimism. He wasn't drop dead gorgeous, but I fancied him immediately. I think it was his eyes, sparkly and blue, with naturally long lashes. Even with mascara my lashes never looked as good as his. He had an ability to impress all who met him as he had knowledge and wisdom beyond his years. Those early days were wonderful… and yet now, as I look back I realise the more I got to know him the more he slipped away from me. It was as though every time he revealed himself, or at least a part of himself, a barrier popped up in its place. We would talk so much and in such depth but the conversations we had were never allowed to be revisited.

Our wedding was lovely. Not a huge grand affair, simplicity was what we both wanted, which made sense as I was already expecting your sister. Adrian was Clive's best man, although he was the worst behaved that day, he got very drunk and passed out in a corner. Things were good as we waited for Maxine's arrival; we were so excited. And then when she finally arrived – she was almost two weeks overdue – I felt that everything was perfect. He doted on her, on us both. We moved here, not this house, but this village. It was where I grew up, as you know. He didn't like being out of London and he was not a fan of the commute. He suggested moving closer to London but I didn't want to do that especially when I discovered I was pregnant again. When you arrived things improved. We settled into a routine that worked, for a time anyway. Then he started coming home late, blaming work, when in reality he had been out drinking. He probably did consider it work as mostly he was out with colleagues and other journos. I think he felt he was missing out on something. It was made worse when Adrian was sent to America to cover the OJ Simpson trial. He was quite envious of that, had it been anyone other than Adrian I don't think he would have cared. There was always an undercurrent of jealousy in their relationship. It wasn't long after that he made the decision to go freelance. There was no discussion regarding this, he just decided and that was that; a done deal. It meant I had to go back to work, part-time initially, thankfully Mum was able to help with you and your sister. That was the beginning of the end though.

Being freelance meant he was away a lot and keeping in touch wasn't as easy as it is today. There were no smart phones, no FaceTime, no Skype. Mobile phones themselves were still in their infancy. So consequently there were periods of time when he wasn't around. When he did come home he had tales to tell, sometimes quite fanciful stories that had clearly been embellished which is why Michael took to calling him Walter. I soon began to doubt him too as he wasn't making any money to speak of. Things became hard and I had to increase my hours. Adrian used to help a lot. He would often visit and would bring hampers of food and presents for you and Maxine. He was good company. And then he went freelance too and went off to join your dad. That was hard, he was a very good friend and I missed him, maybe more than your Dad at that time. Anyway I pushed on but I was struggling, so when Clive did come home we argued terribly, very often causing him to turn around and return to wherever he had come from. Adrian came home more frequently *than your dad and he would often visit. On one occasion he arrived and found me upset and he comforted me and we ended up... We were both sorry after and vowed it would never happen again and it didn't because when Adrian went back that was when they had the accident. It changed everything. Your dad never came home and I never saw Adrian again after he left hospital.*

Samantha looks at her mum who is staring straight ahead, the light on her face shows damp, shiny cheeks, the tears shed as she recounted her story.

"Why don't I remember Adrian?"

"You were very young and you spent a lot of time with your grandparents. My dad was still alive then."

"Did Dad know? About you and Adrian?"

"I don't know. He never said anything. He just didn't come back."

"Not even to say goodbye?"

"No. I think that has always been a big problem for Maxine. She was old enough to notice things and she missed Clive far more than you did. Your relationship developed when he started sending letters to you. He wrote to Maxine too, but it wasn't enough for her, you on the other hand loved the letters."

"I did, I remember. Although he never revealed where he was and the return address was always a P.O. Box."

"Yes, it was that along with Michael's comments that convinced Maxine he wasn't being honest about what he was doing. God, she is going to be shocked when she hears that all along he has been doing exactly what he said."

"Are you shocked Mum?"

"Not really. He always had aspirations to do just this sort of thing. Maybe that was the problem, I quelled his ambition. Where is he now?"

"Still in India I think."

"When will you talk to him?"

"Soon."

Samantha heads to her room. Talking to her mum has been emotionally draining and she needs a bit of time to think about things before Maxine gets home from work. Her mum shouts up to her as she reaches the door of her old bedroom.

"I forgot to say Justin called round while you were away."

Samantha runs back down the stairs. "What do you mean, called round?"

"Well, just that. He came round asking about you. He is quite smitten you know and he was very concerned about you."

"What did he want with you though?"

"I think he was looking for an ally. He is very charming, you could do worse."

"Mum, Justin and I are history."

"Okay. You should give him a call though. Let him know you are safe. He was genuinely worried, especially when I couldn't tell him where you were staying. Made me feel like a bad mother when I had to admit I didn't know where you were but then I reminded myself you're not a baby and…"

"Alright Mum. You've made your point. I'll give you an itinerary next time I go away." Samantha goes back upstairs and flops onto her bed. After aimlessly staring at the ceiling, whiling away some more time she reaches into her handbag and pulls out the phone that Gregory gave her. It takes several minutes for her to muster the courage to press the call button and when she finally does it goes straight to voicemail. Disappointed. Deflated. Dejected. All of that and more. She doesn't leave a message. What she needs to say has to be said to him; allowing him an opportunity to respond. Ideally it should be during a face to face conversation, but unless she flies back to India and locates him that is not going to happen. She will try again later. There are plenty of other things occupying her thoughts at the moment anyway. Not least why Justin doesn't seem to get the message that their relationship is over. His persistence is irritating and visiting her mum is annoying. It's not as if he would just happen to be passing by. Then there is work. There are still some things that she wants to look into regarding what happened in India; the Appleby-Jones connection for a start. And finally Gregory. Her feelings for him are confusing, not so long ago they were bordering on antipathy and now at the very least she cares for him, possibly even more than that. As she thinks of him a lightness inhabits her breath and a smile floats across her face. Life, recently has felt unreal, so maybe this false reality has become inhabited by fake emotion. Her world has been upended and the profundity of it is enormous. Something has shifted. Something has changed. But what has caused it? Circumstance, people, place. Love, hate, fear. It is all of that and more. It is India.

chapter twenty-five

The sun has barely risen when her alarm sounds, no matter, Mahima has been awake for some time. She is sitting by the open window in her bedroom in Nisha's house watching the night fade away. Later today she is to address a gender equality forum and already she is feeling nervous. Watching the sunrise is calming. Its enigmatic beauty is a marvel that cannot fail to enchant, even if you are not a morning person.

As she steps out on to the stage Mahima is astonished to see that the auditorium is full. Because of the lights and camera flashes she is unable to recognise anyone, but the sea of faces looks predominantly female. She takes her seat alongside others on the panel: academics, activists, politicians. Each, she feels has a more legitimate reason for being here than she does, yet they are applauding her and welcoming her as their equal. The woman chairing the panel is a human rights lawyer from the United

Kingdom. She begins the discussion by talking about the recent events involving Mahima. She does this to highlight the fact that human rights abuses are not just India's problem, they are the entire world's problem. She explains that the network behind the trafficking operation included men from across Europe and most likely the rest of the world.

"Why did they operate here, in India?" she asks.

"Because they could, it was easy. Because not all young women and girls are valued. Because not everyone is considered equal..."

Apart from moments of sporadic applause the audience is silent. Listening intently as tales of unloved, unwanted and ultimately unmissed girls are shared with them. Mahima is listening too. She is listening and feeling sad for these girls, for a moment forgetting that she was one of them.

"... she is bravely here today, to tell us her story, in the hope that we can prevent such outrages from continuing in the future."

She knows she is speaking, but is unsure what she is saying. At breakfast she had sought Nisha's advice as she had no idea what to say. Nisha had told her to let her voice come from within. "Do not think on it too much, let your heart talk."

Many questions are asked and Mahima answers them all with honesty and candour. And as the discussion progresses she listens as others share their own tales of abuse and mistreatment; sometimes at home, at work or in the wider community. What they all share though is very often having no means of recourse or justice.

At the end of the talk she notices a familiar figure walking towards her.

"Aisha, how lovely to see you."

Aisha embraces her warmly and introduces her to her mother. "We both thought you were so good up there."

"Yes," adds Aisha's mother. "You are a natural speaker and I think it's so good of you to use your experience to help others.

I am learning, slowly mind, that attitudes must change. Aisha is making me see how things should be, or rather how things should not be."

"That is good to hear. I'm learning that speaking up is actually a positive thing."

During the journey home Mahima reflects on the day. She is relieved it is over, yet oddly looking forward to the next time she is involved in something similar. Opening up and listening to other people's stories has been enlightening; she feels less alone now. The majority of her life so far has been about self-preservation, but now something is happening, and not just to her. Across the country, across the world people are coming together, especially women. The #MeToo movement is gaining momentum and she wants to stand with these women, with all women. Her story and stories like hers need to be told and she knows just the person to do that.

chapter twenty-six

Straight to voicemail for a sixth time. Either her father is too busy to talk or has no desire to talk to Gregory, after all that is who he would think is calling him. Samantha thinks it is the latter; she doesn't see Gregory as her dad's cup of tea somehow. She throws the phone on to the bed and takes her own phone from her bag. She needs to speak to Clive so decides to break the rules and call him. Straight to voicemail. "For God's sake," she shouts, venting her frustration. She is about to try again when she realises she has a new message. It is from Mahima. The message is lengthy and rambling but as she reads it Samantha gets a sense of the excitement her friend is feeling at the moment. After messaging back and forth for a while they schedule a time for a call when Samantha returns to work. Both of them are keen for Mahima's story to reach a bigger audience.

The sound of a car door closing diverts Samantha's attention, her sister is home from work. She had been planning on talking to Maxine after she had spoken to her dad, but as he isn't answering she may as well get it done now. As she walks along the landing she can hear whispered words being spoken at the foot of the stairs. Samantha coughs loudly as she makes her way down the stairs allowing her mum and sister a couple of seconds to end their mutterings.

"Hey," says Maxine.

"Hi. Good day?"

"A long day."

"I don't suppose you fancy a drink?"

"I've put the kettle on," shouts their mum from the kitchen.

"I meant a proper drink," says Samantha.

"Why?" asks Maxine with a suspicious air.

"I thought it would be nice and we haven't had a proper chat for a long time."

"Is everything alright?"

"Yes, I erm… I just want to talk to you."

"Okay. I'll need to freshen up first."

"Sure, no rush."

An hour later the two sisters are sitting opposite each other in the local pub, each nursing a glass of white wine.

"Spit it out then," says Maxine. "I know you have something to say."

"I saw Dad."

"So, you do see him. I don't, and if you've got me here just to persuade me to give him a chance you're wasting your breath."

"I saw him in India," says Samantha, ignoring the barbed comment.

"What was he doing in India?"

"Working."

"Doing what?"

"Doing exactly what he has always said he does."

"Oh please. You don't …"

"Hear me out, just this once." She says this with more force and volume than intended and a few of the locals turn to look at her.

"Okay fine. But stop shouting."

She tells her about India and the part their dad played in it all and that he is in fact a journalist. An undercover journalist with quite a reputation.

"So he has been telling the truth about his work, kind of. But that doesn't excuse the fact that he ran off or that he did not contribute a penny to our upbringing. Mum has had to work bloody hard over the years while he has been swanning around."

"I know. There are things I'm unhappy about too, but until I hear his side I'm not making any judgement. I've listened to Mum and to Adrian…"

"Who's Adrian?"

"Maxine. Have you even been listening to me? Adrian is Dad's partner I suppose. Working partner, they were at university together."

"I heard you say about his friend. I don't recall you giving him a name."

"Okay. Well his name is Adrian."

"We used to have an Uncle Adrian. Not a blood relation, just someone we called Uncle. He used to bring us amazing sweets and biscuits. From Harrods I think."

"Yes. That was him."

"I used to wish he was our dad."

"You didn't."

"I did. Is he? Is that what you have discovered?" Maxine laughs.

"Don't be stupid."

"This whole situation sounds stupid to me. No matter what he has to say, our father has been absent most of our lives. I for one am not going to be able to change how I feel about him overnight."

"Of course not, you've spent a lifetime being hateful and you have it down to a fine art."

"I don't need this. I'm going home to our mum. You know the woman who has fed and clothed and cared for us always. You and I having this conversation about him is unfair to her."

"You are being ridiculous. I am fully aware of the sacrifice and hardship that she has encountered, but this is not about her. It's about him and I think he deserves a chance to explain. And you need to stop hiding behind your loyalty towards Mum and get a life."

"What is that supposed to mean?"

"You are closer to thirty than twenty. You still live at home. Still have the same little job. No sign of a relationship at all. Do you even have friends? And your excuse is always the same, Mum."

"You have no idea about my life. But at least I care about Mum. All you do is cause her endless worry in your pursuit of being more like him. Which is ironic, because clearly you don't know him at all. I wonder if you even know yourself." Maxine stands up, downs her wine and bangs the glass down on the table before swooping out of the pub in a cloud of unrestrained fury.

Samantha doesn't go after her. She empties her own glass before going to the bar to order another from the bemused barman. Two glasses of wine later she makes her way home, her mum opening the front door before she even opens the gate. Samantha smiles at her and is greeted with a stony expression before demanding to know what she said to Maxine.

"I have never seen her so upset. Not upset angry, no upset. Upset and angry."

"Mum it was nothing. You know what she's like. Anything to do with Dad sets her off."

"I think Clive sets us all off."

"I'm going to bed Mum. I want to catch the early train back to London."

As she exits the tube station she recognises the person ahead of her, his regimented stride gives him a gait like that of a professional soldier. She speeds up a little, breaking into a trot in order to catch up with him. When she is level she taps his arm, he slows as he looks to see who has touched him. A smile fills his face as his eyes take her in.

"Didn't expect to see you this morning," they both say at the same time.

When they finish laughing at each other they decide to go for a coffee before heading into work.

"So, how was the trip home?" Gregory asks.

"Not great. I succeeded in upsetting my Mum and my sister and I still haven't been able to get hold of Dad."

"Aah sorry."

"It's fine. How are things with you? I didn't think you were going to come back to work just yet."

"I wasn't, but the funeral isn't until next week and I can't sit around doing nothing and to be honest, I wanted to see you."

"Well, I'm glad to see you too." And as she spoke she realised she really was glad to see him. "Come on, drink up. We had better go and see what Adrian has been up to in our absence."

Adrian watches them come in. It is her he is more interested in. He is wondering what her mother has said, if she has spoken to her father. He thinks she has, that is why Clive is not answering his calls or texts. She seems to be in good spirits, he thinks. He hopes she is. She hangs up her coat and puts her bag under her desk. She is coming over. He pretends to be working.

"Morning Adrian."

"Morning Samantha. Everything okay?"

"Fine." She doesn't elaborate. She knows what he wants, but she is not going to talk about her family today. "Right. I am speaking to Mahima today so I can get her story written up. Hopefully Paul will run it this week."

"I think it might be a good piece for the supplement. Maybe serialise it."

"No, this is a front page story."

"No Samantha it's not. Her tale is the follow on. The story is the corruption and the powerful people behind it."

"Yes and that has already been published."

"Oh Samantha, there is far more to tell. The first piece was just the tip of the iceberg. There is much more to come."

"And who is going to write that?"

"I am, once I have all the facts. Have you spoken to your dad?"

"No, I haven't and I am not discussing my family with you." She turns away angrily, stomping back to her desk.

"Are you alright?" asks Gregory.

"No I'm not alright. Unsurprisingly, Adrian has shafted me. It appears my story deserves no more than a serialisation in the supplement. Nobody reads the bloody supplement."

"That's not true. I read it."

"That's not the point."

"I'll talk to him, if you like."

"For all the good it will do."

Gregory goes across to Adrian's desk, she watches surreptitiously as they talk and is surprised when Gregory drags a chair over and sits down next to him. The two of them look at something on Adrian's computer. Several minutes pass. She notices as they talk they lower their heads and cover their mouths, they must know she is watching them; as if she can lip read from this far away. The more she watches the angrier she gets, until she can bear it no longer. She marches towards them and demands to know what they are doing.

"Adrian was updating me," says Gregory innocently.

"Oh really. And when do I get an update then?"

"I would have brought you up to speed earlier but you walked off in a huff, remember."

"And do you blame me. You have hijacked my story."

"No Samantha, I haven't."

"I found this story and …"

"Yes, you did and that was great, but now you need to realise there is more at stake and much more that needs to be uncovered."

"He's right," says Gregory before she has a chance to say anything further. "Amit and the hotel may have been the start of all this but what lies behind it is far bigger and it is that which needs reporting in the first instance. Anyway, we should work together, there's room for us all I'm sure."

Adrian and Samantha are scowling at one another but both know it's the best way forward.

"Look at this." Adrian turns his computer monitor round so she can see what they are looking at.

She looks at the screen but does not understand what she is seeing. "What is it?" she asks.

"This is the paper trail. This is what I do and I do well. Sit down I'll explain it to you."

"Have this seat, I have things to do," says Gregory.

Adrian's smug manner is adding to the irritation she already feels, but she sits and listens to what he has to say. "I have accessed documents pertaining to individuals we think are connected to this: bank details, diary entries, flight itineraries. Then I have cross-referenced the material and highlighted any correlation."

"And?"

"And I have uncovered payments between individuals, meetings between people who claim they do not know each other and a common account that some of them receive money from."

"Is this actually legal?"

He ignores her question and directs her to look at some of the names. "Do you know any of these people?"

Samantha squeals excitedly as she spots the name Appleby-Jones. Adrian tells her it is not Rupert Appleby-Jones but a cousin, a second cousin. Another descendant of Judge Appleby-Jones who she used to deliver newspapers to.

"Do you think the judge was part of all this?"

"No. But I believe he and subsequent members of his family have amassed considerable wealth by making it easier for certain individuals to avoid justice. He certainly used his position as a judge. Rupert used his position as a high-ranking civil servant in India's High Commission and this one," Adrian taps the name on the screen, "is the best of all. He is a man behind a charitable initiative across the subcontinent that helps displaced women and children."

"Do you have a picture of him?"

"Yes, in that file." He nods towards a file on his desk which she opens. "That's it. It's the board of the charity at a fund-raising event."

She looks at the photograph, but it is not Mr Appleby-Jones she is studying. It is a man standing behind him, looking across his left shoulder. Adrian notices the colour visibly drain from her face.

"What is it?" he asks.

"Him." She points at the man. "He was at the house. He seemed to be in charge, but I only saw him briefly. Who is he?"

"I don't know. The names are not listed, but if he is on the board of the charity it shouldn't be too difficult to find out."

She leaves Adrian to discover who the man in the photograph is and goes over to Gregory's desk to see what he is doing. He says he intends to dig further into the Appleby-Jones family since that part of the investigation is personal as he knows Rupert Appleby-Jones played some role in Simon's death. She goes back to her own desk and calls Mahima.

The two women fall into an easy rapport during their telephone call, as though they have been friends for many years, discussing what they have been up to and the list of events that Mahima is taking part in. They talk for quite some time and although they cover a lot of ground there is still much to be said and so they arrange another time for a further chat.

As soon as she hangs up she gets a call on the internal line. Adrian has learnt the identity of the man in the photograph, the man from the house, her captor. He is an Indian businessman, well respected and liked with many business interests including a large shareholding in a hotel chain.

"But it wasn't his house I was held at?"

"No. As we know the house belonged to another businessman, one with more dubious credentials and links - as yet unproven - to organised crime. My guess is he loaned out his house. He has managed to distance himself from things at the moment, claiming he had no knowledge what his house was being used for. However, the fact that the house Gregory was held at belonged to a colleague of his means the authorities are now taking a closer look at him. I think he is easier to pursue than the man you met."

"So another scapegoat."

"Oh I don't think you can call him that, not entirely. He is a very undesirable sort and deserves to be taken down but I suppose his arrest may be enough to appease some quarters."

"But not us?"

"No way."

"Good."

"So you are beginning to understand that this is not just about Amit?"

"Yes. I am."

"Good. Because if someone doesn't find the people at the top of the tree they will just continue what they have been doing, but somewhere else."

She knows he is right and says as much.

"Okay. This man," says Adrian pointing at the screen once more. "Can you remember anything else about him or recall anything from the house? Overheard conversations, maybe a name dropped inadvertently?"

"No."

"He didn't speak to you himself?"

"Yes he did. It was a bit odd actually. Didn't make sense until I heard that Gregory was free."

"What did he say then, exactly?"

"I'm not sure I can remember word for word. I told him I was there to negotiate Gregory's release."

"Crazy," snorts Adrian.

"Look, if we hadn't done that those girls would all be God knows where by now, doing God knows what."

"Okay, okay. Fair enough. Carry on."

"I told him I could give him who he wants, meaning Mahima. He laughed at me and said I have what I want, you are here. Which made no sense at all, until I learnt that Gregory was actually safe."

"It still doesn't make sense."

"I assumed it was an attempt at intimidating me."

"And did it?"

"Yes, a little."

"Right. Well I need to look into this character a bit more." Adrian's attention switches back to his computer and Samantha knows that is her cue to return to her own desk. Walking across the newsroom floor she sees Gregory walking towards her with a huge bouquet of flowers in his arms. She is unable to stop the grin that takes control of her face; that is until Gregory shakes his head and tells her they are not from him. She snatches at the card that is attached. Sweetpea, jumps out at her and she knows in an instant who they are from.

"Secret admirer?" enquires Gregory.

"Not bloody secret enough," she mutters.

"What shall I do with them?"

"Bin them. Give them to someone else. I really don't care." And she doesn't. She does not care for Justin at all and it is time he understood that. She types out a text to send to him, then deletes it. A text won't do, best to call him, she thinks. Or maybe see him? Face to face might be better. Yes, it will be, she decides to see him after work.

"So, Norma is very happy now," Gregory tells her. Her vague expression tells him she has no idea what he is talking about.

"Norma in accounts. I gave her the flowers."

"Oh good, great."

"I was wondering if you fancied dinner this evening."

"I erm…"

"Nothing fancy. I just think we have things to talk about and…"

"Yes, we do and I, just not tonight. I have something I need to do this evening."

"Fine." He turns away abruptly. His disappointment and irritation are all too plain.

"Friday. How about Friday?"

"Okay. Friday."

ﻉ

Samantha is sitting in the coffee-shop around the corner from Justin's flat. She has decided to talk to him at the flat as it offers privacy should the need arise for her to express herself forthrightly. She is aware that she can be loud and often shouts to make her point and she does not want to cause an unpleasant scene somewhere public. Also, it will give her the chance to get any of her things that may still be there. That should make it doubly clear she has no intention of rekindling their relationship. Sipping the warm caramel latte does not embolden her and she wishes she had opted to wait in the wine bar instead. Spirals of steam swirl in front of her face and she gently blows at the wispy curls as she drinks her coffee.

As she rounds the corner she spots Justin standing on the pavement outside his home talking to someone in the back of a car. A rather fancy looking car. A chauffeured car. As she nears Justin turns his head and sees her. He stands up straight, smiles and nods his head. The person in the back of the car is a man. There is something familiar about him but before she can get a better look the rear window closes and the car pulls away.

"Sweetpea."

Samantha grinds her teeth as she hears his predictable greeting. "We need to talk."

"Yes we do, come inside."

"Who was that?" she asks while following him to the front door.

"Who?"

"The man in the fancy car."

"My father."

That is probably why she recognises him. Although she has never met him, she thinks she must have seen a photograph of him. "So who is he?"

"Who?"

"Your dad. He must be some kind of big shot if he has a car like that and a chauffeur."

"It's a company car, that's all. Look I thought you came here to talk about us."

"Yes, sorry. We do need to talk."

Justin offers her a drink, which she declines, only for him to press a glass of wine into her hand anyway. She places it on the countertop, along with her handbag.

"Did you get the flowers?"

"Yes. Norma loves them."

"Norma?"

"In accounts. They brighten her office."

"Aah."

"Yes, ah. It is over between us. You need to stop calling me and sending me things and visiting my family. That was weird by the way, going all the way to Suffolk to speak to my mum."

"I do have friends in that part of the country."

"Really?" Samantha's disbelief is evident by her sceptical tone.

"Well not exactly there but East Anglia somewhere. Look I miss you and I know you miss me."

"I really don't."

"Why not stay the night and I'll show you what you have been missing."

"I'll pass thanks."

"Look, you have come here to see me. Admit it. If you truly want it to be over you could have sent me a text."

Samantha is beginning to wish she had done just that. "I came here to collect my things."

"Let's go in the other room. You can tell me all about India."

"Don't pretend to be interested in my work. You never were before."

"And that was wrong. So please tell me about India."

"There is nothing to tell. I'm sure you have read the papers."

"Oh come on. I'm sure there is a lot that didn't make the newspapers. Where are all the people who were involved now?"

"What people?"

"That Amit for a start, where is he?"

"She."

"What?"

"Amit is a she."

"Oh yes. And Gregory Johnson and the other journalists. Are they all home now?"

"How do you know Gregory?"

"I don't. I erm, must have remembered his name from the paper. And what about the others. It can't have been just you and him."

"Why not?"

"Oh come on. I'm sure someone more senior would have had to oversee things."

"I go all the way to India, an amazing country and all you want to know is who I was with. That's all you were ever interested in: who I work with, who I speak to, who I listen to. You were never interested in what I do or what I think."

"That's not true. Come on tell me about India."

"Too late Justin. Now I'm going to get my things and go, because we are done."

"Please don't. Stay, drink your wine."

"I don't want the wine. I want my things." Samantha moves toward the bedroom but Justin stops her.

"I'll get your things. Wait in the lounge."

She does as he asks; happy not to have to go into the bedroom. She doesn't sit, instead opting to stand by the window. The lounge feels cold, a feeling not helped by the cool grey décor and clean lines. Everything is crisp and stark. No ornaments, pictures or photos. The walls are bare apart from a giant flat screened television that dominates the room. It is a minimalistic environment devoid of any character or personality. Justin comes in and hands her a bag. He looks at her with doleful eyes, silently pleading for her to change her mind. She doesn't, she won't.

On the tube home she picks through the contents of the bag that he gave her. A t-shirt that she occasionally slept in, some toiletries and underwear are all that is in it. When she exits the underground an email from Justin comes through, with an attachment that he asks her to open. It is a photo of them both, a selfie taken at a rooftop bar. She remembers that day. Although it was bright and the sun was shining, it was windy and she hadn't wanted to go up to the roof. He had insisted as he said it offered one of the best views of the city, and he wasn't wrong, it was a nice day, a fun day and the photograph reflects that. He had said he was going to print it and frame it, he never did. She considers this for a moment and realises he never had any photos on display, not of her or anyone else. So why did she recognise his father, she wonders. She never did meet any of his family.

chapter twenty-seven

Adrian has invited Gregory to the pub. No, he hasn't invited him, he has summoned him, demanded even. Gregory gets a drink for them both and takes it over to Adrian, who has already claimed his regular table. He takes several large sups of his beer before asking Gregory if he or Samantha have spoken to Clive recently. Gregory hasn't. He knows Samantha was planning on contacting him but can't say if she did or not.

"Why?"

"Because I haven't heard from him for a while."

"And is that unusual?"

"Ordinarily no. But as we are in the middle of something I would have expected some contact."

"Have you tried getting in touch with him?" asks Gregory.

"Oh I didn't think to do that," he replies caustically.

"Sorry. Of course you have. Shall I call Samantha and ask her?"

"No. I don't want to alarm her just yet. I'll contact some people I know out there, see if they have seen or heard from him first."

"So you are not unduly worried?"

He doesn't answer, but as he picks up his pint Gregory catches a look that tells him he is worried; very worried.

⅄

The intention is to kill him. He has been a thorn in their side for too long, and now he knows too much. Long has he been on their trail, little by little learning more about their operations and now linking them to others. The scale of it is shocking and it is able to thrive because those who should be trying to stop it are themselves profiting from it. Some are feathering their own nest with bribes and backhanders, received if they look away, turn a blind-eye or forewarn them of possible investigations. Others are right at the heart of it, not only making money but satisfying their own perversions too. He hates them all, but particularly those in positions of power. Those who so many trust to stand up to the criminals, but who instead pave the way for them. He knows he cannot be allowed to live. The names he could reveal will have ramifications here, at home and in other countries too. He doesn't want to die, but he isn't afraid of dying, he doesn't worry for himself. What worries him is the safety of his family. If, as he suspects the connection has been made between him and Samantha she may be in danger. If only she had not inherited his curiosity; that was what brought her here. Perhaps if he had kept Adrian fully apprised of what he was doing, then Adrian may have stopped her. Too many what ifs, no point thinking on them now. What he needs is a plan; an escape plan. Trouble is, he is fresh out of ideas and energy.

The man pushing him forward is his executioner, there is no doubt of that, although it is surprising that only one man has been assigned to this deed. They probably do not foresee him posing a problem following the beatings he has endured. Deeper into the forest they go. The thickening foliage is reducing the light, which adds to the disconsolate drear. Dead man walking, that's him. He thinks of Maxine and Samantha and their mum and Adrian. He thinks of the girls these men take and claim as their own, like a possession. He thinks of himself. He doesn't believe he would be much missed but what he can do, that will be missed. That will be the greatest loss; what he might prevent. An anger fires up inside him, coursing through him. He has to try. Two men walk into the forest, for sure only one will walk out. Why wouldn't it be him?

He staggers forward, emphasising unsteady steps, floundering as his body makes seemingly uncontrolled movements before a violent lurch pitches him forward and he lies motionless on the damp ground. His captor and would-be executioner stops sharply, kicking the bottom of his shoe, telling him to get up on his feet. He walks around him, kicking him some more, prodding and poking him. Dead or unconscious; he cannot tell. He stands astride him, watching carefully; looking for a rise and fall of the chest. Nothing. He should do something to be sure, though but a shot might be heard as they are not yet deep enough in the forest. The guard removes a large knife from the sheath held around his waist and leans forward.

It is now or never. He opens his eyes wide, startling the knife wielding figure hovering above him. Clive raises his leg at speed and his foot connects perfectly between the man's legs causing him to buckle at the knees. Sitting up quickly his head makes contact with the man's nose who shouts in pain as he keels over. Clive springs up waiting for the obvious retaliation but it doesn't come. The prone figure isn't moving. Gingerly Clive edges closer as a wet, sticky pool of liquid seeps steadily out from beneath the motionless body. He rolls him over, to find the man's neck pierced by his own knife.

Inappropriately, he laughs; sheer relief rushing through him. If things had gone to plan it would be his lifeless body lying there. He relieves the man of his gun; not that he has ever used one before but he feels he needs to arm himself but he can't make himself remove the knife from the dead man's throat. He rifles through his pockets, removing his wallet and mobile phone. The wallet contains a driving license, other ID and about 9,000 rupees, a little under £100 and just enough to get him far from here and to someone who can help him, he hopes. The mobile phone is basic but has battery life - although no signal at the moment – so he pockets it.

He buries the body under some leaves and walks back the way he was led in until the thinning canopy of trees tells him he is nearing the forest's edge and where he was held. He needs to change direction. Left or right. He plumps for right.

He has been walking for a few hours and by now he hoped he would have reached a road or some semblance of civilization but instead the trees and vegetation seem eternal. He is worried because by now they would have noticed that the man charged with killing him had not returned and he knows someone else will be sent after him. Clive has to be a long way from here by the time that happens.

With the light fading and despair setting in he's desperate. He is on the verge of giving up when he hears it. He stops. Stands absolutely still and listens again. Yes, he did hear it. It is not his imagination. It is still a way off but it is definitely the sound of a vehicle. If there is a road it must lead somewhere. All roads lead somewhere. And if there is a somewhere, there might be a someone. Hope quickens his step and soon he is rewarded with a glimpse of a road, a track really, but he is glad to be out of the woodland, although now he must be doubly careful out in the open. After half a mile or so the track intersects with a road, a proper road. Left or right. Left this time, he doesn't want to risk going back on himself. It's a good call because a few minutes later he hears a truck approaching. Without any thought or hesitation he starts frantically waving his arms around and when the truck stops he clambers in without even asking where the driver is going.

Just to be moving forward without having to put one foot in front of another is joyous. The driver is going to Ahmedabad and Clive asks if he can go with him, he offers to pay. The driver is happy for him to come along, he is grateful for the company.

"Talking will help keep me awake."

Clive would prefer to get some shut eye, he is feeling rather light-headed but will oblige the driver by staying awake for the journey, which should take about two and a half hours. They arrive late and the driver tells Clive he is going to Manek Chowk to get something to eat.

"You are welcome to come too," he says. Clive agrees, so long as he is allowed to pay for the food. Perhaps food will rid him of this dizzy feeling.

Manek Chowk is a large open square in the centre of Old Ahmedabad. By day it is home to a vegetable and jewellery market, by night it is famous for its food stalls. When they have finished eating they say their farewells and part company and Clive walks off to find a hostel for the night. Somewhere cheap and cheerful will do; he is desperate to lay down now. Without a passport or any identifying documents his first stop should be the embassy, but he is not so sure that's the best idea, he doesn't trust anyone. A good night's sleep will help with his decision making.

He wakes early, fully dressed, his skin feels cold and clammy. His stomach hurts and as he rolls onto his side and raises his knees, a wave of nausea descends. As swiftly as possible he runs to the bathroom down the corridor but doesn't make it, grabbing a wastepaper bin to be sick in. In the bathroom he lifts his shirt and is surprised to see purple patches around his navel, where his abdomen hurts him. Bruising probably a result of the beatings he incurred prior to his escape but the sickness he is not so sure of. He wonders if it is something he has eaten but it's unlikely a cheese sandwich would make him feel like this. Walking back along the corridor to his bed takes monumental effort, the dizziness intense. A pain so sharp, poleaxes him completely and his legs fail, folding beneath him like a collapsed deckchair. He tries to move, but can't. He tries to speak, no sound. Then nothing, but darkness.

chapter twenty-eight

Sleep is eluding her. With her eyes tightly shut she tries to banish the pervading thoughts. Her mind, unwilling to shut down wins out so she switches on the lamp at her bedside and reaches for her phone. Gregory, Maxine, Mum, Dad, Adrian, Justin; all vying for position. Each wants to be the one responsible for keeping her awake. Justin is the victor. Well not Justin exactly; his father. She recognised him from somewhere and it is bothering her that she cannot think where. It is also bothering her that it is bothering her. She doesn't want to be thinking about Justin at all; not even tenuously. It helps to like the person you are intimately involved with and she has come to realise she does not like Justin. He treated her with condescension. And how little does she know of him beyond that he works for an investment company in the city; which pays generous bonuses, allowing him to have a flat in such a great part of London. That, his name and birthday is all she knows for certain. In retrospect she wonders what he saw in her too. They never really had a connection, apart from the obvious. They have nothing in common. It is a relationship that has run its course, and Samantha is sure he feels the same. Which is why the begging and pleading and visit to her mum is hard to understand. Men are strange creatures, she thinks. Even Gregory, - who has ignited something in her – has behaved oddly. For a long time she was convinced he disliked her, such was the disdain he aimed at her.

She scrolls through the many photographs on Justin's Facebook. Most are of him and a bunch of guys clearly enjoying alcohol fuelled activities. She has seen these ones before. When they first met she had of course looked at his social media accounts, but had given up looking at all the pictures as there were so many. She keeps flicking her thumb across the screen of her phone eventually coming to an album titled Cara's wedding where she first finds a picture of his dad, but she is still none the wiser as to who he is. He crops up a few more times but is neither named nor tagged in any of the photos. Cara is Justin's sister so she decides to take a look at her Facebook. One album called Mumbai grabs her attention. As Samantha looks at the images she is reminded again of a country she has fallen in love with despite seeing but a glimpse of it. India has touched her profoundly. The colour and culture. Heat and humidity. People and places. The rush.

The sight-seeing photos end and are replaced by pictures taken at a party or event where one photograph stands out. Its familiarity enough to make her go back and enlarge it. An unease filters through her as she zooms in on the faces. Justin's father, plain to see is standing alongside Appleby-Jones and just in front of the man from Gujarat; her captor. It is familiar to her because it is the same photograph that Adrian showed her.

She needs to speak to Adrian when morning breaks.

ɤ

He should have heard from him. Even with Clive's flippant approach to rules and arrangements, he would have made contact by now. Adrian has called everyone he knows in India; even those hundreds of miles from where he last knew Clive to be. Nobody has seen him or heard from him. On the plus side nobody has heard that anything has happened to him either but that is not allaying his fears. He has called his phone numerous times but it goes straight to voicemail and his texts are unanswered as are his WhatsApp messages with just the one grey tick. Something is wrong. He needs to talk to Samantha. Too early yet, for now he will get hold of someone who can track Clive's mobile. He suspects the battery is dead, but he knows it can be traced to the location it was in when it powered down. That would at least give him a starting point in his search.

They arrange to the meet in the coffee shop up the road from the office, where no one can hear them.

Adrian wasn't surprised to hear from her, he was surprised at the hour; he didn't have her down as a light sleeper. She is there waiting for him, he didn't expect that; timekeeping, especially in the morning is not her thing. Silently he curses her for picking a table in the furthest corner that requires him to manoeuvre his wheelchair between tables and chairs. The serious look on her face stops him from complaining out loud; he wonders if she has already worked out that Clive is missing.

"Morning Samantha."

"Look at this."

He has barely reached the table when she turns her laptop towards him, simultaneously pulling a sheaf of papers from her bag.

"I need coffee before I can function."

"Fine. I'll get you a coffee. You look at that." She points at the screen of the laptop.

He roughly pushes a chair out of his way – he is not a morning person either, he's not an anytime person really, he is consistent though and is always grumpy - the scraping of the legs on the tiled floor reverberates around the almost empty shop. He puts on his glasses and peers at the screen. It's the photo they were looking at yesterday. He looks closer, in case he is missing something. No, same photo.

"I saw this yesterday," he says as she sets his coffee down.

"You're welcome."

"What?"

"I said you're welcome. The coffee. A thank you would be nice."

"Have you brought me here at this ungodly hour to show me something I have already seen and correct my manners?" he barks.

"Do you know this man?" she taps the screen, indicating Justin's father.

"It is Anthony Burchfield."

"How do you know that?"

"I found out. It's what I do. I know the names of most of them."

"Oh." She is deflated.

"Well done for learning who he is, but there isn't much point in us both doing the same thing. I'm already looking into this guy."

"Do you think he is involved?"

Adrian hesitates before answering. Although links to Burchfield have cropped up, they are negligible, but he has come across him before. And more importantly Clive has come across him before. "He could be involved. They might all be. This charity may be fraudulent; a front. I don't know yet."

"I think he is involved."

"What makes you say that?"

Samantha explains about Justin: their relationship, their breakup, his desire to see her again. "He even went to see Mum and he was more interested in who I was working with than India, which I thought odd. And then I saw the photo again and his dad and okay, I know it sounds far-fetched to think he would go out with me because of all this but I'm sure it is the case. Maybe not in the beginning, but definitely now. I think his dad has told him to get back with me. I don't think he would be interested otherwise." Adrian's expression is one of disbelief, she is not surprised. Her ramblings do not make much sense, even to her, but she is sure she is right. "You were the one who told me not to trust coincidences."

He doesn't know what to say. Many years ago Clive did a piece on companies and individuals using off-shore tax havens. Although not illegal, Clive thought them immoral and went on a bit of a crusade, naming and shaming. Burchfield was one of those he exposed. And now Burchfield is linked to this investigation, his son has been messing around with Samantha and Clive is missing.

"Have you spoken to your dad?" he asks.

"What? Oh, I see. You don't want me to be part of this do you?

That's why you're changing the subject. Not very subtle Adrian. Anyhow, I am not talking about my family with you and I am not being dropped from this story."

"Just tell me. Have you heard from him?"

Something in his voice alerts Samantha and from the look on his face she knows something is worrying him and it concerns her dad.

chapter twenty-nine

It is the brightness he notices first. Then the noise. Not loud noise, but continual noise; in the background. A humming sound. Muted chatter. Clip clopping footsteps. Interspersed with beeping and buzzing. He tries to raise himself up in order to properly take in his surroundings; to work out where he is. Barely an inch off the mattress and the effort exhausts him. He is attached to something, a tube he thinks, or maybe a wire. He can hear people. He calls out to them. Nobody replies. He calls again and again and again, until finally, someone comes.

They are asking questions, that he can tell. But they are talking fast and they are not talking his language.

"English," he mumbles.

"Ah okay. It is good to see you awake. How are you feeling?"

"Like I've been hit by a truck."

"Well you've certainly been hit by something, or someone. Do you have a name?"

"I do. I erm... Where am I?"

"The Civil Hospital."

"Why am I here? Am I ill?"

"Yes. You have had emergency surgery. The doctor will explain. If you could give me your name and tell me if there is anyone we need to call."

"There is no one. How did I get here?"

"Ambulance. Your name?"

Clive tries to remember. Not his name, he knows that. He tries to remember what happened, but can only recall bits and pieces, fleeting images, but it is enough to make him fearful. The nurse observes the concentration on his face. She thinks he can't remember his name. He'll go with that, for now, while he works out who he can trust.

The doctor is a woman, a young woman. He is surprised, more by her youth than her gender. She tells him it was necessary to perform an emergency splenectomy as the spleen was ruptured and he was suffering internal bleeding.

"This was most likely caused by a severe blow to your abdomen. Do you recall that happening?"

"No."

"Well, for now you must stay with us. I'm sure things will begin to come back to you. It is not unusual to suffer temporary memory loss after suffering a trauma. I will tell the police that you are not well enough to speak to them at the moment."

"The police? Why do they want to talk to me?"

"Because you have clearly been the victim of a violent and brutal assault."

"How long will I have to stay here?"

"That depends, but I would say at least a week, maybe longer. Now get some rest."

A week is too long, thinks Clive. In a week they might find him and finish what they started. They must have realised their plan failed by now. And how long has he been here, they might be close already. He has no idea what day it is. He could ask to see someone from the embassy, but that could still be risky. He knows some people in India but he has no phone or contact details for them. Who to trust; he has no idea. He needs an ally, a friend. Someone to pass on a message for him.

"Now then. You understand a bit more now you have seen the doctor, I hope," asks the nurse. Clive gives a slight nod and a smile in response. "Still no name though. I have to call you something. Let me see. Frank, that's what I'll call you, after Frank Sinatra. My mum loved Frank Sinatra. Englishman like you."

"American."

"I thought you said you were English."

"Frank Sinatra. American."

"Ah. Yes you're right. You speak the same language though, kind of."

Clive laughs at this, a little. He stops when it hurts. He likes his nurse. She comes across as warm-hearted and honest; direct, what you see is what you get. Someone to trust, she could be.

٤

Gregory looks around at the faces on the tube. Bored and tired expressions tell him these are people who would rather be somewhere else. All silently enduring the morning commute. The tube carriage is a tin can full of people with nothing to look forward to. All of them complete strangers bound by the monotony of the day ahead. But not him; he always has something to look forward to, well someone. Samantha, long held in his affections, always unattainable, or so he thought. Then a twist of fate throws them together and maybe, just maybe... but no. He knows she will cancel their date - once Adrian tells her about Clive - and rightly so. If your dad is missing that has to take priority. And Gregory will help her with this. But then, as each day passes what happened in India will slip further and further from her mind until it occupies no more than a distant corner, where it will become a memory, occasionally recalled until finally concealed by the dust of time. He sighs deeply; back to reality and admiring from afar. At least he has that to look forward to.

The escalator judders as it conveys its load from the depths of the underground to the busy street above. Outside, he is met by a misty and murky morning. London is wrapped in a dismal grey shroud, its beauty hidden. His musings are halted by his phone. Only a text. He will look at it later. It will be her. He strides out, quickening his pace. Today is not a day for a saunter. He suppresses a yawn and realises he has yet to have a coffee this morning and pops into the café near the office.

"So you did get my message," says Adrian. Gregory ignores him and goes straight to the counter to order his coffee. "If you had bothered to reply we would have ordered your coffee," continues Adrian.

Gregory sits on the discarded chair at the end of the table. He smiles at Samantha who is wearing the same worried expression he saw in Adrian's eyes at the pub. She smiles back before reverting her gaze back to her laptop. "What's going on?"

"Have you heard from Clive?" asks Adrian. She raises her eyes and peers above the screen of her laptop

"No, I haven't. I wouldn't expect to though."

"No, quite. I was just checking. I haven't heard from him, neither has Samantha and his phone is no longer active."

"How do you know that?"

"I have had someone trace it and they have located where it powered down." She turns her laptop so he can see the screen. There is a map of Gujarat on it. "The section that Samantha has highlighted shows the area in which the phone died. We are assuming this as Clive's last known location."

"Okay. What can I do?"

"We are trying to establish if there are any places of interest within this area. Any links to what we have been working on. We should contact hospitals, in case he has had an accident. You could do that."

"Sure. Although I think we would have heard if he'd had an

accident. He kept all his documents in a beaten-up old rucksack that was always with him."

"A grey one?" Samantha asks. "Grey with a black trim and doodles and scribbles on the back?"

"It was grey, yes. That much I remember. Scribbles, quite possibly. It was very tatty."

"Maxine bought him one like that and I drew all over it. Boy was she mad and did I get in trouble." Samantha wonders if it is the same one, her eyes glaze over and Gregory places his hand on hers. She allows it to linger there for a few seconds then pulls it sharply away when she notices Adrian studying them.

"I don't suppose you remember his car?" asks Adrian.

"Colour and type, nothing more though."

"Yes, it was a longshot."

"Have you reported him as missing yet?"

"I'll get in touch with some contacts out there before I make it official. See what they can find out first."

Gregory understands. This is Adrian's way of saying he doesn't know who to trust. So far there have been links to law enforcement agencies and the high commission, so they must tread very carefully.

"I could get in touch with Aisha and Mahima. They would be happy to help."

"For God's sake Samantha, that is ridiculous," shouts Adrian. "What could they possibly do?"

"Steady on," interjects Gregory. He can tell that Adrian's outburst has angered and upset Samantha.

"I'm going to the office. We'll meet at The Cheese later and decide what to do next if we haven't learnt anything more." Adrian pulls sharply on the right-hand wheel of his chair and forces himself past Gregory instead of asking him to move.

"Do you want another coffee?"

"Shouldn't we be getting to work too?"

"I don't have to be there this week and you are usually late anyway so I doubt we will be missed."

"In that case I'll have a latte."

When they meet at the pub it soon becomes apparent that between them they have learnt no more about Clive's disappearance. Adrian is still reluctant to contact the authorities but agrees with Gregory when he says it is Samantha's call. Samantha doesn't want to make the decision, she does not want that responsibility. In the end she agrees with Adrian when he suggests they give it until the following morning.

Adrian is glad, because he has learnt something. Something he does not want to share. Not yet. Not until he has more details. A body has been discovered; an unidentified male. Stabbed and left not far from Clive's last known position. His contact will try to find out more, but at the moment the details are far too vague to warrant him sharing it with anyone else.

૪

Physically Clive feels much better. Although the consequences of a splenectomy can be worrying, he is extremely grateful to the young surgeon who saved his life. His improved state has seen him out of bed and moving around the ward, tentatively at first. The nicest thing was being able to have a shower, although it was under the watchful gaze of Sonia, his nurse. He likes Sonia and she likes him, which is just as well as he is going to ask her for a favour.

"What, borrow my phone? And who are you going to call when you don't even know who you are?"

"I don't want to call anybody, I want to look at something online. See the news, from home. Just for a minute. You never know it might jog my memory." He is pleading with her now.

"Alright, there's no need to beg. But just for a minute, that's all or I'll be in trouble."

He doesn't want to look at the news, well, not exactly; just a newspaper website. Facts and figures from years past he can recall easily, but phone numbers or email addresses for some reason he can never commit to memory, he'd like to blame new technology for making him lazy but actually he has probably always been like that. He searches for Adrian's newspaper's website and goes to the 'contact us' page. He types in a cryptic message marking it for the urgent attention of Adrian Miller. Now all he can do is hope that the message is passed on.

chapter thirty

The body isn't Clive's. It is that of a 30 to 40 year old Indian male, not a 50-something white male. Adrian is relieved. But in the absence of any new information regarding Clive's whereabouts it is time to report him as a missing person so he makes the relevant calls and lets Samantha know that it is done. He then sits quietly, contemplating the idea that he may not see Clive again. Despite their - at times - volatile history, this thought is hard, his loss would leave a huge hole in his life, both professionally and personally. On a professional level he is his long-time collaborator, personally, he is as close to him as a brother would be. Adrian shakes his head in an effort to rid the feeling of melancholy that is threatening to overwhelm him.

"Come on man, you have work to do," he mutters to himself.

And he does, because with or without Clive this investigation needs to continue and people need to be brought to account. To this end he turns his attention back to his computer. He has several emails, but decides to look at them later. First he is going to see what he can dig up on Anthony Burchfield.

Samantha is not going into work today and neither is she going out with Gregory this evening. Her dad's disappearance is dominating her thoughts. Acknowledging him as missing is hard; it is one step closer to him never coming home at all. She is grateful that Adrian is the one dealing with the formalities regarding her dad's disappearance. It is enough for her that she has to tell her mum and Maxine.

She hasn't spoken to Maxine since the evening at the pub and she doesn't want to talk to her now. She doubts she'll even care when she hears that dad is missing; so decides to just tell her mum and let her tell Maxine. A coward's way out for sure, but if her sister's reaction displays anything less than concern Samantha will be infuriated and likely unable to conceal her anger.

Ɣ

He knew it would come, he was expecting it, waiting for it even. Yet, when she finally cancelled the disappointment was worse than he had imagined it would be. So instead of preparing for his date with Samantha he decided to head to his parent's home earlier than planned, in preparation for Simon's funeral. He had intended to go the day before the funeral, much to his father's chagrin. His planned late arrival was all about self-preservation; dealing with his own grief is hard enough, seeing his parents cope with theirs is not something he is looking forward to witnessing. Whenever he goes there will be no avoiding it, so putting it off seems futile and sitting at home, alone, mooning over Samantha would be equally as depressing.

The drive is straightforward, no traffic problems or delays at all, so he arrives earlier than he wants to. His childhood home is magnificent, purchased with money both inherited and made, (his father was quite a shrewd investor). It stands quite proudly as a symbol of his family's vast wealth. Although impressive, it is not a house that holds him in its thrall. He has some good memories associated with it but they are few. Boarding school and then university kept him away from here during much of his formative years anyway. As he drives through the imposing wrought iron gates and along the tree-lined driveway trepidation washes over him. The massive wooden door, framed by the ancient wisteria that over the years has wrapped itself around the house vying for position alongside the ivy, opens before he has even turned off the engine of his car.

His father greets him with a handshake and a half-hearted attempt at an embrace which ends up being more than a little awkward. He tells him his mother is upstairs and after a brief chat with his father Gregory climbs the carved staircase in search of his mother. He finds her sitting on the window seat in her dressing room looking out across the garden at the rear of the house. She doesn't realise he is there until he is almost upon her.

"Gregory darling." She grips his hand with hers. Her fingers are thin and frail, her wedding band only held in place by an arthritic bump on the knuckle. "Do you remember playing hide and seek in there with Simon?" She nods towards a small copse of trees. He doesn't remember, but doesn't say as much, only smiling sadly. She enquires about the journey then releases his hand, "I suppose you'll be wanting to freshen up after the drive." This is clearly his cue to leave. His mother wishes to return back to her memories, imagined or otherwise. He stands by the door watching her for a few seconds. She has aged considerably; grief achieving a look that the years had failed to. She doesn't seem to notice as he slips from the room.

After dropping his bag in what was his old room, now a guest room, Gregory goes back downstairs. His father is sitting in the library, a glass in his hand and a book in his lap. The book is unopened. He looks up when Gregory enters the room.

"Join me?" He shakes his glass rattling the whiskey stones

within it. Gregory pours himself a large measure from the decanter, downs it then pours another. He stands with his back to his father looking out of the window across the formal lawn that is edged with sculpted topiary. The house and garden have always remained the same and although well maintained everything about it feels dated, particularly the house. The panelled walls and leaded windows are not to his taste at all, they darken the rooms and create a heavy, oppressive, and somewhat unwelcoming atmosphere. "You can sit with me, if you wish."

"Sorry. I was miles away," says Gregory sitting opposite his father and raising his glass to him. "It's good to see you."

"Likewise. Despite the circumstances."

"How are you doing? And Mum. How is she? Is she…"

"Not drinking. Pills, yes. Valium, or something akin to it I think, mainly to help her sleep. By day she just sits, normally where you found her."

"That doesn't sound healthy."

"Your mother's lifestyle ceased to be healthy a long time ago."

"Quite."

"Now, you are aware of the arrangements for…"

"Yes Dad, I am. I've written the eulogy. Did you want to read it?"

"No that's not necessary. And you're happy to deliver it?"

"Happy? No, I'd rather there were no need, but I am honoured that you think I should do it. Do you have any idea of numbers?"

"I believe there are many people coming. The golf club, the rugby club, ex-girlfriends. It seemed he touched a lot of people. Tony isn't coming though, which is a bit disappointing, after all he is, was Simon's godfather."

"You've hardly seen him in recent years and I'm sure Simon had very little if any contact with him."

"Yes. That's probably true but it would have been nice."

chapter thirty-one

Adrian does not like Anthony Burchfield. He can see why Clive wouldn't have liked him either. Dubious tax practises aside, his business style is often contentious and he has been dubbed a bully among other things. Born in Oxfordshire, he is a second generation heir. His father making a sizeable fortune from property investments. He was educated at a prestigious public school before returning to his hometown and attending Oxford University. He did not complete his degree course and left university to begin working for his father, who gave him a small portfolio of properties to look after. At this time he began to make money of his own and left his father's employ to become a financier. However many of his business dealings at this time saw him labelled by many as an asset stripper, a corporate raider. He always rebuffed these terms, claiming that most companies he worked with increased their value following his interventions. Currently he is the CEO of the investment company that he founded and a major shareholder in several corporations, although some of these appear to be inactive. He and his family own a considerable amount of property, Adrian had to wade through a myriad of documents to establish this. Married twice, he has four children; two from each wife. The elder two work for him.

On the surface it appears that this is a man who bends the law as much as possible without actually breaking it, Adrian is not so sure though. He knows there will be something here that will unequivocally prove Burchfield has crossed the line; probably more than once. There are questions that need answering: Why did he leave university? Why did he leave his father's employ? Why are some of the enterprises he is involved with currently inactive?

By lunchtime he has learnt that Burchfield left Oxford voluntarily. He, along with others, was raising money for good causes, but some suspected not all of the proceeds reached their supposed destination. It was never proved, but to avoid further scrutiny he left the university. Then while working for his father he irritated some of the senior members of staff by trying to implement some questionable practises. They flagged this up and his father reproached him, publicly, which resulted in him leaving the business. He and his father did not speak for a considerable time following this, each side blaming the other. Burchfield was angry that his father did not support him and his father was angry at having to endure the ignominy his son's actions caused. Adrian can see a pattern developing. A pattern of immoral and dishonourable actions that don't quite qualify as unlawful. He hopes when he looks at the inactive businesses he will be able to uncover something. These businesses are most likely shell corporations and although they can have legitimate business purposes they are also useful for tax avoidance or evasion and even money laundering.

Another email alert reminds Adrian that he still hasn't opened his mailbox today. He stops what he is doing and looks through the emails. Some can wait, a couple from Paul requiring answering, then he looks through those forwarded from the newspapers 'contact us' page. These are often nonsense or involve minor news stories that he doesn't bother with, but he likes to look through them anyway; he would hate to miss something. As he thought, most aren't worth a second look, but then something catches his eye. The subject title is crossword puzzle. Occasionally people do email in if they believe there is an error on the crossword and some even enquire about setting the crossword, but why it has been forwarded to him he doesn't know. He enjoys a crossword though, as did Clive. They would often race against each other.

FAO Adrian Miller

Ha, I stop a chill via bad med reorder for my location

Best wishes Dante from Rufus

Adrian reads the email again and again. He lets out a whoop, causing some of those working nearby to look at him strangely. He'll let them wonder. He can't explain that he is reading an email from someone he thought he might never hear from again. Rufus is Clive and he is Dante. They were pseudonyms of their favourite crossword setter and they borrowed them when referring to each other during their crossword battles. The clue is a cryptic one. The first half, up to the word reorder is an anagram. Reorder is the instruction. For my location means the reordered anagram will tell him where Clive is. Adrian is good at anagrams so hopefully this won't take too long to work out. He begins playing around with the letters, re-ordering them, as instructed but after several minutes he is no closer to solving it. He knows he can work this out, although frustration is hampering the thought process. As more time passes he decides to approach it differently. On a map of India he draws a small circle with Clive's last known location at the centre of it. He then lists the major towns within that circle, then works his way through the list to see if any of the places correspond to any of the letters in the anagram. The fourth place on the list is Ahmedabad, it's a match. He removes these letters and starts moving around the ones he is left with. Three or four minutes later he is looking at the words civil hospital on his notepad. That's it, he is at the Civil Hospital, Ahmedabad.

He calls Samantha to tell her the good news. She is overjoyed and says she will call the hospital straightaway.

"No. Don't do that."

"Why not?"

"The manner in which he got in touch makes me think he must believe he is still in some kind of danger." He explains the cryptic clue to her. "Otherwise he would have made contact via more conventional methods."

"Okay, that makes sense. But what now?"

"I'll get someone to go and see him. Someone I can trust."

Samantha knows this makes sense but she doesn't like the fact that control of the situation is not in her hands. After all, it is her dad. "Actually Adrian I'll get someone to go to him."

"And who do you know who can do that."

"Aisha or Mahima. Mahima I think."

"Samantha, I think you should let me handle this."

"I am going to ask Mahima. If I need help I'll get back to you." She disconnects the call before he can respond.

He is not happy but respects that this is her decision to make, not his. However, he lets his guy know that Clive has been found and keeps him on standby should the situation change. For now he will get back to the investigation and establishing any wrongdoing on the part of Anthony Burchfield.

chapter thirty-two

Simon's funeral was a sombre affair. Despite his parents wish that the day should celebrate Simon's life, the sadness loomed large. Anecdotes and stories were shared and an occasional sad smile was raised but the anguish, distress and torment were never far away. In truth nothing had prepared any of them for this scenario. Simon wasn't old and he wasn't unwell. His death arrived suddenly, full of shock and horror at its manner. Murder is truly most horrid.

Gregory has not yet acknowledged his own grief, dealing with the formalities of bringing Simon home, the investigation and writing the eulogy has meant his own feelings have not yet found a place. He has kept them suppressed and hidden but now they claim him; coursing through him, invading every corner of his being like an advancing army. And he is angry: with himself, Simon, everyone. Even the vicar, has angered him. During his sermon he talked of a life lost, it wasn't lost, it was taken. Kindness and sympathy were in boundless supply but did not reach him, not really.

As the last people leave and the door is closed his mother climbs the stairs to go and sit in her spot once again. Gregory watches her. Like his father he feels the exclusion she has imposed on herself is most likely permanent. She turns at the top of the stairs and looks down at him with unsmiling eyes, sorrow etched on her face.

"Goodnight Gregory. Have a safe trip back." And then, with such grace she sweeps across the landing towards her room; her movement at complete odds with her mood. He mutters a goodnight that goes unheard before going in search of his father. He finds him in the library, it seems he too has a favourite spot. He is sitting in semi-darkness, the only illumination, a faint light that remains of the day, coming through the window.

"Drink Dad?"

"No, thank you."

He pours one for himself and takes a seat near his father. He switches on a small lamp on a side table next to his seat, the sudden brightness causes his father to blink. The light also reveals a damp, glossy sheen on his father's cheeks. He reaches into his pocket to get his handkerchief, to offer to his father, but thinks better of it.

"I think it went okay," says his father. "Your eulogy was very good, spot on actually. Good turnout too, more than I had anticipated."

"He was liked and respected by a lot of people."

"Yes." His father pauses before continuing. "The investigation into Simon's death seems to have hit an impasse. I think that's the word they used. I don't suppose you have heard anymore?"

"No. They haven't charged Appleby-Jones yet, but I think that is just a matter of time. As for getting anyone further up the food chain, I'm not sure any progress has been made yet, although I will not rest until I see it done."

"I knew of an Appleby-Jones many years ago. Played in a golf tournament he had something to do with. Family friend of Tony's I believe."

"Really?"

"Yes. Didn't like him much. Right I think I might turn in. What time are you off tomorrow?"

"Early."

"Right. Well, in case I don't see you in the morning have a good journey back. Goodnight."

Gregory won't see him in the morning. He intends to be gone before anybody is up. He needs to get back because he has to find out who killed Simon, and he wants to get back because he has to see her.

chapter thirty-three

Mahima has an excellent memory when it comes to faces, she may struggle to assign a name, but the face she always remembers and more importantly where she remembers it from. So she is horrified to spot a face she recognises outside the civil hospital in Ahmedabad. Thankfully she is not alone. Both Nisha and Aisha have accompanied her and Nisha has also brought along a friend. The four of them watch from the safety of their car as he goes through the automatic sliding doors of the hospital entrance and approaches someone behind a counter who points a very straight arm down the corridor. They watch the man walk away until they cannot see him anymore.

"Are you sure it is him?" Aisha asks.

"I am sure," replies Mahima.

"So now what?" It is Nisha's turn to speak. "What should we do?"

"I will go in," says Mahima. "I'll assess the situation and if, as I suspect he is in danger here we will remove him."

"Not on your own, you're not." Nisha speaks as a mother would.

Mahima does not argue with her, she learnt long ago that it is a waste of time. Nisha always gets her way.

"Okay. Aisha you stay here in the car, in case we need to get away quickly. You two can come with me."

Aisha would rather go in with Mahima but she is the best driver among them so it is best she stays with the car, ready and waiting. She watches the three of them go into the hospital, the doors sliding shut behind them. Mahima disappears from view for a second, then reappears pushing a wheelchair. Nisha sits in the chair and her friend pushes her along while Mahima approaches the counter. Again the person behind the counter points a very straight arm down the corridor and the three of them walk in that direction.

They follow the signs for the men's wards, still unsure what they will do when they get there. Mahima is glad the man she saw in the car park is not around, maybe he is not here for the same reason that she is after all. Outside the entrance to the men's wards is a reception area with another counter. The lady behind it is looking at Mahima enquiringly so she asks if she could tell her on what ward they will find Clive Wainwright.

"Ah. Our mystery man."

"Excuse me?"

"Clive Wainwright. Up until fifteen minutes ago we had no idea who he was. We had been calling him Frank but now we know who he is."

"I see," said Mahima, although she doesn't see at all.

"Are you family?" The receptionist asked.

"Friends."

"I see. Well as I told the previous gentleman, Frank, sorry Mr Wainwright, is having therapy at the moment so you will have to wait in the waiting area until he is finished."

Mahima's heart sank. She had hoped the man from outside would not be here. "Oh okay. Is the previous gentleman in the waiting room?"

"No, I believe he is talking to a member of the medical team, filling in some details; as I said, Mr Wainwright doesn't even know his own name. If you all just wait in the waiting area someone will come for you when he is back from therapy."

Mahima looks at the signs on the walls. The waiting room is to the left, treatment rooms to the right. She heads to the right.

"No, no. Wrong way."

"Oh, I'm sorry."

"Your friend would not want you interrupting his treatment now would he?"

Mahima smiles apologetically but at least she knows where Clive is now. The waiting area is actually a few benches set out along the corridor. It is perfect, because although not particularly comfortable it gives a great view of the reception desk. She hopes that the receptionist vacates her post before somebody else comes along. A few minutes later and that is exactly what happens; good luck or divine providence, whichever it is she is thankful. She and Nisha go round to the treatment rooms with the wheelchair. Nisha's friend stays in the waiting area ready to distract the receptionist should she come back. Only one of the rooms is occupied. They knock on the door but do not wait for a response, instead opening it quickly stepping inside. Clive is being helped from a treatment table by a nurse when they burst in. The nurse lets out a little scream before demanding to know who they are.

"It's okay Sonya, they are friends of mine." Clive recognises Nisha from their meeting at the Bahucharaji Temple and he has seen pictures of Mahima.

"I thought your friend was a man?"

"What?"

"There is a man here claiming to be your friend, he is bad news," says Mahima. "We are here because Samantha asked us to come and I think we need to get you out of here, and quickly."

"Wait just a minute," say Sonya. "He is not going anywhere and who is Samantha?"

"Samantha is my daughter," says Clive.

"Frank, you can't even remember your own name but now you remember your daughter?"

"I'm sorry Sonya."

"You telling me you have been lying?"

"We have to go," interrupts Nisha. "Now."

"As I said, he is not going anywhere."

"I am."

"I can't just let you walk out of here, one, you are not nearly well enough and two, there are procedures to follow."

"We don't have time for procedures. Get in the chair Clive."

"Frank, I mean Clive or whatever. I like you but you can't do this. I'll lose my job."

"And if I stay I may very well lose my life."

"You need medication and care. You are not yet a well man."

"Sonya. I am leaving. I have to."

"Then you have to hit me."

"What?"

"Hit me."

"I'm not hitting you," says Clive.

"Just do it."

"No."

Sonya turns to Mahima. "You do it."

"I can't hit you either."

"Then he is staying with me."

A clenched fist flies forward and connects sweetly with the side of Sonya's face, her legs fold beneath her and she slumps to the floor in a heap. Clive and Mahima turn to look at Nisha who is rubbing the knuckles of one hand with the palm of the other.

"You hit her," says Mahima.

"She wanted us to and besides she was talking way too much and way too loud. Now, let's get out of here."

Clive gets into the wheelchair, Mahima covers him with a blanket and Nisha opens the door and peeks outside. The receptionist is having a rather animated conversation with a nurse, her back is towards them so they sneak out and make their way up the corridor. Nisha's friend spots them so runs to catch up with them. They tell him to go and tell Aisha to get the car ready to leave and when they exit the hospital a minute later Aisha is waiting, doors open, engine running, like a seasoned getaway driver. Between them they shove Clive into the back of the car; he winces as they do. Mahima and Nisha sit either side of him and Nisha's friend sits in the front. Aisha accelerates hard. She glances in her rearview mirror as she heads towards the exit and catches a glimpse of the man they were watching earlier coming through the hospital doors. Another look reveals security officers from the hospital running behind him. She puts her foot down even harder and drives onto the highway without giving way. A chorus of beeps, hoots and honks ensue, but she keeps going, swerving in and out of lines of traffic not slowing down until they reach the safe house that Adrian has arranged for them.

Back in London Adrian and Samantha are on tenterhooks. She is glad Adrian is with her since inevitably she needed his help. Visiting Clive in hospital, removing him if necessary would be easy enough but then what. What next? Where should they take him? When Mahima had asked this question Samantha did not have an answer; thankfully Adrian did.

Her phone rings and she answers it instantly, without even looking at the screen to see who is calling.

"Hi." It is a voice she recognises but not the one she was hoping to hear. "Is everything okay? I'm at work and both you and Adrian are absent."

"We are at Adrian's. You should come over. I need to go, I'm waiting for a call." She disconnects the call and tells Adrian that Gregory is probably on his way over.

Samantha's phone rings again. This time she looks at the screen, it is Mahima. "Hello." The inflection in her voice means that hello is actually a question.

Mahima tells her they are at the house and her father is safe, although he is unwell. She thinks it would be prudent for him to see a doctor. She explains that Clive has no belongings, they were all taken, including his passport. Samantha makes mental notes of the things that need to be arranged in order for her dad to be brought home. Then she speaks to him, he sounds weak but relieved. He then asks to speak to Adrian. She steps out of the room while they talk so she can gather herself together; talking to him was emotional.

When she goes back into the room Adrian is on his own phone doling out instructions to someone. She picks up her phone and lets her mum and sister know Clive is safe.

"Are you alright?" Adrian asks her.

"I'm fine. I will be glad when he is home."

"That shouldn't be long now, someone from the Deputy High Commission in Ahmedabad will go and see him today. They will also arrange for a doctor."

"Can we trust them?"

"We have to."

She looks at him with unease and he explains that there are people at the house with them now who he trusts implicitly, and she should not worry. His guarantee does little to appease her, but she knows it is out of her hands now. The intercom system distracts her from her thoughts; it is Gregory.

Adrian fills him in on what has been happening and it is only after Gregory remarks that a lot has happened in his absence that she remembers where he has been and why.

"Oh Gregory. How was the funeral?" A stupid question, she realises as soon as it leaves her lips.

"Hard. But it has strengthened my resolve to discover who was responsible for Simon..." His voice trails off.

"Well we can help you there," says Adrian.

"I know. So, what do you want me to do?" Gregory asks.

"Right now you could fetch me a sandwich," says Samantha as her stomach emits a low growl.

"I can do better than that. Fancy popping out for something to eat?"

He is surprised when she says yes. He tries to conceal his excitement, after all its only lunch and she has to eat. However, his delight is no surprise to Adrian who tells them to take their time. He can get on with things while they are gone.

They go to a small bistro that is walking distant from Adrian's, choosing a table by the window. As she sits she releases an elongated sigh and rubs her eyes with the heels of her hands, apologises, offering tiredness as her excuse. Gregory reaches across the table and takes her hands in his, telling her she has no need to apologise.

"Your dad will be fine," he continues. "He is a survivor."

"I hope you're right. Anyway, how are you doing?"

He shrugs in response to her question. There are no words and he doesn't want to waste precious time searching for them. A momentary pang of guilt prods him as his feelings for Samantha push aside his grief, but then, surely, that's what should happen. Simon would certainly say so. Gregory can hear him, *'life goes on buddy'*. And he would like her too. This thought amuses him, and his amusement is visible.

"Share," she says.

"Sorry?"

"Share with me, whatever it is that put that smile on your face."

"Oh, I was just thinking about Simon." His smile fades.

"Tell me about him."

"I wouldn't want to bore you."

"I'm sure he wasn't boring."

"No, you're right, he wasn't. He was anything but that."

He was smart and funny, a beautiful man and a joy to spend time with. Although he was younger than me, we were always on the same wavelength. We had a connection that bonded us, made us more than brothers, made us friends. He was my first friend. In fact, when I went away to school I think I missed him more than my parents. He was full of gentleness and goodness and fun; boundless fun. Fun oozed out of every pore and warmth radiated from him. Everyone loved him, not just everyone, everything, too. He had an affinity with animals. Animals always liked him, especially dogs. So much so that we thought he would become a vet. Or if not a vet, maybe a sportsman. He was a fabulous sportsman, annoyingly good at all sports; particularly cricket and golf and rugby and... actually yes, he really was good at them all. He was adventurous too, he would try anything: cliff jumping, bungee jumping, shark diving, caving, mountaineering. He was the first of us to try snow-boarding and then took it one step further by going sand-boarding. His bravery used to astonish me and his wanderlust, I envied. He loved to travel. And I don't mean two weeks in the sun on a sandy beach; proper travelling, mixing with the locals, absorbing the culture. That's how he fell in love with India. Once he went there, he never went anywhere else again. India became his mistress, and he spent every penny on her and every moment he could with her. He spoke of India in such glorious terms.

"I can understand that. It is a fabulous place," says Samantha.

Yes, I thought that too, but to him it was so much more. It captivated him. I would go so far as to say it became part of him. I wish I had travelled as extensively as he did.

"It's never too late."

"I think it is. It's something you do in your youth, before careers and responsibilities become the norm."

"Goodness, you paint a bleak picture of your future if you are ruling out travel."

"I'm not ruling out travel. God knows everyone needs at least one holiday a year, but that's what they will be. Holidays. Breaks from the everyday."

"Not for me," she says. "I still want adventure."

And it is then, in that moment that he realises he has unwittingly highlighted the difference between them. She craves adventure and excitement. He longs for order and calm, obviously fun too, but without risk. This fundamental difference is a reason as good as any why he needs to get over this infatuation.

ᛪ

The doctor is satisfied that Clive's recovery has progressed well and is happy for him to fly, however, he reminds him there is a risk now and in the future of contracting infectious diseases and any travelling should only be undertaken after visiting a doctor for advice. He would also prefer it if he were accompanied on the flight home. The official from the embassy explains that emergency travel documents have been arranged and he can return home as early as tomorrow. He agrees with the doctor and thinks someone should escort him back to the United Kingdom but says that unfortunately the embassy have no staff to spare for such an undertaking. Mahima steps forward and says she is more than happy to travel with him but explains that she does not have the requisite documentation. The official says he will organise it. He and the doctor stand and bid farewell but as the doctor leans forward to shake Clive's hand the sound of breaking glass makes him jump. A scream follows and a popping sound that is unfortunately familiar to them all. The doctor drops to the floor with his arms across his head, desperately trying to protect himself from the gunfire while Mahima pulls Clive behind a sofa, where they are joined by the official. In another room Nisha and her friend are also hiding behind furniture, both are bleeding. And Aisha is outside, she was getting something from the car when the gunmen arrived. There are four of them including the man from the hospital. Three of them headed towards the house, while the driver stayed behind the wheel. They were clearly not expecting any resistance though. Aisha doesn't know who started firing first, but as soon as they did she threw herself down behind a low wall pulling herself further into the shrubbery. The shooting subsides and Aisha watches as the three men try and reposition themselves and she wonders if they have realised that there are only two men in the house who are armed. They move closer and closer to the house and then, just as they look ready to make their move cars sweep down the lane toward them. The would-be assailants scatter as they try to evade capture. One of them is felled by a single shot, the driver has already been dragged from the car, the other two escape. Aisha keeps watching and only emerges from her hiding place when she spots one of the men charged with looking after them.

Thankfully nobody was seriously hurt in the attack, but all are shaken. Nisha and her friend have small lacerations to their face and arms, from the shattered window.

"They threw this rock through the window," says Nisha.

"I don't understand why they did that though, it was the sound of breaking glass that alerted us. If we hadn't heard it I reckon they would have shot us all before we even realised they were here," says Clive.

"I broke the window to warn you," says Aisha.

"What? You cut my face," Nisha shouts.

"But saved your life," says Mahima.

"The other thing I don't understand," says Clive, "is how they knew we were here." He turns and glares at the doctor and the consul official, certain the leak must have originated from one of them. Both begin pleading their innocence. The doctor stressing he had no idea who he was seeing until he arrived at the house anyway and the official claiming it was he who called for law enforcement intervention that probably saved them all.

"Why would I have done that, if as you are implying I am the leak?"

"We can't stay here," says Clive.

"Where should we go?" asks Mahima.

"I suggest you come with me to the embassy. We will keep you somewhere safe until you leave tomorrow."

Clive is not sure what to do, who to trust or where to go. But he knows somebody who will. He calls Adrian, who is horrified to hear that the safe house he arranged has been compromised. Like Clive he believes their whereabouts must have been leaked by someone at the embassy.

"The problem is they are the only ones who can issue you with documents to travel."

"Exactly. So what should I do?"

"You have little choice. You need to go with him."

"I don't like it, but you're right there is no choice. I suppose I'll be safe inside the embassy, just need to get there safely."

Adrian hopes he is right; recent news events have shown that not all embassies are the safe havens they should be. He finishes the conversation and wonders if he should tell Samantha about the attack on the safe house. He decides against it, for now. He will tell her once Clive is airborne and actually on his way home.

chapter thirty-four

The ground below disappears beneath a carpet of cloud and finally Mahima feels she can stop looking over her shoulder. It has been a heart-stopping couple of days and she has had quite enough excitement. Although her anxiety hasn't completely abandoned her, for she has never flown before and she is still concerned for her companion. She looks across at Clive, he doesn't look well. As if reading her mind, Clive looks at her and mouths, I'm fine. She smiles at him and turns once more to look out of the window. The fluffy clouds stretch out as far as she can see, like a giant field of marshmallows. She wonders if this brilliant white vista is what the Polar Regions look like. In her time she has travelled miles, yet she is only just beginning to understand how vast the world is; how different it is, not just landscapes, people too, especially the people. For such a long time she was wary of everyone, then she met Nisha, who showed her kindness and taught her that not everyone was to be feared. And now she has a network of friends that spans continents. A warm feeling spreads through her, before it is interrupted by a bump and a message for passengers to return to their seats and fasten their seatbelts. Instinctively she reaches for Clive's arm. He takes her hand in his and tells her not to worry.

"This is quite normal, a little turbulence, that's all." Mahima nods nervously but doesn't remove her hand. "You should try and get some sleep. We have quite a way to go yet," continues Clive.

"Yes, I will try and perhaps you should do the same. You do look tired."

"Not tired, just old."

"You are not old."

"Old enough to be your father."

"I rather wish you were," says Mahima wistfully.

"No, you don't. I have not been a good father. I wonder if I have even been a good man."

"You are a good man. I am certain of it. And besides, I do not think Samantha would go to so much trouble if you were not. She loves you very much."

"I know she does and it is a love that I don't deserve. But I will make it up to her and her sister too."

"I did not know she has a sister."

"Yes, Maxine. She is a couple of years older than Sammy."

"Is she a journalist too?"

"No, no. She is a, erm… a, you know I can't rightly recall what she does. I haven't actually seen her for a while."

"I see. You're probably closer to Samantha as she does the same as you. You have more in common I should think."

"Yes, I suppose that's it," says Clive. "You know I think I will try and get some shut-eye."

Mahima is the first to fall asleep. For Clive, sleep is just beyond his reach. Despite the weariness of his body, his mind is wide awake, filled with thoughts of his daughters, especially Maxine. He tries to picture her now, as a grown woman. It has been too long since he has seen her. Fixed in his memory is an image of her, she is at the beach filling a small pink bucket with pebbles. She loved collecting stones and pebbles and he would always look out for some while on his travels. She would marvel at them and he would weave fantastical stories about their origins for her. Then, as time passed and his forays home became less frequent, she no longer wanted the pebbles and even less his stories. Consequently, at home, in his tiny studio flat sits a box of pebbles that he still adds to. The happy, playful image of her fades from his mind and is replaced by her screaming and sobbing and begging him to stay. She cried every time he went away. He wants to see her smiling face again so reaches to his back pocket, fingers searching for his wallet. His wallet that holds two small photographs, one of each of his daughters. Of course it is not there, it is missing along with his battered backpack.

A lump comes to his throat as he silently acknowledges his failure as a husband and a father; at the time he thought he was doing the right thing, he truly believed his family would be happier without him. He was sure his unhappiness would infect them all. Ambition, depression, disenchantment, they were all to blame. His need to right wrongs and inevitably his desire to be alone all became more important than his family, but he never stopped loving them.

His daughters have both responded to his absence in different ways. Maxine pretends he no longer exists and Samantha wants to emulate him. He understands Maxine's response more than Samantha's. It is exactly what he did, following his mother's death. He walked away and never returned. As far as he is concerned he no longer has a father, but then his father was an abusive, violent man who made life intolerable. Clive is not like his father, but even so, he still recognises Maxine's anger. How to make amends though, is it possible to remedy the hurt he has caused? He wants to, facing your own mortality does that; atonement becomes a thing, an important thing.

४

Samantha is looking forward to seeing her dad, although his return has created tension between her and Adrian. She resents the way he has assumed control regarding all the arrangements, especially after the attack on the so-called 'safe house'. It means Gregory now has a new role; that of mediator between them. In the end she allows Adrian to organise things - he does have the right contacts – on the proviso that he keeps her in the loop. It's not that she doesn't trust Adrian's judgement, far from it, it's just that it is her dad and she wants to be the one to bring him home. But as Gregory rightly says, it doesn't matter as long as he gets home. She forwards the flight number and other details on to her Mum and Maxine, she is not entirely sure they care but it is right they know what is going on.

Once he has landed and been processed a private ambulance will take Clive to a private clinic. It is likely he may still require medical attention following his operation and even if he doesn't a period of recuperation is not a bad idea. Samantha will see him there. She looks at flight tracker on her phone, his plane has landed. A weight is lifted as she processes this information. A text from Adrian confirms it. She wonders if he has spoken to her dad already. She bristles at this thought, but then tells herself this is no time for the green-eyed monster, jealousy has no place. After all Adrian is only doing as she asked and 'keeping her in the loop'. It's likely that he followed the flights progress just as she did. Her phone goes again, this time it is Gregory offering her a lift to the clinic. She would rather go by herself, but that would involve either an expensive taxi ride or a long journey on two trains and a bus via public transport. She opts for Gregory's offer.

The motorway is particularly slow and her frustration is making her tetchy and short-tempered. He tries to keep things upbeat with idle chatter, but it isn't working. He gives up and they drive along in silence for more than a few minutes. When the traffic comes to a complete stop, Samantha breaks the silence with a loudly spoken expletive.

"Can't we find an alternative route?" she asks impatiently.

"We could, but we need to get off the motorway first. We have been stuck between junctions for almost an hour now."

"What is causing the problem anyway?"

"Roadworks, accident, who knows. Have a look on your phone. See if anything comes up."

She has already started doing just that. She looks up when she feels the car move. Gregory and other drivers are trying to manoeuvre to the side of the carriageway to allow an emergency vehicle through.

"There's your answer," he nods toward the passing police car. "An accident I reckon."

Samantha goes back to her phone, but instead of looking at the map app she logs on to twitter. She scrolls through several tweets before spotting something that catches her eye.

"Oh my God," she says loud enough to make Gregory jump.

"What is it? What's the matter?"

"It's not an accident. It's a shooting."

"What?"

"A shooting."

"Where?"

"Up ahead. It is a shooting that is causing the traffic problems."

"That can't be right," he says.

"Well it's what they are saying on twitter. And some of the news agencies are tweeting about it too. Although they are saying the reports are unsubstantiated."

"Well there you go. It's probably no more than a vehicle backfiring. Shootings here are pretty rare."

"People on here seem convinced about it," she says waving her phone at him.

"It's just an accident. I mean, who would want to shoot someone on the motorway." As the words fall from his mouth he turns to look at Samantha who utters another 'oh my God' before reaching for the door handle. He quickly reaches across and stops her opening the car door. "You can't just get out and run along a motorway. It is illegal and bloody dangerous."

"But …"

"I know what you're thinking, and even if he is involved there is nothing you can do at this moment in time."

"But …"

"No buts Samantha. Just sit tight. We'll get off the motorway and hopefully get some more information."

"I'm going to call Mahima."

He wonders if that's a good idea but doesn't say so. Maybe she will answer and prove their worrying to be unnecessary. Samantha tries several times to call, each time it goes to straight to voicemail. She puts her phone in her lap and stares out of the window. They are moving now, but very slowly.

"Looks like we are being diverted off of the motorway. As soon as we can we will stop and try and find out what is going on. Perhaps we can give Adrian a call."

"Oh yes. Call Adrian. Adrian will have all the answers. He is not bloody God you know. He doesn't know everything."

"Samantha stop being silly. Adrian may know if Clive is at the clinic. If he is we can stop worrying and head over there."

"I never asked you to worry."

"What are you talking about?"

"You said 'we can stop worrying'. I'm just saying I never asked you to worry. He's my dad."

Gregory doesn't respond. He understands she is concerned, but right now her petulance is annoying and upsetting him. He drives a little further along the road before pulling into a layby and calling Adrian. He answers almost immediately.

"Is she with you?"

"Yes," says Gregory, straightaway realising who Adrian is alluding to. "Hold on a minute, it's hard to hear you. I'll move and see if I can get a better signal." He gives Samantha an apologetic smile before getting out of the car and walking to the end of the layby, thankfully she doesn't follow him. "Right, she can't hear me now. What is it? What has happened?"

He is walking differently, as though carrying a weight and she knows he has something to tell her. He gets back into the car and turns to look at her. She blinks hard to stem the tears that are already threatening to fall. The words, your father is dead are in her head but that is not what she hears. She asks him to say again.

"Your dad is fine and so is Mahima. They are at the clinic."

"Thank God," says Samantha as her tears escape despite the good news.

"However," continues Gregory. "There was an incident."

"What sort of incident?"

"According to Adrian, - although all is not entirely clear - it would seem there was an attempt to run the vehicle your dad was in off the road. And possibly shots were fired. But nobody has confirmed that. The main thing though is that everyone is fine. They are all fine."

"Oh Gregory. When is this going to end? Who else have I put at risk?"

"Listen to me. This is not your fault."

"I'm beginning to wish I had never come across the Amit story."

"Don't say that."

"Why not?"

"I'll tell you why, because what that story has led to needs to be exposed and all those involved held accountable. Anything less would be an insult to all the girls that have been caught up in it. Anything less would be an insult to my brother."

"Yes you're right."

"And now I think it will be looked at more thoroughly by our agencies. It's no longer just a situation that occurred in another country."

"You think so?"

"I know so. Possible shootings and attacks on the motorway will get their attention."

"Good."

"Now let's go and see your dad."

chapter thirty-five

The police officer's questions are insulting and Adrian wastes no time in telling him so. However, he knows why he is asking them. There has to be a leak. Clive's movements were only known to a few people. Adrian suspects the leak is from some corrupt official, unlike the police who seem to think the leak is closer to home. He tells them in no uncertain terms that they are being ridiculous.

They in turn tell him, they will be in touch very soon and he is not to go disappearing off anywhere. His phone rings, it's Paul. For a second he considers declining the call but he knows if Paul really wants to speak to him he will just keep on ringing and ringing until he does answer. "Paul."

"What the hell is going on?"

"Regarding?"

"You know damn well what it's regarding. I've had people here asking all manner of questions and I wasn't able to answer any of them. I'm the bloody editor and I know nothing. So I suggest you and your little gang get yourself into this office ASAP and bring me up to speed."

"I can't do that right now. I have to …"

"You will, damn it. You must have pissed off some influential people and quite frankly if it was just about you I wouldn't care, they could do their worst. But, it's not all about you and I will not have you and your pathetic little followers ruining the reputation of this paper."

Paul hangs up without allowing Adrian to respond. Not that there is much he can say. He has known Paul for many years, witnessed his anger and rage but that was something else. The tone he used has left Adrian in no doubt that he is not to be ignored.

Y

Samantha holds her father's hand and tries to decipher the gibberish mumblings that pass his lips. A combination of strong painkillers and recent trauma the most likely cause, although knowing this does nothing to allay her concern. He looks different; undone and defeated. Gregory reminds her that Clive has been beaten, undergone emergency surgery and been shot at, twice.

"He is bound to look different. But you wait, before long he will be back to his old self."

"I'm not so sure," say Samantha. "Shush now Dad. Just rest."

"I wonder if he is trying to tell us something." Mahima who has been sitting silently in the corner, pipes up. "At one point I thought he said a name."

Gregory's phone vibrates. It's Adrian so he steps outside to take the call. He is gone for several minutes and when he comes back into the room Samantha can see he has something to say. He relays to her what he had to say and explains that they have to return to London.

"I can't leave him," she says. She looks back to Clive who seems to be settling down a little.

"You have to. And anyway, he needs to rest."

"I am happy to stay with him," says Mahima.

"And I can bring you back tomorrow," adds Gregory.

She looks at them both, while trying to decide what to do. "Okay. We'll go back. All of us will go back. You too Mahima, you can stay with me. Dad can rest and we can come back first thing tomorrow."

The traffic is kinder to them on the return journey and they make good time. They go straight to the newsroom, taking Mahima with them, after all she has been at the centre of this story the entire time. When they get there Adrian and Paul are already engaged in quite a heated debate.

"Finally," says Paul when he spots the three of them approaching. "And who is this?" he asks jerking a thumb in Mahima's direction. Samantha introduces her and insists that she stay and be part of any discussion they may have. Despite raising his eyebrows at the suggestion, he doesn't object. Adrian tells them that he has brought Paul up to date.

"Okay, right," says Samantha tersely. "So what exactly is the point of us being here if we are no longer needed?"

"Well young lady, the point is you are here because I said you need to be here and don't question me again." Paul's measured tones highlight his barely concealed anger. "I want to know what you three intend to do next and I want to know what you have said to the police. I need to know how their investigation will affect the paper."

"Samantha and I haven't been formally interviewed yet," says Gregory.

"You're lucky. I have and it wasn't pleasant," says Adrian.

"Oh? They just asked us a couple of questions at the clinic and said someone would be in touch."

"And they will be, seeing as they have it in their heads that one of us is responsible for the shooting."

Samantha and Gregory exchange bemused looks. "Why on earth would they think that?"

"Because they don't want to acknowledge that the leak came from someone on their side of the fence; an official, someone who should be on the right side of the law but instead thinks themselves above it."

"Is that what you think?" Gregory asks.

"It's what I know."

"So corruption is a problem here too," states Mahima.

"Sadly it's a global problem," says Adrian. "Don't let your perception be fooled into thinking that rich countries are honest and poor ones are not. The poorer countries are less able to hide corruption, so people believe it more prevalent. Not so, if you look hard enough you will find corrupt practices in some of the richest organisations."

"Are you sure you are not over-stating the corruption theory?" asks Paul. "I'm sure if someone on high wanted rid of Clive it could have been done far less visibly."

"So who do you think it is then? One of us?"

"Don't be ridiculous. Maybe we have been bugged again."

"I didn't know we had been bugged before," replied Adrian with more than a hint of sarcasm.

"You know very well what I mean, the email thing, the hack."

"We haven't been using email."

"Maybe your phones are tapped."

Adrian shakes his head in despair. "We are not the leak. They are." He waves his hand and points angrily in no particular direction, yet they all know to whom he alludes. His distrust of the establishment and all associated with it is well known.

"Okay, whatever you say Adrian. Now, let's get on. I need you to give me all you have, pictures, documents, the lot. We have to hand it over to the police."

"Not bloody likely," shouts Adrian.

"Look, it's a police matter now."

"You're one of them, that's the problem. You've been seduced by the prestige and power that is served up alongside the champagne and canapés at those ridiculous events you go to. You've lost sight of what is important."

"You know that is not true."

"Isn't it?"

"No it is not. I have to look after the interests of the newspaper and that means staying within legal boundaries. I don't like it but that is the way it is. Also anything you write regarding this will need to be looked over by the legal team too, but I would guess that we won't be able to run anything else until their investigation is concluded."

"And by then it will no longer be news."

Paul dismisses them all from his office. He has heard enough and is more than a little insulted by Adrian's assertion that he has been seduced by the rich and powerful. Yes, he has made friends with one or two of them; some offer useful connections. He moves in those circles now so what can he do, and besides he would much rather be in the circle than outside of it. And then there are his golf buddies, who are good company and useful business allies. Anthony being one of the latter. He has put a lot of business

Paul's way, which has almost doubled the papers advertising revenue. He has also introduced him to many notable contacts: influencers, people to know, people who make his address book look impressive. Taking all this into account Paul owes it to him to let him know his name has cropped up during this investigation and that the file is now with the police. Not that he need worry, there is either a simple explanation or a mistake has been made. Anthony is certainly not involved in anything as sordid as this, not wittingly. Tax avoidance, creative accounting – possibly. Exploitation of young women and girls, attempted murder, – absolutely not.

chapter thirty-six

Traffic on embankment is flowing nicely this evening. The Thames is lit by an opaque white glow from the distinctive streetlamps that line the embankment. The lights -colloquially called the dolphin lamp posts - consist of two dolphins or sturgeons wrapped around the base of the post, a fluted column leads to the light which is topped by a crown. He has always liked them, that's why he has replicas of them in the garden of his London home; a home he may have to leave for a while, at a rather inconvenient time. There are deals going through that he would prefer to oversee personally. Bloody journos. Nothing more than interfering busy-bodies and one in particular he should have taken care of a long time ago. Of course, there are some who are advantageous to know; a tip he passed on to his son. And thankfully he took his advice, because the information Justin has gleaned has been useful. It's just unfortunate the people he employed to act on the information have let him down every time, either that or this man has nine lives. He considers this and decides it is time to take control of this situation himself. It requires a hands-on approach, so to speak, and despatching this particular man would give him immense pleasure. It's no longer just about business, now it is personal.

ɣ

"So, is that it?" Samantha asks as they leave Paul's office.

"No it bloody isn't," spits Adrian. "We will need to be discreet though. Also we need to sort out what happens to your dad next."

"What do you mean?"

"He can't stay in the clinic forever, but I don't know that he should be on his own straightaway. He really should stay with someone until his recovery is complete. What about your mum? Would she let him stay with her? Or would that be weird?"

"**Mum might be persuaded, but Maxine. Well that's a different** matter entirely."

"Perhaps you should ask. You never know it might give Maxine and Clive a chance to reconcile."

"Maybe." While growing up she wanting nothing more than all her family together and she always thought Maxine was the one preventing it. But as she got older she realised that wish was one **that would never be fulfilled and she was okay with that.** She hasn't spoken to Maxine since that night in the pub, she hasn't even been in touch to ask how dad is. Mum would have told her, Samantha is sure of that.

"Okay. Well, be careful please and I'll speak to you all tomorrow."

"Why be careful?" asks Samantha.

"Because I am concerned that your dad may not have been the only target." Adrian's whispered reply alerts Gregory who pulls him to one side to ask what he means. Adrian raises his eyebrows in Mahima's direction and he understands. Outside the building Gregory suggests to Samantha that she and Mahima come and stay with him.

"I have a spare room that Mahima can have and you can sleep in my room." He smiles before quickly adding that he will be on the sofa. Samantha agrees, not least due to Adrian's warning but also because she has just the one room in a shared house with inquisitive housemates. And the nosey person in her would quite like to see where Gregory lives, although she can well imagine what it is like.

She expected it to be bigger, his house. And grander: flashy, gaudy, screaming wealth. She is sure it is worth something, quite a lot of something - a mews house in Notting Hill doesn't come cheap – but it is not flashy at all, it is actually rather beautiful. Understated and tastefully furnished without a trace of ostentation. It is luxurious, yes and sophisticated, yet comfortable. And he is completely at ease here, she can see the house suits him. She must stop making assumptions based on stereotypes, it is a fault, she knows. For a long time she had Gregory pinned as a big-headed show-off, a spoilt rich boy, but he continues to surprise her and little by little the differences between them are proving to be irrelevant. She casts her mind back to India and that kiss. She wasn't sure what it meant at the time. She is still not sure, and yet, as she watches him pour drinks for each of them she acknowledges for the first time that she does have feelings for him. Feelings she would like to explore. He brings their drinks to the coffee table, carefully placing each one onto slate coasters that he has spread in front of them and sits on a chair opposite the large over-sized sofa that Mahima and Samantha have occupied. Mahima looks as if she will fall asleep any second, Samantha is on her phone. She glances up and notices him looking at her, she explains she is texting her mum.

"I've asked her to put Dad up for a while."

"And?"

"It's not going to happen. Although she isn't saying as much I know Maxine is the problem."

Justin resents it when his father issues orders, especially when they are directed at him. He has been summoned to the house, commanded no less. No please, no will you, just get here now. It must be important though because he wouldn't tell him on the phone why he needs to see him. They are both well aware of the possibility of someone listening to their calls or reading their messages.

His father is pacing when he arrives; a sure sign that something has got him riled. Justin hopes he is not the cause. He listens as his father rants about incompetents and how 'if you want something done you should do it yourself'. When he finally sits Anthony explains to his son that he has to leave the country for a while.

"How long is a while?"

"Can't say, but its fine. I'm always prepared for this scenario. But I need to do something before I go."

His son shakes his head when he hears what his father intends to do. He questions why he can't forget about Clive Wainwright.

"Because he has been a thorn in my side for far too long. Constantly poking around in my business. In the beginning he was just looking for financial irregularities, he was one of those who resented the successful. You know the type, full of envy and animosity towards anyone who is doing better than them; think they are the only ones who work for a living. More recently he has been looking at the type of businesses I'm involved with, particularly in Southern Asia and now he and that wheelchair bound sidekick of his are claiming that the hotels and other investments are nothing more than a cover for an elaborate trafficking racket, of which they have placed me front and centre."

"Dad. It is a trafficking racket," Justin sniggers. His scornful laugh is a red rag to his bullish father. Anthony grabs the lapels of his son's jacket, shaking him as he hauls him out of the chair before pushing him roughly against one of the bookshelves that line the walls of his study.

"It is not, do you hear me. It is not. We are service providers. That is our business. And we take damn good care of all the girls: they are fed, clothed, housed, even schooled. You know what their lives would be like without us. You've seen it, living hand to mouth on the streets, begging for scraps others don't want, sleeping in gutters. We give them a better life and provide a service at the same time. That is not fucking trafficking."

"Okay, okay. I'm sorry." Anthony relinquishes his grip and Justin smooth's his crumpled jacket. "What's the plan then?"

"That is why you are here. I am hoping you will help me come up with one."

This makes Justin uneasy. His father has always been the man with a plan. He always knows what to do. Then he gives the orders and it is done. Justin prefers it that way really, because if things don't work out he can't be blamed. His own ideas have never been good enough anyway, so he stopped offering them as solutions a long time ago. He knows what his father wants though, he wants to be in a room with Clive so he can beat the shit out of him, or worse. But how to achieve that. At the moment he is in a clinic; a very public place and where he goes from there nobody knows, yet.

"Well boy, what are you thinking?" barks Anthony.

"We need to wait until he is moved from the clinic," replies Justin.

"I don't have the time to wait. Any intel from that girl of his?"

Justin goes to his father's desk. The rich, dark red piece of furniture is as imposing as the man who normally sits at it. He is careful not to knock anything out of place as he wakes up the computer and types a code into the browser that allows him to access Samantha's phone. In an instant the details of her conversations and texts and emails are on display. Anthony looks over Justin's shoulder and together they read through them.

"This is brilliant son. And she has no idea?"

"No she doesn't. Not that there is much here that helps us."

"Oh I don't know. I think this situation with the mother can be exploited. Doesn't she live in the countryside somewhere?"

"What? Yes, she does but I don't see…"

"We need to persuade her mum to change her mind."

"About what?" asks Justin.

"THIS." Burchfield bellows in his son's ear as he points to the screen. "Let's persuade the mother to look after the father."

"How and why?"

"Is that all you can do, ask questions?" says Anthony despairingly. He wonders about his son; sometimes the lights are on but nobody's home. "The how, I am working on. The why, is because her house will be a good place for an ambush." He begins pacing again, but this time each step is fuelled by an idea that is forming. "Her mum can text Samantha, say she has had a change of heart and will look after him. But when he gets to the house he will not find his ex-wife waiting to fuss over him, instead he will find yours truly."

He is not convinced it will work and says as much. Anthony dismisses his concerns and begins putting his plan into action. Half an hour later they are joined in the study by Anthony's head of security, a man of dubious background who Justin has never warmed to, but he is someone his father trusts implicitly. He is also discreet, wears a forgettable face and his vicious tendencies mean he can be very persuasive. Which is exactly what is required for this task. After he leaves Anthony tells Justin to pay Adrian Miller a visit.

"My source at the paper says he has all the documentation. However, I'm quite certain a man like Mr Miller will have made copies and I'm also certain he will keep them close at hand. You can pay him a visit and relieve him of them."

Justin is about to ask how but hesitates and then decides against

CAST NO SHADOW

it. He does not want to do this but won't waste his breath saying so; nobody argues with his dad, least of all him.

Y

Mahima has gone to bed. The flight and the drama that followed has caught up with her. Neither Gregory nor Samantha are feeling tired, despite another long and emotional day. Gregory fixes them both another drink and as he hands her hers his stomach growls loudly. "Hungry?" she asks.

"I am rather. You?"

"A little."

"Fancy some toast and marmite?"

"Yes please."

"Good. My favourite late-night snack," he confesses.

"And mine," she smiles. "Although not only late at night. And actually, not just as a snack. I have been known to have marmite on toast for dinner on more than one occasion."

"Me too," he laughs. "I don't enjoy cooking for one. A pause in the conversation is halted by the pop of the toaster. "And it's so much quicker," he adds pointing at the perfectly browned bread. She watches as he spreads the warm slices with lots of butter and a generous layer of marmite. She devours it greedily, much to his delight and amusement. "Would you like some more?" She grins at him and nods. She spots a photograph on the windowsill behind the sink. It is Gregory and another man who bears a similarity to him, they are sporting wide grins and holding beer glasses aloft.

"Is that Simon?" she asks, pointing at the photo with a greasy, marmite marked finger.

"Yes, at Twickenham, watching the rugby."

She tears off a piece of kitchen roll and wipes her fingers. "Do you have anymore?" she asks.

"Are you still hungry?"

"Photographs not toast, of Simon and you, of course."

"I do."

Sitting close to her, hearing her laughter at his boyhood photos reminds him that he is still very much in love with this woman.

Despite their many differences they also have much in common. She shares his love of marmite for a start.

Looking through the photos is something he hasn't done for a long time and certainly not since Simon's passing. They evoke such happy memories although still tinged with sadness. He wonders if that ever passes. He selects another album, this one contains photos from the many family parties they had. His mum loved to throw a party; any excuse. And they were always such fun, until alcohol became part of her daily diet; then the fun stopped. Samantha stops turning the pages and points at a particular photograph.

"Who is that?" she asks.

"That's Simon. At his 21st."

"No, the man with him."

"His godfather. Ha, look at that one," he points at a picture on the opposite page. "What am I wearing?"

But she doesn't want to look at that one. She doesn't want to look at any more.

"You know I think I will go to bed. I'm feeling tired all of a sudden. Goodnight Gregory."

And before he even has a chance to respond, she is gone. Her vacating the room pulls the joy from it and he feels cold. He wonders if he said something wrong, was he sitting too close, perhaps invading her personal space. He has no idea but a change has occurred; a sudden, swift change that is quite inexplicable. A bewildered Gregory clears away the photo albums and takes the spare duvet from the ottoman.

Samantha is lying in his bed, staring at the ceiling. She is not tired, in fact she is more awake now than she has been all evening.

Her mind is racing with possible explanations and scenarios, none of them favourable to Gregory. She can't believe he hasn't said anything, but then he wouldn't if he was one of them. But what about Simon, he surely wasn't party to his brother's murder.

No, she doesn't believe that. His grief is genuine. Then what, just a coincidence. If that's the case why not say. He must be the leak. But why. Maybe he is being blackmailed. Maybe he has been bought off. Maybe this, maybe that. Maybe, maybe … She eventually falls asleep despite the possibilities running through her head.

chapter thirty-seven

He parks the car on a different street, but still close enough in case he needs a swift getaway. In the absence of a balaclava he wraps his scarf around his face and pulls the hood of his top down over his forehead before pulling the drawstring on it tight to ensure it does not slip away from his face. He pulls on a pair of gloves before carefully climbing over the rusty iron railings that lead to the rear of the property. He scans the building to see if any windows have been left open. One has, but it is on the first floor. Adrian lives on the ground floor. No matter, he is rather adept at getting into buildings without the aid of a key. He walks slowly across the courtyard garden, making sure to avoid the gravelled areas as the crunch of gravel may alert someone. Also, the small pieces of stone may get stuck in the tread of his trainers. The kitchen looks out onto the garden and he notices that one of the fanlights looks a little proud compared to the others. As he nears the window, he can see that although it has been shut the catch has not been fastened properly. He can also see that the key to the main window is on the windowsill. So many people make the mistake of doing that; lock all the windows but leave the key visible. He won't fit through the fanlight, but he can probably lean in and get the key to open the window below it. First, he needs something to stand on. He looks around, there are a couple of seats, but he needs something a little taller. He spots a row of wheelie bins, one of them will do. Although a tight fit he is able to lean in and use the key to open the larger window. Within a couple of minutes, he is standing in Adrian's kitchen; grateful now for his time at boarding school, where he honed his breaking and entering skills during night-time forays to the kitchens and other out of bounds rooms. On the worktop he spots Adrian's phone charging. He unplugs it and slips it into his pocket. It may have something useful on it, although probably not the file he is looking for. He tiptoes across the tiled floor towards the door.

Adrian may have lost the use of his legs but the rest of him works perfectly well, particularly his senses. That, coupled with the fact that he sleeps very lightly - if at all - means he is well away that there is someone other than himself in the flat. The question is what to do about it. Should he stay in bed, keep very still and pretend he is asleep? Should he call the police? Or should he try and do something to said intruder? The third option is stupid, but he likes it. After all he has the element of surprise.

The uninvited guest slowly makes his way through the flat. The doors to all the rooms are open, a blessing, no squeaks or creaks to contend with. He passes the bathroom and the living room, he doesn't think either will have what he is looking for. There are two more doors at the end of the hallway, one is presumably a bedroom. With the lightest of steps now he ventures forward. He peers around the first door and smiles to himself when he spots a desk sitting beneath the window, its silhouette visible thanks to the streetlight outside. He gingerly approaches the messy desk. It looks like everything has been dumped on it in a hurry, papers and files and many things that have no right to be on a desk. Atop of all the chaos is a laptop and a couple of memory sticks. He doesn't have time to go through everything so hopes what he is looking for will be there. He puts the memory sticks into his pocket and unzips his hoodie and slides the laptop into it. As he pulls the zip back up the room is suddenly flooded with light. He spins round to see Adrian propelling himself across the room in his wheelchair. Too slow to move he is rammed by the chair and struck on the arm with something. He loses his balance and topples backwards, before he can get up again Adrian has launched himself from the chair and is upon him. When the initial shock has passed he fights back, and with arms and legs flailing he throws Adrian from him. Adrian's face connects with the leg of the desk and he feels his chin split. Ignoring the intense pain he reaches out and grabs the intruder's legs. He can only hang onto one and the other leg comes toward him at speed. Adrian's face takes the brunt once more and he relinquishes his grip. As the intruder scrambles to his feet and heads for the door. Adrian can do no more, he is spent and his eyes close as the intruder flees.

When Gregory gets the call from Adrian he is tempted to go alone, allow Mahima and Samantha to lie in. But he knows Samantha will be cross if he does that, so he wakes them and together they head over to Adrian's.

His face is a mess and requires attention but Adrian is adamant he is not going to the hospital. Samantha takes on the role of nurse and begins bathing his face.

"Not anyone you recognise then?" Gregory asks.

"Look, you just keep rephrasing the same question. As I've already told you, he was dressed in black or dark clothes, his face was covered and he wore gloves. I didn't hear him speak, we didn't exchange pleasantries or take time to strike up a conversation. Ouch."

"Okay, sorry. It's just that sometimes we think we haven't noticed anything when actually we have."

"Well I didn't. Apart from the fact he was tall, had extremely hairy legs, I know because I had hold of one, and he was wearing odd socks."

Samantha drops the small bowl of warm water she is using to clean Adrian's face. "For God's sake will you be careful," shouts Adrian.

"Sorry."

"What is it? Are you alright? You look like you've seen a ghost. You're not going to faint are you?"

"No. I'm fine." Samantha goes into the kitchen for a cloth to clear up the spilt water. She takes a moment to consider Adrian's description of his assailant. Although vague and not much help to most people, it has told her exactly who is responsible. Her phone vibrates in her pocket, several times, four text messages, all from her mum. She reads through them. The contents are a surprise but pleasing; her mum will take her dad in after all. Samantha tries to call her back but she doesn't answer, she sends a text instead then goes and tells Adrian the good news.

"Can you arrange for someone to take him to Mum's?"

"I can," says Adrian. "Probably in a day or two."

"Today. It has to be today. Mum was quite clear about that."

"I don't know if that is possible."

"If you can't sort it, I'll do it myself."

"Samantha, he may not be fit enough yet."

"In case you've forgotten Mum is a nurse and perfectly capable of taking care of him." She will not be dissuaded.

"Fine. I'll see what I can do."

"Thank you. I need to go somewhere now, let me know when it's sorted. Mahima you can come with me."

"Where are you going?" Adrian asks.

She doesn't answer, but takes Mahima by the hand and heads out.

Adrian shouts after her, he reminds her he doesn't have a phone and shouts out his landline number. Gregory follows her and also asks where she is going. She ignores him too, walking away quickly without turning back. When they have turned the corner Mahima pulls her hand free and asks what is going on.

"We are going to see the person who attacked Adrian."

"What? No. You know who it is?"

"I do."

"Why didn't you tell them?" Mahima points her arm back the way they have come. "Gregory should come with us."

"No, no."

"Why not?"

"Because he is the leak."

Mahima brings both hands up towards her face and her eyes widen as the shocking news sinks in. "Are you sure?" she whispers through her palms.

"Yes. I think …"

"Samantha, you have to be sure."

She tells Mahima about the photographs, about Anthony Burchfield and Justin. Mahima listens but is not convinced. She asks why he would have gone to India, why go to so much trouble if he was part of it. Why protect the man responsible for his brother's murder?

"Maybe he wasn't part of it at first, maybe he found out and wanted a piece of the action or maybe he is being blackmailed. Maybe he was told he would end up like Simon if he didn't help them."

"That's a lot of maybes."

"I don't want to be right Mahima."

Disconsolately, Gregory goes back inside. "I don't get her," he says. "One minute she is laughing and joking with me, the next she doesn't want to speak to me."

"What's that?" asks Adrian.

"Oh Samantha. She can be so damn…" he searches for the right word. "... fickle."

"Not fickle, female. Right I had better see if I can sort transport for Clive. I reckon it will have to be a taxi."

"Forget the taxi," says Gregory. "I'll do it."

"Really? You don't have to. There are other ways of getting in her good books."

"I'm happy to do it."

"Okay then. You can take this file with you. I want Clive to look over it when he is able."

"You printed off copies?"

"Of course. I'm old school. I still like hard copies of everything. You might want to have a look at it too, make sure you are up to date. You were away for a couple of days."

"I will. Are you sure you're okay? I still think you should get that face looked at."

"Stop fussing. My face is just fine."

Samantha has left Mahima in the coffee shop around the corner from Justin's flat. She was not happy at being left and said she would call the police if Samantha did not return within half an hour. She reluctantly agreed before heading off. She is not afraid of Justin, despite seeing what he did to Adrian's face and she marches up to his front door confidently. She presses the buzzer several times before he answers. Even though he is surprised to hear her voice he admits her straightaway.

"Sweetpea. What brings you here?"

She hesitates before answering. Anger is not far away but she needs to play it cool. It won't do to throw accusations at him based on his footwear. She needs to convince him she knows what he did and make him realise that the best thing for him to do is to confess his part and offer up his dad in exchange for leniency.

"I wanted to see what you've been up to."

"Ha. Finally missing me are you?"

She doesn't answer his question, choosing to ask a question of her own. "Last night for example. What did you do?"

He turns away from her. She thinks she saw him swallow. "Last night, I erm, watched the footie and had an early night. Early for me anyway. Why do you ask?"

"Because I saw you. In Hoxton, near Old Street tube station."

This time she definitely saw him swallow. "Must have been my doppelganger. They say we all have a double somewhere."

"Perhaps. This one was driving your car though."

He spins around to face her. "What are you saying Samantha? What are you accusing me of?"

Bravely she steps towards him and pulls up the legs of his sweatpants. "Still like to wear odd socks I see."

"And."

"I know where you were. I know what you did. And, more importantly, I know why." She stands her ground and stares at him, hard. He can't look at her and she knows she has won. He flops onto the nearest chair and puts his head in his hands. He cuts a diminishing figure and she almost feels sorry for him. "The question is, what happens next."

"What do you mean?"

"Do I call the police or do you?"

"I can't do that and neither can you. You don't know the sort of people you are dealing with."

"Like your father, you mean. The likes of him do not scare me. I'll make the call then." She takes her phone from her pocket, but before she has even unlocked it he is on his feet and knocks the phone from her hand. For the first time since arriving she is disquieted.

"I'm sorry," he says. Her shocked face upsets him. "I'm not going to hurt you. I'm not even going to stop you. But you cannot use that phone. If you insist on calling the police you must use a different phone."

"Why?"

"Because he will know."

"What?"

"Every phone call, every email, every text, photos, web history. He can see it all."

"How?"

"You have a spy app on your phone." She looks at him with incredulity and he realises he will have to explain. "I put it on your phone. The photo I sent you, it contained the app, so when you downloaded it … Bingo. We could see exactly what you were saying and doing."

"Oh my God. It's not him, it's me. I am the leak." It is Samantha's turn to flop onto the nearest chair. She is pale and shaking. Utterly ashamed to think she ever thought it was Gregory. But the photograph, his brother and Burchfield. Did he know? She shakes her head, so much of what has gone wrong can be attributed to her. From Simon's death to the attacks on her father to the assault on Adrian. "It's my fault. It's all been my fault." Justin watches her. She appears deflated. The bravado and confidence she had on display when she challenged him has slipped away. His chance to take control and at the very least save himself and perhaps even buy his father enough time to do what he has to. He squats down beside her.

"Sweetpea. Don't beat yourself up." He strokes her cheek gently with his index finger. "Let's work out what to do together for the benefit of us all."

It takes but a split second for her to realise what he is doing. This time though, he is wasting his time. She is finally immune to his charm and wastes no time in telling him so. She gets to her feet and asks for his phone and what he took from Adrian's. His reluctance to do as she asks is testing her patience. "Justin you have five minutes. I have a friend waiting for me with instructions to call the police if I do not return when I said I would."

"Yeah, of course you do." His scepticism is evident.

"You know what I'm happy to let her do that." She sits back down, casually crossing one leg over the other. "We'll wait."

He sits too, mirroring her actions and also crossing his legs. "Yes. Let's wait. In the meantime you are in danger of losing both your mother and your father."

chapter thirty-eight

Gregory picks up Clive from the clinic and is glad to see he is looking better. He helps him into the back seat as he thinks that will be more comfortable for him. Both men hope that this journey will not be as eventful as Clive's previous one. The two fall into easy conversation.

"Have I missed much? Any further developments?" asks Clive.

Gregory tells him about the break-in at Adrian's.

"He is okay though, Adrian, he wasn't hurt?"

"A bit bloodied and bruised but otherwise okay."

"What was taken?"

"His phone, laptop and a couple of flash drives."

"Oh no, what about …"

"It's fine. Adrian has copies of everything you and he and the rest of us have been working on," says Gregory, pre-empting what he was going to say.

"That's something I suppose. Although whoever has the laptop will now know exactly what we know."

"That's assuming they gain access. I think Adrian has a lot of security in place, and if necessary he said he can remotely remove the files."

"That's good. This is a nasty bunch of people we are dealing with."

"There is a copy of the file for you and me to look over. It's in the pocket behind the passenger seat."

Clive leans forward and stretches the elastic pocket so he can slide the folder out. "I'm grateful to you for driving me today.

Although, I had hoped Sammy would be with you."

"She is doing something with Mahima today," says Gregory. "And this was all rather hastily arranged."

"Yes it was. But there's no arguing with my ex. If she said it had to be today then so be it. I'm still trying to assimilate the fact that she is prepared to let me stay with her. It's totally unexpected. The vagaries of women, eh."

४

Samantha is alarmed by what Justin has said, obviously concerned for her parents, but she is not going to give him the upper hand. Mahima will call the police. Samantha hopes that doesn't happen though. If she can tough it out for a couple of minutes, maybe he will crack and tell her what is happening.

Justin expected a reaction, he needs a reaction; but nothing. Perhaps she isn't bluffing after all, the police could be on their way already. He runs his fingers around the neck of his t-shirt and his eyes flit towards the window as he hears a siren. The sound fades and he breathes more easily again. He looks back at her, she is unnerving him and she knows it.

"It's tragic how one bad decision, one wrong call can ruin a life," she says. "Worse still when one is relatively young. Hopes and dreams all vanish as your life comes tumbling down, unravelling in a microsecond. Are you going to make a bad decision Justin?"

"I cannot betray my father."

"I know you are scared of him but I reckon prison is scarier."

"Make the right call and you'll be protected."

"I doubt that, my father's reach is long."

"Justin. It is over, make it easier for yourself." She eyes him carefully waiting for a response. Nothing. She looks at her phone. "Time's up."

There is a lot in the file. As usual Adrian has been very thorough. Clive decides to start at the beginning, even though much of the first few pages is nothing new to him. It doesn't hurt to recap though and it's a welcome distraction. He and Gregory appear to have run out of conversation and the view of the M25 from the car window is less than inspiring. He yawns, the gentle rocking of the car and regular movements of his eyes as they follow Adrian's words across the page are making him feel sleepy. He puts the file down and looks out of the window. The monotonous motorway has gone and they are now on the A12. Still a little way to go yet, wouldn't hurt to have some shuteye then, he thinks. It will pass the time and the rest may fortify him before he sees Andrea.

He loved her, loves her. He always will, and not just because she is the mother of his children. She was, is the love of his life; if there is such a thing. Nobody else has ever come close and they never will but the life they shared was not enough. Not enough for him. He had things to do and thinks to say and doing and saying them became the most important thing to him. She said he was off chasing rainbows. He said he wanted to make a difference; do something meaningful. She said she didn't need to live her life on such a grand scale. She could make a difference right here, at home and to her nothing was more meaningful than bringing up their daughters. She was right, of course, but in the end he had to go. If he had stayed he would have ruined them all. He left for them as much as for himself. He said that to her one day. She said, keep saying that to yourself and eventually you'll believe it. She was right again. Ultimately they were two divergent personalities. No matter how hard they tried it was never going to work. And they did try; they tried to make each other a better fit. But doing that would eventually erase the people they were to start with; rob each other of their true self. To say goodbye to the person you thought would be by your side forever is hard. But when compromise means saying goodbye to yourself... in the end there is no choice. Saying goodbye to her was the worst thing for his heart, and yet the best thing for his soul.

Gregory can hear a soft rumbling sound coming from the back of the car. A glance in the rear-view mirror tells him that Clive is responsible for the noise. The rhythmic snores begin to get louder and louder and soon are more than a little irritating so he turns on the radio. He can still hear him a couple of minutes later so turns the volume up on the radio. The gravelly voice of Joe Cocker comes on and finally drowns out his companion's imitation of a freight train. He sings along, not caring that his own not so dulcet tones may wake his passenger. Thankfully they don't, Clive is in a deep sleep and oblivious to everything apart from his own dreaming. Gregory is also in a world of his own and his rendition of Unchain my Heart fills his ears so he can hear nothing else, not even his mobile phone.

ℵ

She didn't write down Adrian's landline number so can't call him. She gets the number of the clinic and calls it on Justin's phone. Her dad has gone, picked up by a Mr Johnson they believe. She tries calling Gregory. No answer. She tries several times before throwing Justin's phone across the room.

"I'm taking your car," she tells him.

"You can't, I need it. You said I could go."

"You can. In a taxi, on a bus, train, plane. I don't care, but I'm taking your car."

Reluctantly he hands over the keys, they are barely in her hand before she is out of the door. Once she has gone Justin goes online. He books himself a flight and calls a taxi. He goes into his bedroom and begins filling a holdall with some essentials. A look at his wristwatch tells him he has less than two hours to get to city airport. He is planning to join his mother at her house on Malta and if necessary plead his case from there. He knows he will have his mother's support. He just hopes Samantha keeps her word and allows him enough time to reach the island.

She curses herself. She should have taken Justin's phone too. Too late now. She comes to an abrupt stop outside the coffee shop and begins honking the horn of the car. Eventually Mahima spots her and comes running from the shop.

"Get in, quickly," yells Samantha. She does as she is told and nervously puts on her seatbelt as Samantha drives the car at speed through the narrow street. Another crunching of the gears causes her to ask Samantha if she has forgotten how to drive.

"I'm sorry. It's a matter of life and death," she says looking at Mahima.

"Yes, ours if you don't keep your eyes on the road."

She smiles apologetically and fills her in while she tries getting to grips with the workings of Justin's car. She gets her to put a postcode into the sat nav system, hoping it will find the quickest route out of London.

"Why can't we just call Gregory?"

"I've tried."

"I will keep trying while you drive."

Samantha puts her foot down. As she leaves the North Circular Road and joins the M11 she wonders how far behind they are. She figures around forty minutes or so based on the time the clinic said her dad had left. Justin's car may be fast but she doubts she can make that time up. Still, she doesn't have to beat Gregory she just needs to reach the house before Anthony Burchfield. Justin said his father would go there once he knew Clive had arrived. Or better still Gregory will answer his bloody phone. Beside her her friend is muttering something.

"Is that Gregory?" she asks.

"No. I am praying."

Samantha wishes she believed in the power of prayer because right now she would pray for the A12 to be its reliably slow self.

chapter thirty-nine

Maxine is watching her mum's house again. Like she has every day since the argument. She needs to know she is okay even if she won't talk to her at the moment. She cares enough to sit outside in her car but is still far too angry to go back home yet. Following her fallout with Samantha she began asking her mum questions and was shocked and dismayed by what she learnt. They say all families have secrets, but she didn't think there were any between her and Mum. And now it seems there is another. A man arrived at the house late last night, clearly someone her mum knows because she invited him in. Today the car he arrived in is still parked outside.

What grates most is that she has stayed by her mum's side when everyone else left. Yet everyone else seems to know more than she does. Of course, by everyone else she means Samantha. She is tempted to go over and knock on the door or even let herself in; she still has her key. Demand to be introduced to Mum's 'friend'. She won't though. She will just watch and wait and wind herself up even more.

४

He had forgotten how picturesque Woodbridge is. In his mind he pictured a dismal, soulless place because it is synonymous with his heartbreak. But that image is so far removed from reality it astounds him. Perhaps he never viewed it properly, or as Andrea said, he never gave it a chance. As they drive through the town memories begin to stir; jolted from their hiding place by reminders of places and things he visited long ago. Signs for Sutton Hoo and the Tide Mill remind him of days out when they were still a family. A barking dog reminds him of days walking along the Deben with his in-law's dog when they were off on one of their cruises. A mother with two small children brings a lump to his throat. He blinks back tears and hopes Gregory doesn't notice. They turn the final corner and he can see the house. The house that was once his home, yet never truly felt like it. He wipes his eyes, blows his nose and runs his fingers through his hair. And then takes a very deep breath. He needs to compose himself before he sees Andrea. Time to remove the rose-tinted spectacles.

ɣ

Maxine watches as a car rounds the corner; quite a fancy car and not one she recognises. She wonders where it is going. It is moving slowly, readying itself to stop. She knows most people on this road and plays a game with herself, trying to predict who the occupants of the car will visit. Both of mum's next-door neighbours are at work, so not them. Maybe it's Doris and George, an elderly couple who live in one of the bungalows. Or perhaps they are visiting Ana and Pavel, a polish couple. He is at work now, but she is home with their young son. The car has stopped behind her mum's visitor's car. The driver gets out, a tall man who she doesn't recognise. He stretches his arms up and arches his back; long drive, she suspects. He opens one of the rear passenger doors, he is helping someone out of the car, it is another man, not as tall as the first. When he is out of the car the second man points. For a second she thought he pointed at her house. The first man goes to the back of the car and opens the boot. He takes out a small suitcase and puts it on the pavement. While he is doing this his passenger is leaning on the car and having a look around. She watches as his head slowly moves around, there is a familiarity about him. A familiarity that becomes recognition when their eyes meet. She gets out of the car, her gaze fixed. It can't be, she says to herself, but there is no mistaking him, despite the years since they last saw each other.

Her mind is racing, yet it cannot find a single reason to explain his presence. And then there are the others. Her mum has not had gentleman callers for, well ever, and now there are three in quick succession, like proverbial buses. Maxine shakes her head before marching across the street. She wants an explanation.

"What are you doing here?"

"Hello Maxie."

"What are you doing here?" she repeats.

"I've come to stay for a few days."

"Yeah, like hell you have."

"Really I am. It's all arranged. Your mum didn't say…"

She looks at the suitcase sitting on the kerbside, then at Gregory. "And you are?"

"Gregory Johnson," says Gregory thrusting a hand forward which Maxine declines to take. "I'm a friend of your sister, Samantha."

"Yes, thank you, I know who my sister is and I might have realised this would have something to do with her."

"Can we talk about this inside, please Maxie?"

"No we bloody can't. You can get back in the car and go back where you came from. I don't know what line Samantha has been feeding you, but you are not welcome here."

"Your mum knows about this. It's all arranged."

"That's not true. And I know that because one, she would have told me and two, her boyfriend is here."

"Boyfriend?"

"Yes, boyfriend."

"I didn't know she had …"

"Why would you? It's nothing to do with you. You left, remember."

"Sammy didn't say."

"Clearly Sammy doesn't know everything," barks Maxine.

Clive wants to weep. His daughter hates him. He doesn't blame her. He hates himself for what he did. He had hoped that while recuperating he may have been able to explain and possibly rebuild their relationship. He turns back toward the car and as he reaches for the door handle he hears a voice he recognises. A voice he hasn't heard for some time.

"Are you coming in or not?"

He follows the voice and sees her. She is standing in the doorway of what was once their home together.

"Am I going in?" he asks Maxine.

"It looks like it," she replies through clenched teeth.

With faltering steps Clive goes in the direction of the house. Gregory picks up his suitcase and follows but Maxine steps in front of him. "Not you," she says, and takes the case from him. He doesn't argue with her; it is clear they have a lot to talk about. He'll wait in the car for now.

Clive's stomach tightens in anticipation. Thus far the welcome has not been what he had hoped for. Not that he had expected the red-carpet treatment, but he had not imagined things would be as tense as this. As he walks up the path he can see her clearly for the first time. She is wearing a baggy jumper and jeans. Her long blonde hair is cut short and flecked with grey. She looks nervy, on edge, but then under the circumstances that's not surprising. An ex-husband coming to stay and a boyfriend in the house. He wishes he had known about that.

"Hello Clive."

"Hello Andrea. It's good to see you."

"Shouldn't you be at work?" Andrea is addressing Maxine.

"I came to make sure you were okay. Just as well I think."

"I'm fine. Go to work." Andrea tries to close the door but

Maxine puts her foot across the threshold. "Go to work, please."
Andrea is imploring her with wide eyes.

"Bring her in," says a gruff voice from behind the door.

Gregory watches the door close and hears shouting and what he thinks is a scream. He stands still and listens, nothing. It was probably Maxine kicking off. He gets into the car, he may as well let Samantha know that they have arrived. He takes his phone from the centre console and sees over forty missed calls. That can't be right. He looks again, yes forty-two, six from one number the rest from another. Both numbers unknown. He will deal with that in a minute after he has called her but her phone rings a couple of times then goes to voicemail. He tries again, same thing. He is disappointed that she doesn't answer. She seemed a little off with him this morning and he was hoping that had passed, still he could be making too much of it and there may well be another reason she is not answering. He sends a text instead:

Thought you'd like to know your dad is safe and sound at your mum's house. G x

He doesn't elaborate on the situation with her sister, it's not his place to comment, so instead he turns his attention to the unknown numbers. He tries them both, no answer. It would appear nobody wants to talk to him this afternoon.

The two women are little more than ten minutes away when Gregory's text comes through. Her heart is hammering in her chest. She is beginning to panic. What awaits her? Is she too late? Has she actually made the right call; should she have let the police handle this? So far her decisions have worked out, but she concedes sometimes down to luck rather than judgement. If only she had left the Amit story alone. Simon would still be alive, her parents would be … She looks at Mahima and remembers what this is all about; women like her. Tens, hundreds, she doesn't know how many. Young girls without a voice or the freedom to choose what sort of life they live. They have to stop it, but first they have to save her parents. She presses her foot as hard as she dare on the narrower roads.

Gregory is a little fed up sitting in the car and considers knocking on the door of the house. He just hopes they haven't forgotten he is still out here. The town centre looked nice, he decides to take a walk back there but as he rounds the corner at the end of the road he is astounded to see two familiar figures climbing out of a fancy sports car. Samantha spots him first and promptly bursts into tears, leaving Mahima to explain.

"That is why your sister knew nothing of the arrangement."

"My sister is here?"

"Yes and your mum's boyfriend."

"She doesn't have a boyfriend."

"Your sister says she does."

"She doesn't have a boyfriend," says Samantha very sternly.

"Okay. Well, then there is an unknown man in there with them. We should call the police."

"NO. There isn't time. Burchfield could be in there now. I'm going in."

"Who?"

"Burchfield. Anthony Burchfield. Your brother's godfather." Samantha watches as Gregory registers the name. His face contorts as he grapples with the notion that one of his father's oldest friends and his brother's godfather is one of the people behind this sickening organisation. "You really didn't know?" He shakes his head.

"What's the plan?" asks Mahima.

Samantha has an idea. She explains that you can get into her mum's back garden from an alleyway in the next street and there is a key to the backdoor behind the water butt. She suggests that Gregory knocks on the front door, after all they probably know he is out there and she and Mahima will get into the house from the back while he causes a distraction. He doesn't like it but in the absence of a better idea he agrees. He gives them a couple of minutes to get into the garden before knocking on the door. Andrea opens up and Gregory tells her he is Clive's driver and wonders if it is okay to come in and use the toilet. A large hand reaches forward and pulls him into the house.

"The more the merrier," says the hand's owner before roughly pushing Gregory into the living room and onto the floor. Gregory looks up to see Clive sitting in an armchair. He looks like he has been roughed up a bit. Maxine is on the sofa where she is joined by her mum. Both women have tear-stained faces. Gregory scans the room, it is long and narrow, running the length of the house with two doors, the one he was pushed through near the front door and one further along. There are patio doors at the end of the room, he thinks he saw someone run past them. The man holding them doesn't appear to be armed. He tries to raise himself up from the floor but the man tells him he can stay where he is and to emphasise this he pushes him back with his foot. That's when he spots it; a knife strapped to his leg. Gregory protests at his treatment and demands to know what is happening. "You'll see soon enough. And then you'll wish you had stayed outside."

"I wish that already," says Gregory. "Come on mate, whatever is going on here is nothing to do with me. I'm just the driver. Let me go. I won't say nothing."

"Yeah sure. We're all just drivers. Now shut up."

He doesn't shut up, he persists, being as loud as possible so the girls can get in without being heard. When he realises Samantha is outside the door he starts getting up again.

"I told you to stay put." A leg is raised once again but this time he grabs hold of it and tries to unbalance the man who stands his ground and reaches down his leg sliding the knife from its sheath. He pulls his arm back and lunges at Gregory before a crack resounds and he falls to his knees, slumping to the ground. Gregory looks up to see Samantha standing over him clutching a baseball bat.

Gregory and Mahima drag the unconscious man into another room while Samantha tells her confused and terrified family what is going on. Andrea says she is calling the police and is about to when there is a knock at the door. Gregory peeks through the window to see the upright figure of Anthony Burchfield standing on the doorstep, another man standing by the gate. Gregory grits his teeth. His fury fermenting; anger rising like mercury in a thermometer. He moves away from the window and positions himself behind the door. He nods at Andrea who opens the door.

"I believe you are expecting me," says Burchfield as he steps inside.

"We sure are," says Gregory as Andrea closes the door behind him. He grabs Burchfield by the neck. Burchfield tries to call out but his cries are lodged in his throat, held there by the pressure being applied by Gregory's hands. He forces him to the floor and continues to squeeze. Burchfield's face has turned a nasty shade of red and the blood vessels in his head are beginning to bulge. His eyes are glassy, wide and full of fear. He looks like he is wearing a grotesque mask, like that of a gargoyle atop a gothic cathedral, as he claws at Gregory's hands, desperate to free himself.

"No," shouts Samantha. "This is not the way." She pulls at Gregory, who refuses to relinquish his vice-like grip. "Please stop." Mahima tries to help her but Gregory is too strong for them both. Shouts can be heard outside and suddenly the front door crashes open – Maxine screams as the house fills with more uninvited guests. These guests, however, are armed.

chapter forty

Samantha was never more grateful for Adrian's interference. Without the police's timely arrival the outcome may have been quite different. She asked how he knew to send the police to

Woodbridge but he refused to tell her; saying he would never reveal a source. She realises now that what she viewed as someone trying to take control because they wanted her story was actually someone wanting to take control so he could keep them safe. He was looking out for her; for them all. When the dust settled the story did run, the whole story. And the by-line was hers. It will be her last though, maybe not ever but certainly for a while. When she said goodbye to Mahima at the airport her longing to revisit India returned. As she drove away from the airport it was all she could think about and by the time she reached home she had decided. She was going. Her mum expressed concern but gave her blessing anyway, her dad was not surprised and Maxine said she would miss her. Adrian thought she was throwing away a promising career, but she wasn't convinced he was being altogether honest. And Gregory. Well Gregory said nothing. Even when she said 'come with me'.

It didn't take long to make the arrangements. Maxine took over her room in London as she had registered with an agency and was looking to work in the city. In his capacity as acting editor - following Paul's fall from grace for passing information to various individuals, including Anthony Burchfield – Adrian allowed her to leave the paper without having to work out her notice. Her dad, despite having made a full recovery, was still lodging in Samantha's old room in Woodbridge enjoying long walks and real ale. Her mum seemed happy for him to be there, for now. Everybody was fine. No reason not to go. Her mum wanted to throw a going away party for her, but she declined, choosing instead to go out for dinner. Mum, Dad and Maxine came, her grandmother too and Adrian, Uncle Michael was not invited and Gregory declined. They had a lovely evening but Gregory's absence was keenly felt. Samantha realised it was time to accept that she had obviously misread what had passed between them. It was indeed just circumstances that had thrust them together.

The minute she disembarked she felt it. Whatever it was about India that held her in its thrall before now held her once again.

The air is different, sweet and heavy with floral scents but bitter too; a pungent mix of fires, flowers and fervent heat.

Aisha - who is now one step closer to her dream - has expanded the family business and now spends some of her time in Delhi. Samantha will stay with her for a while and together they will visit the sights of Delhi, Agra and Jaipur; India's so-called Golden Triangle. The Golden Triangle is a well-used tourist circuit and although she wants to get off the beaten track and explore she knows there are certain things she must see; boxes she should tick.

"I thought we could spend three, maybe four days here in Delhi before heading to Agra," says Aisha. "Is that okay?"

"Absolutely," says Samantha. "You have no idea how good it feels to be back here."

"Yes and this time you're not running from anyone or looking for someone."

In the end they spent six days in Delhi. Samantha didn't mind. She is in no hurry and it gave her the time to explore parts of the city she may have otherwise missed. At the end of her first week they boarded an early train to Agra. The train blew into the station in a cloud of smoke, chugging and whistling. It was just as she imagined, just as she had hoped it would be. The journey was faster than she expected and the rapid movement of the train made taking pictures difficult but she enjoyed looking out of the window watching as the city gave way to beautiful countryside. The train would slow as they passed through stations and then she was able to watch the people walking along the trackside carrying their loads. The women wore colourful clothes and open smiles. Samantha noted that since arriving she had only been met with smiles; something not so in London.

Aisha spent most of the journey on her phone for which she apologised when they arrived in Agra. She also explained that she would be unable to stay with Samantha as something had come up and she had to return to Delhi.

"I have arranged for someone, a guide to meet you. He will accompany you to the Taj and wherever else you wish to go."

Samantha hid her disappointment well. She enjoyed Aisha's company but she always knew that they would have to part at some point and she was not worried about travelling alone. In fact she would prefer to be alone than meet Aisha's guide but it was already arranged. Together they went to a cafeteria just outside the station. The guide would meet her there. They ordered a masala chai while they waited.

"What are you grinning at?" Samantha asked Aisha who had a huge smile across her face.

"It is time for me to go," replies Aisha, ignoring the question. She stands but tells her friend not to. "I hate goodbyes and we will see each other again soon. You wait here for your guide," Aisha grins again.

"How will I know him? What is his name?"

Aisha puts a hand on her shoulder and whispers, "You will know him."

Samantha turns her head, expecting her eyes to follow Aisha's exit, instead they are astounded to see someone she knows walk through the door.

"Namaste," says Gregory.

Shock. Surprise. Delight. Amazement. Glee. Joy. Elation. Bliss. Happy. She felt them all and more. She flung her arms around his neck, her fingers entwined so tightly he thought she would never let go. When she did he sat down where Aisha had been sitting and ordered them both another drink.

"I can't believe you came."

"Neither can I to be honest, but the need to be with you

outweighs any reservations I have about being here."

"Well I'm glad, but what reservations? Can you not see the wonder of this place?"

"I want to and I think I will if I see it with you."

"What about your job?"

"Extended leave. Courtesy of the new boss."

"Ha and how is Adrian?"

"The same. Exactly the same."

"That's good. I wouldn't want him to change."

"I saw your sister. She gave me this." Gregory hands Samantha a postcard. It's from Valletta and scrawled across the back is one sentence: 'Where is my car?'

"It's from Justin."

"I figured as much," says Gregory.

"Are there any updates?" she asks.

"We don't really want to talk about that. Do we?"

"No, no of course not. Although, there is just one thing that is bothering me. How did he know?"

"How did who know what?"

"Adrian. How did he know to send the police to Mum's?"

"Mahima."

"Mahima?"

"Yes. When you left her and went to see Justin she called Adrian and then Adrian sent someone to see Justin."

"How could she call Adrian? She didn't have his number and his phone had been taken."

"She memorised his landline number. She apparently has a rather good memory."

"Yes she does."

"So. What now?"

"Well I haven't anything planned I haven't even booked a hotel. Aisha has been arranging things."

"I arrived here yesterday. I have a hotel... they have vacancies.

We could get you a room or we could visit the Taj. They say it's very beautiful."

"Let's go to the hotel," she says taking his hand. "And one room is fine. The Taj can wait."

Acknowledgements

Thank you to all at Urbane publications for their continued support of my work, particularly Kerry-Jane Lowery and Matthew Smith. Matthew also deserves further recognition for helping to turn my raw material into this book. Thanks also to the advance readers and friends who have offered advice and support; your help has been invaluable. Closer to home thanks must go to my family: to my parents, siblings and most of all to Richard, Tom & Hayleigh.

And finally thanks to the wonderful people I met during my visit to India. Their pride and love for their beautiful country was plain to see and utterly understandable. It is indeed a most extraordinary and very special place.

Julie was born in East London but now lives a rural life in North Essex. She is married with two children. Her working life has seen her have a variety of jobs, including running her own publishing company.

She is the author of the children's book *Poppy and the Garden Monster* and two novels: the psychological thriller *Beware the Cuckoo* and gripping urban tale *The Kindness of Strangers*. Each of her novels have carefully crafted central characters through whom Julie raises key questions around topical and often controversial social themes.

Julie writes endlessly and when not writing she is reading. Other interests include theatre, music and running. Besides her family, the only thing she loves more than books is Bruce Springsteen.

URBANE

Urbane Publications is dedicated to
developing new author voices, and publishing
books that challenge, thrill and fascinate.
From page-turning thrillers to literary debuts,
our goal is to publish what
YOU want to read.
Find out more at

urbanepublications.com